"Are y...

Julia asked the quest... concern.

"Fine," Jesse lied quickly, not wanting to see her concern turn to pity. "I'm drunk." Another lie.

"Jesse," she breathed, her smile hesitant and somehow beseeching. He knew what she wanted. She wanted him to *remember* what he was trying so hard to forget.

He made the mistake of looking into her endless blue eyes, and he saw exactly what he had seen when he met her the first time, months ago in Germany.

A million missed opportunities. A thousand unanswered prayers and unspoken wishes.

He'd been kicked in the gut when his best friend had opened that door and introduced the woman of Jesse's dreams as his wife.

And now fate had brought her here to finish him off.

Dear Reader,

My husband and I welcomed our son into the world in February 2006 and soon after I was right back to work on the rewrites of this book. I had no idea when I got the idea for *His Best Friend's Baby* (months before even getting pregnant!) how one of its themes would resonate in my life—the need for a support system.

After giving birth (my water broke at a book signing—how about that for dramatic?) I found myself with an infant who didn't care much for naps and some serious work to do. As much help as my husband was, I needed more. I needed support. And I found it in spades. Writing, like motherhood, can be lonely at times and I am blessed with friends, a mother-in-law and my own mother who provided me with baked goods, laughs and a couple of hours every day to get the work done.

I felt as though I belonged to a tribe. Sleeplessness, worry and a joy I'd never experienced before were my entry into that circle of mothers.

It made me feel even more for Julia, the single-mother heroine in this book. She came to life for me during these rewrites in a way I never would have dreamed. I hope you enjoy her path to happily ever after as much I enjoyed discovering it.

Happy reading!

Molly O'Keefe

HIS BEST FRIEND'S BABY
Molly O'Keefe

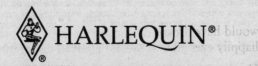

TORONTO • NEW YORK • LONDON
AMSTERDAM • PARIS • SYDNEY • HAMBURG
STOCKHOLM • ATHENS • TOKYO • MILAN • MADRID
PRAGUE • WARSAW • BUDAPEST • AUCKLAND

ISBN-13: 978-0-373-71385-1
ISBN-10:   0-373-71385-1

HIS BEST FRIEND'S BABY

Copyright © 2006 by Molly Fader.

This edition published by arrangement with Harlequin Books S.A.

® and TM are trademarks of the publisher. Trademarks indicated with ® are registered in the United States Patent and Trademark Office, the Canadian Trade Marks Office and in other countries.

www.eHarlequin.com

Printed in U.S.A.

ABOUT THE AUTHOR

Molly O'Keefe is thrilled to add Harlequin Superromance author to her résumé. And even more excited to add her new role as mother. She lives in Toronto, Ontario, with her husband and son. She loves hearing from readers, so drop her a line at www.molly-okeefe.com.

Books by Molly O'Keefe

HARLEQUIN SUPERROMANCE
1365–FAMILY AT STAKE

HARLEQUIN FLIPSIDE
15–PENCIL HIM IN
37–DISHING IT OUT

HARLEQUIN DUETS
62–TOO MANY COOKS
95–COOKING UP TROUBLE
    KISS THE COOK

Don't miss any of our special offers. Write to us at the following address for information on our newest releases.

Harlequin Reader Service
U.S.: 3010 Walden Ave., P.O. Box 1325, Buffalo, NY 14269
Canadian: P.O. Box 609, Fort Erie, Ont. L2A 5X3

For all the Mothers in my life:

Tracey Fader and J.K.,
who kept me laughing. Leslie Millan and
Sarah Drynan, who kept me sane.
Cindy and Carole Mernick, who made the
revisions of this book possible. And especially
to Mom, who made all of this possible.
You left me very big shoes to fill in the
motherhood department—I love you.

CHAPTER ONE

JESSE FILMORE lifted his fingers from the bar, signaling for another drink.

"Liquid lunch, huh?" the bartender asked with a nervous laugh as he poured Jesse another cup of coffee. Black.

"What time is it?" Jesse's voice sounded like something that had been dragged behind a horse. His whole body felt that way—sore and beat up.

"Twelve-thirty." The bartender leaned against the polished wood bar. "We don't get a lot of coffee drinkers in here. You want a beer or a sandwich or something? We've got—"

"What's your name?" Jesse asked. He didn't lift his head, just stared at the bartender from under his eyebrows. His neck was killing him. Moving it would send an electric shock through his body.

"My name? Billy. This is my—"

"Billy? I'd like to drink in quiet."

Billy looked stunned, no doubt used to a friendlier sort of drinker in this crappy sports bar. "Yeah, ah, sure. I'll be down here if you need me." Billy backed toward the other end of the bar where two guys shared a pitcher of beer and a plate of nachos while they watched yesterday's sports recap on the screen in the corner.

When Jesse was a kid, this bar used to be a serious drinking place. No music. No darts. No pool tables. No damn ESPN. It had been a bar where men swaggered in after work and stumbled home at midnight, then fell into bed and slept without dreams.

Jesse wasn't doing any drinking. The pain meds the docs had him on were bad enough, he didn't need to let go of any more reality.

But a little peace and quiet wasn't too much to ask for.

He'd come here to get out of the sun, stall for time before going to see what was left of the old house.

He'd come in here because he was a little bit scared.

He blocked out the noise of the television and the buzzing neon lights and drained half of his coffee mug before setting it down precisely on the damp circle that stained the napkin.

"Holy shit. Jesse Filmore!"

Jesse turned his head as much as he comfortably could and saw Patrick Sanderson barreling down on him. In high school, Patrick had tried, briefly, to keep up with Jesse and his best friend, Mitch Adams. But the kind of trouble Jesse and Mitch had gotten into wasn't for the faint of heart and Patrick had definitely been faint of heart.

It was probably for the best. Jesse recalled the night that Patrick had gone out with them. *We got arrested for stealing that car.*

"How have you been, man?" Patrick slapped a clammy hand on Jesse's back. Jesse fought the urge to shake it off. It wasn't Patrick so much—though he had never liked the guy—as it was anyone and everyone getting too close. Even alone in a room he felt crowded. Too many ghosts.

Jesse shrugged and the gesture apparently satisfied Patrick. "We haven't seen you in town since…?"

"My mother's funeral," Jesse said carefully, his throat a solid throb of pain.

"God, right, three years ago. I thought you were still over in Iraq." Patrick slid onto the stool next to Jesse. "I heard about Mitch. Terrible news. Just terrible." Patrick's belly strained against his yellow golf shirt. He ran his hand over his thinning hair. "Agnes and Ron are all messed up over it."

Jesse didn't smile, didn't in any way encourage this intrusion, but Patrick didn't seem to need encouragement.

"I'd steer clear of that house if I was you. She'd probably skin you alive if she saw you." He laughed, as though what he was saying wasn't the heartbreaking reality of Jesse's life. Luckily, Jesse had grown a thick skin, from years of letting the casually hurtful and completely stupid things people said roll off him.

Billy sauntered over and threw a cardboard coaster on the bar in front of Patrick.

"What can I get you, Pat?"

"Draft and whatever Jesse here is drinking—"

"No thanks," Jesse declined. "I'm good."

Billy shot Patrick a look indicating what he thought of Jesse's manners, before walking away to get the beer.

"So are you on leave or something?" Patrick asked, turning back to Jesse.

"Something." Jesse took a big gulp of his coffee, eager to get out of this place.

"I tell you, that war…" Patrick shook his head. "Lots of good boys dying over there. Mitch Adams, I still can't believe it. He always seemed to have a horseshoe up his ass or something—luckiest damn guy. Did you ever see that girl he married?" Patrick whistled through his teeth and Jesse had the sudden and powerful urge to smash in those teeth.

"I heard she was gorgeous," Patrick continued.

Time to leave.

Jesse shifted, digging into his back pocket for his wallet.

"Guess old Mitch's luck ran out." Patrick's well of insight was seemingly bottomless. "The whole town thought it was nuts when he went into the military after you. He could have done anything, football scholarship, anything. His mother…" Patrick wrapped his fat fingers around the pint Billy slid over.

"Will never forgive me. I know." Her name was at the top of a long list of such people.

I shouldn't have come in here.

Jesse threw a few bucks on the bar, drained his mug then made an attempt to stand. But his bum knee buckled. Too many hours in the car.

"Whoa there." Patrick laughed, putting up a hand to brace Jesse. "What'd you have in that mug?"

Jesse's arm jerked instinctually. He stood frozen, knowing exactly how he could kill Patrick with an elbow to the windpipe or the heel of his hand to the nose.

Jesse didn't do it, of course, but he was capable of it and that was somehow worse.

"Hey, man, sorry if talking about Mitch—" Patrick looked nervous but there was something else in his small eyes, a certain morbid curiosity. The rumors had made it home. "Terrible accident."

If Jesse stood here long enough, maybe Patrick would just come right out and ask what he clearly wanted confirmed. But Jesse didn't have time to pussy-foot, he had a house to get rid of and a life to get on with, so he took pity on Patrick.

"I killed him." Jesse said. "I killed Artie McKinley and Dave Mancio. I put Caleb Gomez in the hospital. And I watched Mitch Adams burn up in his helicopter." He patted Patrick on the back, like the good friend Patrick had always wished him to be, and limped away.

Mitch ghost dogged Jesse out the door.

The bright sunshine blinded him. Jesse blinked and gave himself a second to adjust before tackling the steps down to the asphalt parking lot.

A hot wind blew down from the mountains, carrying the smell of tar and sun-warmed grass. The scent of the southern California desert reminded him all too much of being a boy.

He'd grown up in this town on the edge of nowhere, and if it weren't for the damn house his mother left to him in her will, he would never have returned. The war had kept him occupied for three years, but now, thanks to the discharge papers, he could no longer ignore this little obligation.

All he had to do was get rid of the house and he could leave. Chris Barnhardt, a buddy from before the war, waited for him in San Diego with more construction work than he could handle and an interesting proposition that included the word *partner.*

If Jesse were a smart man, something he'd never claimed to be—he'd be halfway down Highway 101 on his way to the rest of his life. A life he could taste like clean, cold water after years choking on dust in the desert.

Instead he was in New Springs. Just him, more dust, the dumb dog he couldn't get rid of and the ghosts.

The bright spot of reflection bounced off his Jeep's windshield sitting the corner of the parking lot. A small woman stood next to the vehicle. Her brown hair blew out behind her like a flag. Like a warning.

He lurched to a stop.

Not this, Jesse thought, panic kick-starting his heart. *Not her.*

She pushed away from the Jeep and Jesse forced one foot in front of the other, inching his way toward his sister.

She had a lot of nerve. A lot of goddamned nerve tracking him down this way, ambushing him when he hadn't been in town long enough to get his bearings.

"Hello, Jesse." Rachel took a few steps closer. He tried not to notice the chin she thrust out as though she were ready for whatever he might throw at her.

It was exactly the way he remembered her. Even at

thirty-four, she still looked like that eighteen-year-old girl who'd been so damn fired up to take on the world.

"How'd you know I was here?"

"You know small-town gossip. Mac and I got word the second you drove into town." She tried to laugh, but it came out all wrong. Broken in all the important places.

She tucked a strand of hair behind her ear and he was struck by how short she was. How fragile she appeared. He almost laughed as he thought it. *Fragile? Rachel?* As a boy he'd believed she was the biggest, tallest, strongest thing on earth.

But now she didn't even come up to his shoulder and he could easily snap her in two.

He never figured his perspective would change.

He opened the driver door only to have Rachel slam it out of his hand. She slid along the side of the vehicle until she was right in his face. "You're not going to run from me like you did at Mom's funeral."

"Get out of the way, Rachel," he growled, not necessarily on purpose, but the effect was good.

"No." She crossed her arms over her chest. "Please just listen to what I have to say."

He didn't care what Rachel had to say, so he turned and started walking back to the bar. He'd take Patrick and his barely veiled insinuations over his sister any day.

She darted around him and Jesse stopped, attracted and repelled by his sister's magnetic force. "Why didn't she leave you the damn house?" he demanded.

"Jesse," she whispered. He kept his eyes locked on the *y* in the Billy's Final Score sign over the door of the bar rather than succumb to Rachel's plan. Her voice was thick with emotion and he was not going to stand here and watch her fight tears. "Before Mom died I wrote you letters, Jesse. Didn't you get the letters I sent?"

"I got them."

She had written almost every week since the day she'd left after her high school graduation. Once he turned eighteen and joined the army, he'd finally written her back and told her to stop. And for a year, she respected his request. Then the letters had started arriving again—with a vengeance. He now knew that was about the time she and Mac Edwards had finally gotten together.

There had been cards from Mac, boxes of cookies from Rachel and funny pictures from Amanda—Jesse's new niece thanks to Rachel's marriage to Mac.

He'd opened all letters that weren't addressed in Rachel's handwriting. The rest he sent back or burned. Except the cookies—a man could only be so mad.

But he'd never responded to Mac's letters, and only once to Amanda's. There was never a reason for them to continue sending him stuff. But they had.

The whole family was just so stubborn.

"We're hoping you might come up to the farm. Amanda is dying to see you again and Mac can't wait." She smiled again, all the hope in the world rolling off her.

"I didn't read your letters, Rachel."

"Jesse." She reached out to him as though to touch his arm, and he stepped out of the way. His eyes met hers and he saw what his rejection did to her, the light that it killed in her eyes.

Let it go, Rachel, he urged silently. *You keep coming at me like this and you're only going to get hurt.*

Her hand curled into a fist and fell to her side. "I know you're mad. But I tried—"

"Stop it." Jesse struggled to find that cold dark center of himself, that place where simplicity reigned. "I was a kid when you left. You don't know me and I don't want to know you. Just leave it alone." He watched all that hope crumple in her, like wadded-up paper.

Good. Now, stay away.

He moved past her to his beat-up Jeep and she didn't try to stop him.

"Where are you going?" she asked.

"San Diego," he told her. He winced as he swung his aching leg into the vehicle. Damn bum knee. "After I take care of Mom's house."

"So you're just gonna run again?"

Everything in him went still.

"Running's your deal, not mine. I stayed until the old man died. What did you do?"

They both knew the answer all too well—she'd left, when he'd needed her most.

She was a little late if she expected forgiveness now.

Wainwright, the ancient black Lab he'd somehow inherited in the last two weeks, lifted his head from the duffel bag he'd been using as a bed.

Take the dog, Artie McKinley's folks had said. *He's old and we're moving to an apartment in Nogales. We can't have pets.* Artie had been their only son, so there had been no one else to take care of Wainwright and they refused to put him down.

What could Jesse do?

So he'd taken the aging dog and now, every time he looked at the animal, he remembered why Artie hadn't come back to claim his dog.

Wainwright spied Rachel and barked. She flinched.

"I hear you, boy," Jesse muttered. He turned over the engine and peeled out of the parking lot without once looking back.

DAMN IT.

Jesse braked at the deserted intersection of Goleta Road and Foothill after having driven around aimlessly for an hour. He leaned forward in the driver's seat and looked right down the long stretch of road that would lead him down to the coast and Highway 101.

He could drive to San Diego, be there by tonight.

He turned and looked left down the length of asphalt that would lead him back to New Springs.

"What do you think, Wain?" The dog struggled to his feet and climbed over the console to sit in the passenger seat. He barked once at a passing bird. "That's not much help, buddy."

Jesse's knee throbbed from all the walking and driving he had been doing the past week and even though he was steering clear of the pain meds in his bag, the relief they offered seemed pretty good right now.

Jesse eyed the waves of heat rising off the blacktop

and Wain nudged his thigh with his snout. Jesse patted the dog's head and wished again, as he had a million times in the past, that his genetic makeup was different.

It would be so damn easy if he was the kind to run away like his sister.

But no, Jesse took after his mother. He had Eva's black eyes, dark hair and the same stubborn chin. Despite heavy drinking and hard living, his father had looked like a young man when he died, but Eva had looked every one of her fifty-six years, as if all her disappointments and heartaches had been pressed into the lines on her face.

Jesse wondered briefly what was written across his face. What details of his past were visible?

He and Eva were the same beasts of burden, carrying everyone's troubles and responsibilities like stones around their necks. When everyone else had deserted they had both stayed—in that house, in this town—long after the time they should have left.

Just do what you are supposed to do, he told himself. *You're in this little shithole for a reason.*

He pulled his cell phone out of the faded green duffel and dialed Chris's number.

"Inglewood Construction," Chris answered after two rings and Jesse's dark mood lifted at the sound of his friend's voice.

"Hey, Chris. It's Jesse."

"Jesse, when the hell are you going to get down here? I am up to my pits in work." A saw buzzed to life on Chris's side of the line. "Watch the damn floors!" Chris yelled and Jesse could practically smell the sawdust; he could almost taste it. "Seriously, man," Chris said. "I need you here, like, yesterday."

"Yeah, I'm sorry, Chris, but it looks like I'm stuck in New Springs for a few days."

"Well, the sooner you get here the faster we can drink some cold beers and start making some money."

"Sounds good," Jesse said. It sounded like heaven, like the furthest possible thing from the life he'd lived for the past three years. "Sounds real good."

"Keep me posted," Chris said. "I gotta run. The guys are pouring the basement floor and I swear if someone doesn't watch them, they'll make a swimming pool out of it."

"See ya, Chris." Jesse hung up and threw the phone back in his duffel.

Wishing was for fools, something he learned the day his sister walked away from him, so he stopped wasting his own precious time. He was who he was and he had to take care of his responsibilities.

He gave Wain a pat on the snout.

"See what you're getting me into?"

Wain farted and sighed.

Jesse jerked the wheel to the left and kicked up a lot of dust heading toward New Springs. He took the winding mountain road too fast. Wainwright put his nose in the air and howled and Jesse knew exactly how he felt.

He drove through Old Town, past the Royal Theater and the Dairy Dream ice-cream shop. He took the left after the Vons grocery store, toward the south side. With every twist and turn through his old neighborhood, the pressure in his chest built.

There weren't any railroad tracks in New Springs, but Jesse never questioned which side of the proverbial tracks he was from. There had been a grit and a filth that came from this part of town and sometimes he could still feel it.

When he was a kid, this particular street had been made up of single moms with kids they couldn't control. Big, once-beautiful old homes—the first built in the town—had been falling to ruin or divided into apartments while people with money had chosen to live in the newer homes by the rec center on the other side of town.

He shifted gears as the pressure in his chest started to feel like panic.

The turning point of his life had come when Mitch and his family had moved into the neighborhood. Mitch's mom liked old houses and apparently she'd never noticed the filth until her son had come home after school with Jesse in tow.

Then she'd noticed.

Since those days, however, the old neighborhood had clearly changed. The lawns were now green and nice, the tiled roofs repaired, the houses painted.

It freaked him out. He wiped one sweaty palm on his thigh. He felt like the boy in the fancy shop who security watched—a feeling he hadn't had since he was a kid.

The old house must be the eyesore on this street.

Mom had died three years ago and the house had been a nightmare then. Jesse could only imagine the damage raccoons and high-school kids looking for a place to get drunk had done since then.

Truth be told, the idea appealed to him—the old homestead a broken-down disgrace among these refurbished houses. All the neighbors once again cursing the Filmore family over their repaired and whitewashed back fences.

Just like the good old days.

But at the corner of Wilson and Pine, where the ruins of his childhood home should have sat, was a house newly painted a creamy yellow color. There were red flowers in window boxes and a shiny white front porch.

"What the hell…?" His mouth fell open as he peered through the open passenger window at the vision.

His heart squeezed uncomfortably.

Man, I wish Mom could have seen it like this.

Jesse pulled up to the curb, and stared, stunned, at 314 Wilson.

That was his old house all right, but it looked nothing like it once had.

Years ago, he'd thrown a rock through the front picture window after a fight with his father. His mom had covered the hole with cardboard because they couldn't afford a new piece of glass that size.

Now, the cardboard was gone, the replacement window surrounded by flowers nodding in the breeze.

The porch where his father used to sit many nights drinking Scotch and getting mean no longer sagged, threatening to fall away from the house. And the hole Jesse had used to crawl under the porch on nights when

Dad kicked him out was covered over. He'd learned later that his mother had kept the back door open for him the way she had for Rachel, when his sister had been the one thrown out into the cold desert night.

All of his surprise and regret quickly boiled down to something much more familiar. Anger.

His mother had left him the damn place as some kind of chain, forcing him back here. Worse, Rachel had been repairing it and shining it up pretty.

Wonderful. A gold-plated chain.

If Rachel thought she could stop him from getting rid of it—tearing the damn thing down if he had to—she was wrong. Rachel could dress up the house all she wanted, repair it and cover up the ugly parts, but underneath it was still the violent and angry home of his youth. There was not enough paint in the world to cover that.

"Let's go, Wain." Jesse climbed gingerly out of the Jeep.

Wain barked with an enthusiasm Jesse was far from feeling and trotted ahead to sniff and urinate on a hydrangea bush.

Jesse pulled the key from around his neck, where it hung with his dog tags.

He bent and picked up one of the solid decorative rocks that lined the walkway. He tested its heft and then hurled it through the front window. The glass shattered and Jesse smiled.

Now, it looks like home.

CHAPTER TWO

JULIA ADAMS managed to eat three bites of the cinnamon roll she had grabbed from the motel vending machine then tossed it in a garbage can outside the Vons grocery store. She took another sip of the stale coffee from the motel lobby and dumped that out as well.

She couldn't get food past the slick bitter taste of nerves at the back of her throat. The anxiety had gathered steam as she and Ben walked into town from the motel and now she was a kettle about ready to blow.

"I think Momma has made a mistake, Ben," she said to her two-year-old son, even though he was sound asleep in his stroller.

One mistake? How do you figure just one? The voice belonged to Mitch, her dead husband, always there to count her failings.

She hit a crack in the sidewalk and the stroller under her hands swayed, thanks to the loose screws she'd tried repair a million times—the whole thing was just about shot.

The streetlights blinked on and the world past the street receded to shadows. Dusk arrived to the desert town with a beauty Julia had never seen. The enormous sky turned purple and blue and the temperature finally cooled to a tolerable level.

She and Ben had missed the worst of the heat, having spent most of the day inside their motel room. Ben had napped and fussed, confused by the time change, and she'd stewed—replaying Agnes's phone call in her head, wondering if she'd gotten the invitation all wrong.

The smell of eucalyptus filled the air and Julia, trying to calm the twisting of her stomach, pulled off one of the flat round leaves and rubbed it between her fingers. The oil soaked into her skin, but it wasn't enough to calm the raging nerves.

She turned left and the reality of what she was doing came down on her like a hammer.

She was about to knock on Mitch's parents' door. Her in-laws, who had never liked her, and say...

"What?" she asked herself aloud. "Surprise! Can I stay a while? Here's your grandson. Do you mind if I take a nap?" She took a deep breath. "Remember when you asked me to come for a visit? When you said you would be here for me?"

I've finally lost it. I'm talking to myself!

"Your mother's a lunatic," she told her sleeping son, just to prove the point.

With Mitch gone, Julia only had her own mother, Sergeant Beth Milhow. Julia and Ben could have gone to live with her mom and continue the life she had known forever.

A military daughter. A military wife. A military widow.

But she couldn't do it anymore. She wanted a family. Friends who had more in common with her than what their husbands did for a living. She wanted more than duty and loneliness so sharp it sliced at her. She had to try and find a better way, which was why she'd come to New Springs.

What she really wished, if she were completely honest with herself, was that Jesse Filmore would be here. Last she had heard he was in the hospital in San Diego, which was close enough that he might head home if he still had family in the area. She'd settle for any kind of anchor that would pull him back to New Springs.

This was her new life—a fresh start, and she wanted desperately to have Jesse in it.

She was being foolish. She had enough on her plate dealing with her in-laws. The very last thing she needed to do was cloud up her head with romantic illusions… or delusions. Particularly about her dead husband's best friend.

But if she closed her eyes, she could still see Jesse's dark eyes burning bright through the shadowy dawn.

She pulled the envelope from Agnes and Ron's last Christmas card out of her jeans pocket and checked it against the numbers on the houses. She turned at the corner at Wilson and Hemlock, walked down half a block until she found 12 Hemlock Street, a two-story brick house that was triple the size of the small army house she and Ben had called home in Germany for the past two years.

She swiped at the sweat that beaded up on her forehead. *Oh, God, why didn't I call? What if Agnes changed her mind?*

She turned up the beautiful slate path toward the house. Her heart clogged her throat and with every heartbeat she saw spots in the corners of her eyes.

The last thing she needed was to faint on the Adams' doorstep. She tried to focus on the concrete reality: the flowering vines clinging to the red brick, the overgrown garden filled with jade plants and gorgeous lupine that were nearly choked out with weeds.

Losing a son must put you off lawn work for a while.

She clapped a hand over her mouth to stop the hysterical giggle that was nearly a sob. She was coming unglued. She stopped at the door—a wooden one, simple and solid with a small window at the top.

She tried to smooth her short, dishwater-blond hair to get the worst of the haywire strands to settle down. Julia never bothered with makeup, and now she wished she had at least put on a little blush.

Yeah, she laughed at herself, *because your hair and makeup are really going to make her love you.*

She leaned down and looked at sleeping Ben. He'd woken up a few hours ago but his internal clock was screwy from jet lag.

Julia tried to see her son with unbiased eyes, to find imperfections, but she couldn't detect any. Even dead to the world he was still the cutest kid she'd ever seen. He had Mitch's thick, white-gold hair with just a little curl. His eyes, when they were open, mirrored her own big blue ones. And, thanks to a genetic hiccup, he had a dimple in his chin.

"Grandma Agnes is going to love you, Ben," Julia whispered. "Even if she can't stand me."

She didn't give herself time to think, or change her mind or even imagine the worst possible outcome. She charged ahead and rang the doorbell.

The seconds between pressing the small illuminated button and hearing someone on the other side of the door stretched unbearably. Slowly, the door swung open and an older, sadder version of Mitch wearing a faded plaid shirt stood there. He peered over the top of a pair of thin gold glasses. "Hello?"

"Hi, um, Ron."

He flipped on the light over the door and Julia blinked, jerking back from the brightness. Ben woke up with a cry and clapped his hands over his eyes.

"Oh, my," Ron whispered.

"Ron? Who is it?" a woman's voice called from inside.

Ron smiled and Julia felt every bit of tension and worry slide right out of her.

"It's Julia and Ben," Ron replied, his smile growing until he started to laugh.

"That's not funny, Ron."

"I'm not kidding, Agnes."

Silence. And then the clatter of a pan hitting the sink and Agnes—a short, round woman with a curly nimbus of gray hair and a tea towel trailing like a silk scarf behind her—was running down the hallway toward them.

"Oh, oh!" she cried, barreling past her husband to

wrap her arms around Julia. Julia was awash in the scent of garlic and roses. Agnes's strong wet hands gripped Julia's back and she felt all the air rush from her body. Agnes dropped her arms and knelt in front of Ben.

"Hello, hello, little boy," she cried, tears running down her round cheeks.

Julia shut her gaping mouth. This welcome was simply more than she could have hoped for. More than she'd ever dreamed.

Careful, Mitch's snide voice whispered. *You always believe the things that are too good to be true.*

Julia, exhausted and emotional, ignored her dead husband's voice. If this was too good to be true she would figure it out later, as she always did. Right now, she was swept up in the tide of the moment, helpless to stop this strange homecoming.

"He looks just like Mitch, doesn't he, Ron?"

"Yes, he does," Ron agreed, lifting his glasses to wipe his eyes. "Let's get them in the door, Agnes."

"Of course." Agnes started to get up and Julia held out a hand to assist and found herself back in her mother-in-law's arms.

"We're so glad you're here," Agnes murmured. "Thank you for coming to us."

The icy silences between Julia and Agnes had seemingly melted away after Mitch had died in the helicopter crash. Julia had gotten a call from an inconsolable Agnes, who'd begged Julia to come to California, to bring Ben so they could get to know him—the only thing left of their precious son.

Come, she'd said, *we will be here for you.*

It had been a spell, an enchantment, *we will be here for you.* Words so foreign to Julia they might have been a different language.

A million things rushed to Julia's throat but all she could manage to say was a tight, "Thanks for having us."

"Are you hungry? Did you just get in? Do you have a place to stay? You have to stay here. We insist, don't we, Ron?" They stepped through the foyer into a small dining room that opened into a large living room with a fireplace and bookshelves crammed with books.

The dining-room table was freshly wiped down, the streaks still damp on the oak finish, and the smell of garlic and potatoes filled the air.

Julia's stomach roared to life.

"I guess she's hungry," Ron said.

Julia pressed a fist to her stomach. "You know, airline food," she said with dumb chuckle. The truth was the rubbery airline sandwich was probably the best meal she'd had in weeks.

Ron crouched, his knees cracking, to get a better look at Ben, who blinked owlishly at the old man. "Hello," Ron said in a soft voice and everyone seemed to hold their breath, as if this were a test that they could all fail.

After a moment, Ben reached out a curled fist and dropped a handful of raisins in Ron's hand and smiled his heartbreaker smile.

Ron and Agnes sighed in adoration.

Nice one, Ben. Julia ruffled her son's blond hair. *They're goners for sure.*

"We got in this morning." Julia unhooked her son from the stroller and he pitched himself from the seat with his usual enthusiasm. "We're over at the Motel Six on the highway."

"Oh, no," Agnes gasped as if Julia had said, "We are living in trees."

"You have to stay here, we can't have Mitch's bab—"

"You are welcome to stay here," Ron interrupted. "We could go pick up your stuff and bring it back."

Julia and her overextended bank account heaved a sigh of relief. She had hoped they would offer, but the motel had been a necessary plan B. "That would be nice, thank you."

"We have so many questions." Agnes took a deep breath and seemed about to launch into all of them and Julia braced herself with the limited reserves of energy she had left.

"Agnes, the girl is asleep on her feet. Let's get her some food and let her rest for a minute," Ron cut in reasonably and Julia's affection for the man leaped off the charts.

Ben put his hand in Ron's and pulled him toward the other room as though he wanted a guided tour.

"You're right. I'm sorry, I'm just so excited."

Julia smiled. She didn't have the energy to do more.

"I've got roasted chicken and some potatoes," Agnes offered. "It's not very fancy but—"

"That would be wonderful, thank you," Julia whispered. Tears of relief and gratitude filled her eyes. Agnes ran off into the kitchen. Ben toddled toward the shelves and all of the books and magazines he, no doubt, could not wait to rip to pieces. Ron followed, his eyes glued to Mitch's son.

Suddenly alone in the room, Julia collapsed into a chair. All of the fear and hunger and worry that had been keeping her upright since getting the call that Mitch was dead disappeared.

Thank you, she said silently.

Her life, irrevocably diverted when she'd bumped into Mitch on that beach, might somehow end up back on track.

AFTER DINNER, Agnes led Julia, with a sleeping Ben in her arms, up the staircase to the bedrooms.

"You can use Mitch's old room," she said with a sad smile. Agnes pushed open the door to a room that had been frozen in time. Posters of Michael Jordan—back when the basketball shorts were shorter—covered one wall. A prom picture of a young Mitch looking uncomfortable wearing a pink bow tie sat on the dresser.

"This will be great," Julia said. Her bags, which Ron had kindly picked up from the Motel 6, sat at the foot of the bed.

Agnes backed out of the room, but stopped before shutting the door. "Thank you," she said fervently for the hundredth time in the few hours Julia had been there. "Thank you for bringing Ben to us."

Julia smiled and reached out to squeeze Agnes's hand. It was hard to believe that this was the same woman who almost three years ago had called Julia a gold-digging whore.

Goes to show how some people can change.

Agnes left and Julia put her son down on the bed and took off the Spider-Man shoes that were getting too small for him. Once he was settled, she dug through her purse for her cell phone. She checked her watch—9:00 p.m. in California meant that it was midnight in Washington, D.C.

Julia said a quick prayer—*please Mom, be home*—and dialed, needing desperately to hear her friendly, if firm, voice.

"Sergeant Beth Milhow," Julia's mother said by way of greeting.

"Hi, Mom."

"Julia? You made it okay? I was getting worried."

"We had some delays, but we got to New Springs this morning."

"You must be tired."

"I am so past tired, I can't even see straight." Every time her eyes fluttered shut she could feel herself falling asleep.

"How was Ben on the flight?"

"He was great." Julia couldn't quite make that half truth totally believable. "Well, he was as great as could be expected. A minor meltdown somewhere over Denver and a larger one on the bus, but mostly he slept and stared at every new face."

"How are you?" Her mom's voice dropped and Julia rubbed her forehead. Her mind was slippery and clouded from too much worry and too little sleep. "I'm—" *nervous, tired, freaked out* "—all right."

"Oh, honey, you don't have to do this. You can come back here and—"

Live in a big empty house all alone, Julia finished her mother's sentence. *You can continue doing everything by yourself.*

"I know, Mom," Julia interrupted. "But I really need to do this."

Her mom made a skeptical noise and Julia brushed her fingers through Ben's fine hair that was so much like Mitch's. She leaned down and kissed the top of his head, smelled the distinctive powdery-fruity scent of her son and hoped she was doing the right thing.

"Mom, they want to get to know Ben. They've never even seen him. We just spent two weeks with you, plus you came to visit us in Germany, but they—"

"They never bothered."

Ben woke up with a whiny cry and rolled toward her. He had fallen asleep during supper and she knew the poor guy was probably hungry. Julia winced and tried to stop Ben from smashing her kneecaps as he crawled over her legs. He was two, but he weighed thirty pounds. She grabbed a Thomas the Tank Engine toy from his diaper bag and wiggled it in front of him. He took the bait, wrapping his little fingers around the toy. Sleepy, but determined to stay awake, Ben ran Thomas up and down her legs like railroad tracks. "Choo choo," he said and Julia found a smile from somewhere in her weary body. She jiggled her legs under him so he bounced around. He laughed and buried his face against her.

Oh, God, she prayed again, *please don't let this selfish decision hurt Ben.*

"They only want to get to know you now because Mitch is dead," Beth said and Julia flinched, swallowing the taste of copper and bile. It had been five months since the accident and she still felt raw.

"What's wrong with that?" Julia asked, pushing aside her own doubt. "So they're two years late? Should I punish them forever?"

"Well, I don't think you should go running into their open arms. They were nothing but terrible to you."

"They weren't terrible," Julia muttered. "They just weren't nice."

But they are here and they are solid and they aren't going anywhere. They aren't going to fight in any wars or move every two or three years. Their roots go so deep that maybe Ben and I can stand close and pretend those roots are ours.

"Oh, sweetheart, you are too nice for your own good," Beth said, her voice soft like a hug. She was prickly and stubborn to the point of blindness, but Julia never doubted that her mother loved her.

"Probably," Julia laughed.

"So, how are they? Is that woman civil?" Julia smiled at her mother's loyalty. Ever since Agnes had so singularly rejected Julia, Beth referred to her as "that woman."

The petty parts of Julia that were still wounded by the things Agnes had said sort of liked it.

"They've been really nice to me and nothing but sweet to Ben."

"But don't you go forgiving that woman too soon. You are a strong mother, you don't need their help."

Julia clapped a hand over her mouth to stop the incredulous laughter. Beth, as usual, had no clue what Julia needed.

Julia was a twenty-four-year-old widow. She had a two-year-old son who only knew his father from photographs. Her own father was dead and her mother, though loving and involved in Julia's life, was still an active engineer in the army. And when the United States wasn't at war, Mom was home in Washington, D.C., for only about half the year. For the past three years, Beth had spent eleven months out of twelve in Iraq.

No one had ever truly *been there* for Julia and Ben. And she needed that to change. Ben needed family, people in his life on a daily basis. Not twice a year for a few weeks.

"Do you have enough money?"

An excellent question, Mother. "I'm fine," she hedged.

"Okay, I'll let you get some rest." Beth's deep breath echoed down the line. "Remember, sweetheart, you can always come here. I leave to go back on Saturday to help the Brits with their water problems so my house will be empty."

Another empty army house. Exactly what I am trying to avoid.

"I know, Mom, thanks. I love you."

"I love you, too."

They hung up and Julia's spirits bobbed upward. She smiled at her son, who was nearly asleep where he lay against her legs.

"Everything is going to be okay," she told him and hoped with every last thing in her body that it was true.

THE DREAM CAME as it had for the past five months. She stood at the front door of the small apartment in Germany she and Mitch shared briefly before he went to Iraq. She was dressed in her favorite white skirt and a sweater that Mitch said made her eyes look like the sky. She knew she was opening the door to something special. Excitement danced over her skin and she was happy, the way she'd been for the first few months of her marriage. But when she opened the door there was only fire and smoke and the sound of someone screaming.

She ran into the smoke, sure that someone needed her. Just her, no one else could help. The smoke shifted and on the floor of the hallway sprawled Mitch, bloody and hurt.

"Hey, baby," he said with a smile she recognized from the days when he was trying to get her in bed.

She dropped to her knees beside him, looking for the source of all that blood, but she couldn't find it.

"Is this a trick?" she asked, angry.

"No trick," a voice said behind her and she turned and Jesse, Mitch's best friend, stood there with a hole in his chest that she could see through. His dark eyes seemed to burn and smolder, the way they had the day she met him. "I can't stay here," Jesse said and turned away into the fog. Julia wanted to tell him to wait, to take care of that wound, to stay. But she didn't.

She remained silent in the middle of a war with her husband.

CHAPTER THREE

JULIA WOKE to the smell of pancakes and coffee and—
she took another sniff of the air. Oh, boy. Bacon. It
wasn't so much the food that had her eyes flying open,
it was that she didn't have to make it. All that food
waited for her.

She stared at the ceiling and luxuriated in the faded
blue sheets. She had slept like a rock on this soft
mattress with all the extra pillows. It was heaven.

This was definitely the right place for Ben. She could
feel their roots growing already.

Growing up as an army brat, Julia had worked hard
for years to never form material attachments. But one
night in this room and she coveted everything—the
mahogany bed frame that matched the old washstand
in the corner and the five-drawer dresser on the far wall.
She wanted the mirror hanging over the dresser that re-
flected the small window and the perfect California
day outside.

Everything was so beautiful. So permanent and
substantial.

She'd even take the Michael Jordan posters.

This is a brand new day. Opportunity was here, glimmering like dust motes in the sunlight. She could shed the past and try something new. Try to be someone new.

Try to figure out who I am.

She rolled over to see how her son had slept, but he was nowhere to be found. She sat up and searched the floor around the bed. Where did he go? How could he have woken up and left the room without her noticing? She didn't trust him entirely on his own with stairs, and they had followed Agnes up a steep wooden flight last night to this bedroom.

Julia rolled out of bed and ran downstairs, her bare feet slipping across the polished hardwood floors on her way to the kitchen. She burst into a scene right out of Norman Rockwell.

Ben sat in an ancient high chair, cheerfully shoving blueberries in his mouth.

"Airplane!" he cried. "Big airplane."

"And what else?" Agnes asked.

"On a bus."

"You were on an airplane and a bus in the same day?" Agnes asked, her eyes wide as though no one had ever done such a thing.

Ben nodded.

"Such a big boy!" Agnes cooed and Ben smiled, his teeth blue. He lifted his hands above his head to show her how big he truly was. Julia loved this game, loved wondering if he was broadcasting how big he felt, the size of his cheerful spirit.

Ron laughed. "All done?" he asked.

Ben nodded, his blond curls waving, and Ron leaned in to wipe Ben's face and hands. "Let me atcha."

Agnes picked up a camera and took a couple of pictures of Ron attempting to clean Ben up.

"Smile, Benny," she cooed and Julia tried not to cringe at that nickname.

Julia had only sent them one picture of their grandson. A family shot of her, Mitch and Ben taken six months ago—the night Mitch was on leave from Iraq.

Jesse had taken the picture.

Shame and regret trickled through her.

She should have been the bigger person, tried harder to breach the gaps between her and the Adamses. But she was too much like her mother, maybe. Too proud.

New beginnings, she reminded herself.

"Momma," Ben cried, dodging Ron's washcloth. Agnes and Ron turned toward her, their smiles radiant.

"We heard him wake up and knew you needed your rest so we brought him downstairs, hope you don't mind," Agnes said with a bright smile before focusing on her grandson again.

"Of course not," Julia croaked, her voice rusty from nearly twelve hours of sleep. Despite her assurance, something in her chafed at the idea that they had come into her room while she slept.

Really, you're gonna get mad because they let you sleep an extra hour? She tried to relax. Clearly she had been on her own for too long.

Ben struggled to lift himself out of the chair with one hand and reached for Julia with the other.

"Stay there, Ben." She walked over to kiss his cheeks and his hands, rub her nose with his damp one. All of their morning rituals. He laughed and clapped in response.

"Hog heaven, huh, buddy?" she asked, letting him put his hands on her face leaving sticky handprints on her skin. "Pancakes and blueberries."

"Nana," he said, pointing to Agnes, but watching Julia.

"That's what I told him to call me," Agnes said with an embarrassed laugh, pulling at the neck of her yellow T-shirt. "I've always wanted to be a Nana."

"Sounds good." Julia swallowed a lump of emotion.

"Ron." Ben pointed to Ron and everyone laughed.

"Grandpa is for old men," Ron said with a grin. The metal frame of his glasses caught the sunlight and winked, making him seem particularly merry. "Besides, Ron is easier to say."

He looked young, trim and healthy with his blond hair shot through with a little silver. He appeared younger than his wife and Julia wondered if Mitch would have looked that way. Respectable. Dependable.

She doubted it.

"Ron, it is." Julia nodded definitively as if she were checking that off a list. What to call Grandfather—check.

"Ron," Ben mimicked Julia's nod and tone.

"He's such a sweet baby," Agnes said.

"The sweetest," Julia said, smiling in agreement. She ran her fingers through her son's hair to try and work out a knot of maple syrup near his ear.

"Look at us, forgetting our manners." Agnes stood, suddenly a flurry of activity.

"Would you like something to eat, Julia?" Ron patted the chair next to him at the small kitchen table. "Some coffee?"

"Coffee would be a dream." Julia sat and an uncomfortable silence blanketed the room. They had covered the basics last night. Weather. Flights. How they must just be exhausted. This morning all the unsaid things and the hurt they had caused each other in the past pulled up chairs and sat at the table.

Julia curled her bare toes into the braid rug under the table and folded her hands into her lap, trying to look the opposite of a gold-digging whore. She felt shabby in Mitch's old army T-shirt and pajama bottoms.

I should have worn something nicer, she thought, when unease and doubt slipped under her guard. *I don't have anything nicer.*

"How did you sleep?" Ron asked.

"Like a rock," Julia said brightly and wondered how she could stretch that answer for another hour of conversation. "Very well, thank you."

More silence.

"You have a lovely home." She hoped that didn't make her sound like a gold digger. She was only telling the truth. Every room was filled with books and art and warm rich colors, rugs, beautiful wood floors, light stucco walls with dark wood support beams across the ceiling.

"Thank you." Ron nodded and took a sip of coffee.

Kill me now, Julia thought.

Agnes cleared her throat and Julia looked over to where the woman, short and round, stood in a pool of light from the window above the double ceramic sink. Tears glittered on Agnes's cheeks.

"I am sorry, Julia," she whispered and shook her head. Squeezing her eyes tight. "I was horrible to you and—" She stopped and a single sob came out.

Julia leaped to take the coffee mug out of her mother-in-law's hands. She wrapped her arms around Agnes's curved shoulders. "I wasn't the best, either," she said.

"I was just so upset that you got married without telling us," Agnes went on. "Mitch is—" another sob escaped "—*was* our only son and I know we expected a lot but it was just such a shock. The marriage and then the news of the baby—it was just such a shock."

"Tell me about it," Julia said dryly, relieved when Agnes gave a watery chuckle. "Trust me, getting pregnant and marrying a helicopter pilot was the last thing I expected to happen." *Or wanted to happen,* she didn't say. Her life tended to be made up of things she had to make the best of.

"You know how your son was," Julia said softly. "He was so—" She stopped, at a loss for words, trying to remember exactly what it was that had attracted her so ferociously to Mitch Adams. "Bright, you know? Shiny and bold. Like the world was there just for him to enjoy."

"Yes," Ron agreed. "He was like that."

"He just swept me off my feet." *Swept* wasn't even the right way to describe the sensation. It was as if she had been blinded by the light that always shone around Mitch.

"When I got pregnant—" she cleared her throat,

uncomfortable with the topic "—we hadn't known each other very long."

"A month," Agnes said, obviously casting judgment on Julia's loose morals. Julia swallowed the protestations of her innocence. They seemed pretty stupid, in light of what had happened. What did it matter if Mitch had been her first? She'd been so completely paranoid about pregnancy that they'd used two forms of birth control.

She'd gotten pregnant anyway, after only knowing Mitch for three weeks. She had been so stupid and silly with lust and love.

"I was twenty-one—"

"So young," Agnes said, lifting watery brown eyes to Julia.

"Mitch didn't hesitate. He wanted to get married. He wanted to give our child what you guys gave him."

He just never managed to be around enough to do it.

Agnes, who had been weeping silently, buckled a little and put a hand on the counter to brace herself.

"We wasted so much time with him." Agnes sighed. "Three years. I would give anything to have them back." Her face twisted in agony that struck a chord in Julia's own grief. "*Anything.*"

"Nana!" Ben yelled. "Don't cry!" Ben hated when Julia cried. He got angry and fussy. But when all three of them turned to the little boy he looked away, confused and embarrassed. Julia wondered if he'd ever had the undivided attention of three people.

"You want more pancakes?" Agnes asked Ben and he broke into a beatific grin, revealing all of his little teeth.

"That's a yes," Julia translated needlessly.

"Well, sit and drink your coffee," Agnes said, drying her eyes with a dish towel. "I'll make some more pancakes."

Agnes put a steaming mug of coffee in front of Julia and darted a quick look at Ron. It was a cue of some sort and Julia braced herself. Not for any particular reason; it was the conditioned response of a woman who had never felt as though she really belonged anywhere.

"Julia," Ron started uncomfortably. He drummed his fingers on the table briefly and cleared his throat. There was a glacial undercurrent in the room suddenly and she was not so sure of her welcome here. "What are your, ah, your plans?"

"Plans?" she croaked. This was it. This was "the good to see you, don't be a stranger, but could you move on?" speech. Her stomach churned bile. Maybe Mitch was right. She was a fool for believing in the good things.

"I mean, how long will you be—" Ron and Agnes shared a look "—in California."

Julia put her mug on the table. "I don't have any plans," she said coolly. "We can be on our way today."

Agnes gasped and dropped a plate in the sink, a discordant crash that made all of them jump and Ben fuss. Julia turned to her son and tugged on his ear.

"Nana's bringing you more pancakes, buddy," she whispered, staring at her son to stall for time.

No rest for the weary. She quickly shifted to survival mode. She had the money that the army gave her each month as a widow, but she was still paying off most of

Mitch's debts. The remainder might cover rent some place, although she wasn't sure she wanted to live in a place that could be rented for next to nothing. She'd need to find a job. She would have to get daycare for Ben.

She'd come all the way to New Springs and now didn't have enough money to leave immediately. She'd have to stay until next month's check—

"Do you have to go so soon?" Agnes asked, her hands clenching the counter. "I mean it would be wonderful to have you stay."

"Stay?" Julia asked, not sure she'd heard correctly.

"As long as you like," Agnes insisted. "You can stay here however long. Ron used to teach at the community college over in Lawshaw. I'm sure he could talk to someone there. Get you enrolled in the fall and you could get your degree. I remember Mitch saying something about you wanting a degree."

And another lie from Mitch. Thank you, sweetheart.

"I hadn't given it much thought," Julia said and she really hadn't. Mitch's death, the phone call from Agnes, getting out of Germany, all of that had taken up every minute of her life.

"Well, you can be here and think about it. This house is so empty with just the two of us," Agnes said. Ron stared at Julia levelly, his eyes warm and steadfast.

"You can get your associate degree for just about anything at Lawshaw, can't she, Ron?"

"We would like you to stay," Ron said, cutting through his wife's chatter. "We would like to get to know you and Ben."

"You know," she said with a bright smile, solace like a cool stream of water sliding through her, gently eroding the tension that had built in the last few moments. "You had me with the coffee." She lifted her mug and took a sip while Agnes and Ron laughed.

"What do you think, buddy?" Julia asked her son. "Should we stay?"

Ben smiled, his face radiant and beloved and threw his arms in the air. "Pancake!"

"Sounds unanimous," Ron said.

Julia watched her son clap his hands and she took a big sip of coffee, using both hands so that she wouldn't do the same.

CHAPTER FOUR

JULIA INSISTED on doing the dinner dishes that night and spent a long time with her hands in the warm soapy water, washing Agnes's great-grandmother's china.

Her fingers traced the faded vine around the edge of a dinner plate and she tried to imagine owning something so old. So precious. There was such a feeling of solidity and permanence in this house that she craved to be a part of.

She put Ben to sleep after finishing the dishes and Agnes retired a few hours later, declaring herself pooped. But Julia was too awake to go to bed. In Germany she'd put Ben in daycare three days a week for two hours because she'd been worried that seeing only her day in, day out would stunt him in some way—make him a social outcast in kindergarten. So while he'd learned to share toys with other kids, Julia had taken long runs to drive out her worry, to banish her fears. It seemed a good tactic to use now.

"I am going to go for a walk," she told Ron, who read in his easy chair. He and Agnes had accepted Julia so quickly, had taken care of her and Ben so readily, that she felt a little blank. *What am I supposed to do?* she wondered. She wanted so badly to believe that this comfort and family was real. Was hers. She could settle in, put her feet up and stop treading water. But part of her was still braced—ready for the rejection she still wasn't entirely convinced wasn't going to come.

"Ben is out like a light," she said assuring Ron that she wasn't going to run out and leave him to entertain her toddler.

"Of course, Julia, it's a lovely night," he said with a smile. "Grab my sweater there at the door."

She took the beige cardigan, then stepped outside. The cool twilight embraced her as she admired the low stucco homes that made up the neighborhood. The sweet scent of night-blooming jasmine filled the air and somewhere nearby a dog barked and another answered. Julia gave herself a moment to imagine a life here. A family. Ben and a dog and a man who was honorable. Everything that she'd thought was possible when she married Mitch.

Mitch had loved New Springs—or at least his boyhood. That had been part of the attraction for Julia at first, what drew her to him like metal shavings to a magnet. He'd seemed so grounded, so focused. He'd told her all about this beautiful, fairytale-childhood with adoring parents and a best friend with whom he'd gotten into nothing but trouble.

Jesse.

More importantly, Mitch had claimed to want to recreate that experience with his own family—right down to the best friend and the trouble. She almost laughed at the spectacular failure he had made of that.

She remembered everything Jesse and Mitch had talked about that night in Germany. Every word was imprinted on her, including the directions for the shortcut between Mitch's home and Jesse's.

In this foreign territory, she longed for a trace of something familiar, even if it were only a tidbit from a story she'd heard months ago.

It had not been her intention to seek out Jesse's house when she set out for her walk. But standing on the sidewalk with nowhere to go, her heart became a compass.

She looked around to get her bearings. Mitch's street ended in a forested dead end and she walked toward it, then cut left across one dark lawn and another before finally jumping over a ditch to arrive at the next street. She turned right and saw a small house on the corner with a broken front window.

Jesse's childhood home. Interior lamps cast a shallow pool of light on the porch through the damaged glass and a ladder leaned against the side of the house.

Her heart faltered, her breath clogged in her throat. Her skin pricked as blood rushed through her veins and the world seemed to swim.

Someone was home.

The house surely belongs to someone else now, she told herself, but her feet suddenly had wings. She crossed the street, hoping that somehow Jesse was there.

The sidewalk ended abruptly and she stood on the grass in front of the house.

On the porch, a man sat in a rocking chair with his head in his hands. She couldn't see his face, but chills ran down her arms, across her chest.

He leaned back in his chair, resting his head so he could look up at the sky. The light from the house that fell through the broken window illuminated part of his face—a long straight nose, and a strong chin, hair that gleamed black.

Jesse.

He was here.

She could have dissolved with relief while joy and hope nearly lifted her off her feet.

A dog lying beside him lifted his nose and barked once.

"Rachel?" Jesse said, but his voice was a harsh whisper, practically a growl, and Julia realized he stared at where she stood in the shadows.

He laughed, a weary broken chuckle and again something stirred in her memory. "Just come out, Rach. I'm too tired for this."

"I'm not Rachel," she said as she crossed the dark lawn. She took a step into the pool of light and smiled. "Hello, Jesse."

He stood quickly and the chair tipped sideways. He took a lurching step to the left and looked as though he were going to fall, so Julia leaped forward to help him, but he caught himself against the railing.

"Is this a joke?" he barked.

JESSE BLINKED and shook his head, horrified that the pain meds had managed to crack the lock on this particular fantasy.

Julia Adams.

Close enough to touch. Her short blond hair gleamed in the low light and her skin looked like velvet, cream velvet.

No wonder people get addicted to these drugs. He wondered what he could do with this vision, if he could spend the rest of his life high enough to keep seeing this woman.

"Jesse?" She put her hand on his arm and the touch of her cool skin against his overheated flesh slammed him back to reality.

He pulled away, limping backward, his fantasy now a nightmare. "What are you doing here?"

Her brow furrowed. "I'm, ah," she stuttered and wrapped an oversized brown sweater around her lithe body, as though it would provide protection against him. "Ben and I are visiting Mitch's parents."

Ben. Right. The kid. Mitch's kid. Another life he'd ruined.

"What are you doing *here?*" His voice grated through his throat—every effort to talk hurt. The doctor had told him he shouldn't overwork his damaged larynx. He wondered what the good doctor would think if he started screaming. "On my porch."

Rachel. The house. And now this.

"I was just out for a walk—I—Jesse?" She smiled,

clearly trying to get this little reunion back on track. "I can't believe that you're here. This is amazing."

She took a step toward him, her hand out. But if she touched him, he would shatter. He took another staggering step backward.

"Are you okay?" she asked, her head tilted in concern.

"Fine," he lied quickly, not wanting to see her concern turn to pity. "I'm drunk," he lied.

"Jesse," she whispered, her smile hesitant and somehow beseeching. He knew what she wanted. She wanted him to *remember* what he was trying so hard to forget.

He made the mistake of looking into her endless blue eyes and he saw exactly what he had seen when he met her for the first time.

A million missed opportunities. A thousand unanswered prayers and unspoken wishes.

He'd been kicked in the gut when Mitch opened that door and introduced the woman of Jesse's dreams as his own wife.

And now fate had brought her here to finish Jesse off.

Just in time, the drugs kicked in with a vengeance, the world wavered and he felt himself sliding along with it, carried on the sudden wave of painlessness.

"Sit down," she urged, picking up the rocker he'd knocked over.

Defeated by the pain meds and the appearance of every damn ghost he was trying to outrun, he dropped into the old wooden chair like a stone.

"Last I heard you were still in the hospital," she said, once he was seated.

"I left two weeks ago," he whispered.

"Are you okay—I mean, all right? Your knee and—"

"I'm fine."

She smiled and then laughed nervously. The sound lifted him up, made him weightless.

I'm doing better than Mitch, he thought just to remind himself who was the bad guy in this scene.

"Do you mind if I sit? Just for a minute."

He couldn't say no. She was the way she'd been in Germany—so hungry for company that she'd sit down with the devil just for some conversation. He simply nodded, worried that if he opened his mouth, words he barely allowed himself to think would fly out.

When she sat on the step and wrapped the sweater around her legs, resting her chin on her knees, Jesse let himself go. He let go of all the mistakes he had made and the ghosts that were catching up with him. He left the broken and battered shell of his body and allowed himself to be a man on a porch enjoying the evening with the woman of his dreams. He let possibility and hope hover close. The what-ifs he refused to think about settled on his shoulders like snow.

What if she were here to give him a second chance? What if life weren't as cruel as he had always thought? What if it were possible for him to be forgiven?

"I didn't know you'd left Germany," he said, engaging in conversation even though he knew it was a bad idea. He remembered everything she'd said in

Germany. All the small hints and gifts of herself she'd made during those brief twenty-four hours. He knew she hated mushrooms, couldn't sing, loved to run.

He knew she was so lonely she cried most nights.

"There was nothing keeping me there," she sighed. "I didn't have many friends and my mom was back and forth between Iraq and D.C., so I decided to come here."

"Looking for a family?" he asked, the drugs making him loose and careless.

She smiled at him. "Constantly. You want to adopt us?" She joked but it fell flat in the thick air.

No, sweetheart, he thought, reminded of all the things he really wanted to do to her.

Wain stood up from his spot at Jesse's side with a groan and shuffled over to Julia. He sniffed her, must have decided she was okay and collapsed on the step above her.

She smiled and scratched the old guy's ears.

"Nice dog," she said.

"He's yours if you want him," Jesse said, though his hand itched with a sudden desire to scratch those old ears.

Wain curled up into a ball and soon started to snore.

"Have you heard anything about Caleb?" Julia asked quietly. "I called the hospital a few times to check on him, but then I got so busy with—"

"Still in the coma." He was reluctantly touched that she would keep tabs on the survivors of the accident that had killed her husband. Touched, but not surprised. Julia was a good person. Good in a way most people never were. In a way he never dreamed of being.

He'd stopped checking in on Caleb, mostly because

he, Jesse Filmore, was a coward. He'd already killed three men in that accident, he didn't want to know about the death of another one added to his conscience.

"I got your note," Julia said. She referred to the stupid, morphine-induced lapse of judgment that had resulted in him asking a nurse to write a note to send to Julia. A sympathy card. He couldn't even remember what he'd said. "It really helped." She sighed heavily and smiled at him.

He looked away and said nothing. What could he say? *I've thought of you every day for months. I wish I'd never met you.*

"That night in Germany seems like a million years ago, doesn't it?" She rested her cheek against her knee and watched him, her blue eyes glowing with things he refused to recognize.

Seems like yesterday, he thought but didn't say.

"I couldn't believe it when Mitch showed up out of the blue, and with you, no less." She chuckled and rubbed her nose on her knee as if she were scratching an itch.

The desire to touch her was so strong he could taste it, bitter and hot in the back of his throat. Thanks to meds, everything had a rosy sort of glow, a sparkle, and she was so damn gorgeous—although she would have been so even without the effect of medication.

"We didn't get a lot of warning about the assignment," he told her, his tongue seeming to function its own. "It was real quick."

"I'll say. It was all real quick." She sighed.

Their briefing had taken all of two days and then they were gone. And Mitch was dead. Real quick.

"We had fun though, didn't we?" she asked.

"It was the wine," he said, though Mitch had been the only one who'd drank it.

"It was the company. And the stories." She pulled at a thread in the hem of the sweater. "Those stories Mitch told about you guys growing up and all the trouble you got into."

"Mitch got us in trouble, I was just the cleanup." The official blame-taker. No one had believed the troubled kid with the drunk for a father and everyone had believed the star football player who could always outrun the cops.

"Come on," she teased. "Mitch said painting the water tower was your idea."

He smiled, remembering. "Yeah, you're right."

There had been good times with Mitch. His wild streak had called out to Jesse's own and in high school there was nowhere he'd rather have been than causing trouble with Mitch.

Mitch, however, had adopted that wildness as his life mission. Jesse found that, by default, he'd still been expected to clean up after his old buddy, long after the thrill had worn off for him.

She wrapped her arms around her knees and lifted her feet a little off the step so she balanced on her butt.

"Mitch told me you were a dancer," Jesse blurted.

Julia shook her head, her eyes suddenly darker. "My husband said a lot of things…most of them not true."

"He wasn't known for his honesty."

Julia's eyes got sadder and Jesse could feel sympathy churn through his gut. The silence stretched and he watched her profile, the sweet line of her cheek, her nose. The perfect rose of her mouth. He was the only other person in the world who knew what Mitch was really like—and high on painkillers he couldn't deny her the small bit of comfort she clearly needed.

"He was hard on the people who loved him," he finally said.

She turned wide eyes on him. "You sound like a man with experience." She tried to smile, but failed, and that told him so much about what being married to Mitch had cost her.

His hands itched to stroke her narrow shoulders, but not for comfort. Not as further cleanup after Mitch.

Jesse wanted to touch her for himself.

"Everybody in this town loved him, but no one knew him. There was only one guy stupid enough to be his best friend."

She bit her lip and he wondered if he'd gone too far. If he'd read her wrong and her emotions for her husband were stronger than he thought. Maybe she didn't know what a bastard Mitch was.

"He was pretty good at keeping the worst of himself hidden. Until it was too late."

"Remember that when you get tired of all the Mitch stories this town can tell. These people never knew him like we knew him."

He met her crystal gaze and they were suddenly knit

together, not just by that morning in Germany, and not by the terrible, forbidden things he felt for her, but in their knowledge of Mitch Adams.

The Mitch the whole town refused to believe existed.

"I thought I married someone else," she said. "The way he talked, I thought… Well, I thought he was a different person."

"I understand," he said. An expression of gratitude spread over her features.

"It's been a long time since someone has said that to me."

The moment stretched taut and then snapped. He looked away with a cough—hot and uncomfortable with how much he still wanted his best friend's widow.

She laughed nervously and wiped at her eyes. "Look at me," she said. "I arrive out of the blue to start crying on your porch."

"Go ahead. Cry away."

She turned aside and studied the stars while he studied her. Birds called and dogs barked and Jesse lifted himself from the chair and stupidly, foolishly, was about to lower himself onto the steps so he could touch her, smell her. Press his lips to the quick pulse that beat in her neck.

"Do you know Mitch's parents real well?"

The air went cold, dousing the flames in him.

"Yeah." He sat down heavily.

"What are they like?"

"They hate me," he said, getting right to the point. "They'd hate you sitting on this porch with me."

"Because of the accident?"

The word shattered the serene picture they made like a pane of glass. His intentions, his desire for her, turned to ash. They weren't two strangers engaged in warm conversation, carefully scoping out the edges of their feelings for each other.

Mitch was between them. Mitch and his death and the accident.

He almost laughed. *Accident?* People could be so stupid. Didn't anyone realize there were no such things as accidents?

"Among other things," he said and shrugged.

She must blame him, at least a little, for Mitch's death. How could she not? Her husband was dead while Jesse was alive. In his head the math was simple.

"Jesse?" She looked at him warily. The pressure in his chest grew unbearable. "That morning in Germany when you—"

"Don't." He groaned and shook his head. The honesty in her eyes and the ache in his chest defeated him so, like a coward, he looked away. "Don't say anything. I'm sorry. I'm…sorry."

"Sorry?"

He refused to look at her, willing her to get off his porch. He had been stupid to let her stay. Drugs or no drugs.

The silence built like a wall between them. Brick by brick, until he wasn't even sure he could see her.

Finally she stood, swiped her hands over her butt and took a step toward the shadows of the lawn.

"Good night, Jesse." She took another step, all but disappearing in the dark. "I'm so glad you're here. I never expected a friend—"

"We're not friends, Julia," he said, from his side of the wall of silence and lies. "Don't come back."

JULIA DIDN'T SLEEP WELL. She was plagued by Jesse's ravaged face and the sharp-fanged nightmares Mitch's old room seemed to spark.

She had to put Mitch's prom picture facedown in the hopes that she'd stop seeing it when she shut her eyes. But it was useless, Mitch's ghost lived in this room, lived in these quiet moments of doubt that came at night. He mocked her and reminded her of how much she'd fallen out of love with him. Of how badly she'd wished he'd been more like Jesse.

In fact, that night in Germany with Jesse and Mitch, she'd wished he *was* Jesse.

And to make it all worse, there was nothing she could do to shake loose Jesse's words. They ran on a loop whether her eyes were closed or not.

I'm sorry.

She'd carried the memory of that morning in Germany with Jesse in her heart for months. She'd lived on it when food tasted like dirt. She'd breathed it through Mitch's funeral and through all the long nights.

And he was sorry. Sorry it ever happened.

We're not friends. Don't come back.

She flopped over on her back and stared up at the

ceiling where the shadows of the maple branches danced and that morning rushed back to her in painful detail....

"All done," Julia whispered to Ben. She held out her hands as if to prove she wasn't holding anymore puréed peaches. "All gone."

Ben mimicked her, shouting her words back to her in his gibberish.

"Sh," she whispered. "We have to be quiet. Daddy and Jesse are sleeping."

Jesse Filmore—the much-boasted-about friend of Mitch's youth—slept in the living room, draped over the too-small couch. And Mitch slept on in the bedroom, smelling slightly of the wine he'd drank last night and the uncomfortable, lousy sex he'd attempted before dawn. He'd come to bed late, full of drunken apologies and tears. There'd been another girl. A reporter or a contractor or something. She'd meant nothing, he swore.

None of them meant anything.

Julia wiped Ben's face, holding his head still so she could get the cereal from under his chin, and pulled him out of the makeshift high chair she'd rigged on the kitchen counter.

She filled his sippy cup with juice and water and walked behind him as he toddled over to the table she'd set up next to the only window in the apartment that let in the morning light.

She sat in her chair and Ben tried to pull himself up into her lap.

"Up you go," she whispered, giving him a boost.

He repeated the tone of her voice, if not her exact words.

She had a few toys on the table and he played while she rested her chin on his head and looked out the window to the street of duplicate houses, covered in Christmas lights and snow that made up the family housing on the barracks.

Houses filled with women just like her. Alone. Lonely. Worried half the time. Scared the other half. They filled their time with book groups and sewing circles, coffee klatches and grief-counseling sessions.

She went, dragging Ben and bad pasta salad, wearing the mask of a woman still in love with her husband. She wore that mask until she thought she'd scream.

She rested her head against the window.

"Jesse," Ben whispered and her heart squeezed tight at the mention of the handsome stranger her husband had brought home last night. It had been a surprise, not just Jesse, but Mitch's appearance as well. She'd had no notice of their leave. No chance to prepare herself.

Not that she could have.

Not for Jesse Filmore.

He'd walked into her home, he'd shaken her hand, he'd smiled at her, played with her son. He'd even gone so far as to compliment her spaghetti and she knew she'd found the very limit to her foolish heart.

She'd watched him all night from the corner of her eye, from beneath her lashes like some lovesick teenager.

Maybe that's what I am.

Maybe that's what this feeling is.

He was a good man—it was the clearest thing she'd ever seen. As real as the sun behind the window. He'd walked into the room and she'd known him. Known him as though she'd been beside him his whole life. Jesse was the kind of man she'd imagined Mitch to be. The kind of man she wanted Mitch to be and it burned her like acid to have him in her house.

"Jesse," Ben said louder and Julia turned finally to shush him, only to find Jesse standing in the doorway to the kitchen. A bright and dark angel brought into her life to remind her of the mistakes she'd made, of the things she'd never have.

His black eyes were a hot touch on her face.

She opened her mouth, but there was nothing to say. No empty chatter in her head to fill up this moment. She wanted to stay this way with this man's eyes on her— intense and dark and so knowing she felt naked.

Ben scrambled off her lap and ran past Jesse into the TV room.

"There's…" Her mouth was sticky, dry. But before she could try to finish her sentence Jesse crossed the kitchen in three steps, stopping only when he was right in front of her. Less than a foot away. She could have reached out to touch the hem of his gray T-shirt.

You're married, she told herself—a stupid reminder of the vows she'd taken, binding herself to a man who had never meant them.

Jesse crouched in front of her, until his face was level with hers.

She grasped her hands in her lap until her knuckles went white.

"You deserve better," Jesse whispered, and her lips

parted on a broken breath. He reached out and his fingers, the very tips of them, brushed her face in a nearly imperceptible touch. Her cheek and the curve of her jaw. As though she were diamonds and gold to him. Precious.

She shut her eyes and hated herself for wanting him so much.

Jesse stood, jammed his fingers through his short military hair as if he wished he could pull it out.

"I can't stay here," he said.

Julia didn't stop him and when she heard her front door click shut the tattered, threadbare life she'd managed to hold together split at the seams, falling in terrible ruin around her.

Julia closed her eyes wishing the memory away. Wishing it on another person. She'd arrived in New Springs looking for a family, to set down roots…and finding Jesse was like a dream come true. She was so close to all she ever wanted, only to have it ripped away.

Don't come back here.

It's because you expect other people to make you happy. Mitch's voice revealed her worst fears about herself, the bitter truth she'd always suspected but never wanted to admit. *You expect other people to do everything for you. You're useless. You're worse than useless.*

The pain burrowed into her chest and made a home in the soft tissue surrounding her heart. She'd thought she was tougher than this, that Mitch's lies and infidelity had turned her cold and hard. But she was wrong. That pain was nothing compared to what she felt right now.

Jesse's rejection ruined her.

Such a fool. Such a sucker.

She rolled to her side and punched her pillow, trying to get comfortable. The wonderful mattress that had cradled her last night now seemed too soft. Lumpy in places. Hard in others.

You're impossible to please. You want too much.

Ben sighed, murmured something in his sleep and rolled toward her, curving himself into her body, into that little space against her chest that had been made for him.

She had to get her act together. She had to make a life for her son. She couldn't expect other people to help her with this anymore.

"No more," she whispered.

What are you gonna do? Mitch's voice asked and she could practically see his sneer, the snide superiority in his eyes that had made her feel two inches tall for most of her married life. *Live off my folks? Sleep with my best friend? You heard him, he's sorry for that morning. It was a mistake—*

"No more!" she said, louder this time to shut up the voices in her head. To convince herself that she meant it.

Things were going to change.

She was going to get a job. Tomorrow. And she'd only stay with the Adamses as long as was absolutely necessary, until she'd paid off the last of Mitch's debts and could save some money for a place of her own.

And she'd stay away from Jesse—just as he'd asked. She'd remove her heart, set it someplace else where she couldn't feel its pain.

JESSE DIDN'T SLEEP. He was no fool, he knew the nightmares waited on the other side of consciousness. And frankly, tonight he had no taste for fire and the crash and Mitch's knowing eyes.

He sat on the porch for a good long time, his eyes open and the image of Julia—sitting so close…right there…within arm's reach—burned into his retinas.

He leaned his head against the old rocker he'd made in high-school shop class and imagined standing up on two good legs, walking down the street, jumping the ditch, crossing the yards. He imagined circling the Adams' house and climbing the rainspout up to the roof of the kitchen. From there he could walk up to Mitch's second-floor bedroom window. It was easy. He'd done it a thousand times.

It would be so simple to open that window, to ease into that dark hushed room, warm and alive with the scent of Julia, sleeping on that old bed. There'd be moonlight and silence and—

Jesse stood and the rocking chair slid backward, crashing into the house.

This has got to stop.

The world swam from the drugs and he gave himself a moment to get his knee under him before he stalked into the dark house.

He had been right to tell her to stay away. She had to or he wouldn't survive. He was moving on with his life, putting the accident and Mitch and this town behind him.

So he grabbed another bottle of water and headed out

the rusty aluminum back door that had not been changed in all of Rachel's meddling renovations.

He'd been here two days and one night and so far all he'd been able to get done was write a list of all the things that needed to get done. The roof, the back porch, the kitchen floor—the list was a long one. And he was more tired than he'd thought. His long stay at the hospital had worn him down. The weakness was aggravating, but there wasn't much he could do about it. Slowly, each day he felt a little better, a little more as though he could get the work done.

The only reason he'd needed the painkillers tonight was because he'd spent most of the day on the roof, climbing up and down the ladder.

His knee was getting stronger and the work helped. He thought of it like conditioning for San Diego and the construction he and Chris were going to do. Preparation for his real life.

The night was cool, the sky clear and deep, and the air seemed damp. Everything seemed damp after the Middle East, where the desert turned everything into grit. Human beef jerky is what Dave Mancino used to say.

That's all I am, walking beef jerky.

Jesse smiled—Dave had been a funny kid. Cocky as all get-out, but funny. Five months after the accident and Jesse was just now getting to the point that he could remember anything about those boys other than their deaths.

A million times a day he wished he'd backed Mitch instead of listening to his gut.

The one time in my life I decide not to do things Mitch's way and the guy dies.

Jesse didn't know whether to laugh or put a bullet in his head.

He stepped onto the long grass and left footprints in the dewy lawn as he crossed the backyard to the garage nestled back amongst some pines and more weeds. The door had once been red but now was the faded gray of weathered wood. The whole structure leaned slightly to the left and Jesse figured gravity would soon take care of the rest.

The garage had never housed a car. Inexplicably, his dad had once come home from the bar driving a golf cart and it had stayed in the garage for a week until the cops had come looking for it.

They'd all laughed over that.

What had always been housed in the garage—and Jesse was half hoping had been sold or lost or stolen over the years—were Granddad's old woodworking tools. The planers and awls and chisels fit Jesse's hand as though they had been born there. He had spent a lot of years in this garage with the tools, pretending that the world outside the sweet smell of fresh oak didn't exist.

He could do with a little of that pretending right now.

The heavy door slid back on the nearly rusted rollers and the odor of sour, rotting wood poured out. He reached for the light switch, and was surprised when it flickered on, illuminating the cracked cement floor.

Along the back wall was the workbench he'd made himself a million years ago and on the wall above it, still as neatly arranged as he'd left them, were the tools.

When he was younger they'd offered him, if not a way out of his family and his home, a way to survive.

Jesse took a deep breath and stepped into the musty familiarity of the garage looking for something, anything, that could be saved.

CHAPTER FIVE

"YOU'RE A KILLER," David Mancino's father said. "We trusted our boy with you and you brought him home in a body bag."

"But look." Jesse tried to show Mr. Mancio what he'd brought in exchange for Dave. He held out his bloody palms and tried to give Mr. Mancio the still-beating heart.

"What the hell is wrong with you, boy?" Mr. Mancio smacked Jesse's hands away and the heart fell to the ground. "We heard you were crazy!"

It's ruined, Jesse thought, watching the heart pump blood into the dirt. No one is going to want that now.

"Wait, wait. I brought more, just a second." Jesse waved over the thin blond woman with the haunted blue eyes he'd never been able to forget and she, in turn, led Wain and a man in a black hostage mask. "See, you can have the dog, and the—"

Jesse woke to the sound of a key sliding into the lock on his back door. The dream vanished and he traveled from sleep to battle ready in seconds—another little gift from the United States Army. He could kill a man in a hundred ways and he hadn't fallen fully asleep in over six years.

The pain meds he'd popped last night made his brain feel thick and stupid, but the well-honed instinct in him was still razor sharp.

He crept from the couch, barefoot and in his blue jeans, toward the back door, where he had heard the distinct sound of a lock sliding open.

Wainwright snored on his pillow.

Some guard dog you turned out to be.

He fully expected Rachel to be busting in, and he relished letting her know in no uncertain terms that she wasn't welcome. Her days of coming and going in this house were over.

But he yanked open the door only to find Mac Edwards, his arms filled with grocery bags. Jesse rocked back on his heels.

"Help a guy out, would you?" Mac asked over the perforated edge of one of the bags. The look in his light blue eyes went through Jesse like a knife. It was the look his men used to give him—respect and a general gladness to see him.

"I don't—" Jesse started, but Mac stepped in and pushed the bags into Jesse's chest. Instinctively, Jesse caught Mac's burden and Mac used the opportunity to barge in.

"Nice one," Jesse growled, his throat rusty.

"Old trick I learned from a nine-year-old," Mac said over his shoulder. He walked past Jesse, through the small mudroom and into the kitchen.

The nine-year-old Mac referred to was him. Jesse had used the trick to dog Rachel and Mac's every step.

Jesse shut the door with his foot and followed his old friend to dump the groceries onto the counter. He yanked opened the refrigerator door and began shoving the bags' contents into the nearly empty fridge.

"Just as we suspected, you're living on road trip food." Mac reached around Jesse to hold up a turkey sandwich Jesse had gotten from the gas station out by the highway. "Not fit for human consumption."

"Works fine by me," Jesse said. He'd been avoiding the grocery store and all of the good citizens of New Springs.

"Good to see you, man." Mac pulled Jesse into a hug before he could say two words. "It's really good to see you." Mac thumped him on the back, which hurt but, for some reason, Jesse didn't say anything. He stood motionless, like a scared animal in the hard grip of Mac's arms. Emotion leaped in him.

I missed you, he thought.

"It's good to see you, too," he finally managed to say. He squeezed Mac tight across the shoulders and then pushed away.

They both laughed awkwardly and Mac held Jesse out at arm's length. It had been three years since they'd seen each other at his mother's funeral and Jesse had kept his distance that day.

The moment stretched and Jesse took in the changes time had made in his old friend. Mac was big, thick across the chest and through the arms. His work in the sun had turned his skin brown and given him wrinkles and creases at the corners of his mouth and eyes. But his smile was still quick and his eyes sharper than ever.

"You look old," Jesse joked.

"You look like roadkill," Mac shot back and Jesse felt as though he were soaking up the warmth of the sun.

"I see you've made yourself at home." Mac pointed at the broken front window.

Stupidly, excuses came to Jesse's lips but he stopped himself in time. He didn't have to explain anything to anyone. Not to Rachel and not to Mac.

Even though he did owe Mac a lot.

"Well—" he grinned like the old troublemaker he'd been "—she did leave the house to me."

Mac laughed and scratched at the day-old whiskers on his face. "Man, you know, that's what I always remembered about you." He pointed at Jesse. "Every time you got into trouble and I had to go down to the police station, you'd be sitting in lockup with this sly grin on your face like everything was going according to plan."

"What else was I supposed to do?" he asked. "I was so scared half the time I could barely see straight. Which is why I called you instead of the old man."

"I was too good to you. I should have left you there, might have scared some sense into you."

"Probably," Jesse agreed. "But you were always a sucker for strays."

They both smiled, but the rosy reunion scene soon faded away. They were two men with only the past and his sister in common—both of which Jesse was trying to forget.

"What are you doing here, Mac?"

"I would think that was obvious." Mac's laughter was gone, replaced by a sad earnestness in his eyes. "You come back into town after all these years, and you think I'm not going to come by and say hello? Come on, Jesse, you're smarter than that."

Jesse shrugged. "I'm leaving in a—"

Mac walked into the small living room before Jesse could finish. He had to follow. What else could he do? This was Mac. He couldn't hit him.

"Amanda's in the truck. I practically had to tie her down to keep her from following me." Mac pointed out the broken window at a gorgeous teenager staring at them from the passenger seat of a truck.

Amanda lifted her hand in a slight wave.

"Wave to her," Mac insisted, lifting his own arm in a big salute.

Jesse raised one finger. "She sure grew up," he whispered.

"You're telling me. Seems like yesterday I was teaching her how to ride a bike." Mac turned to him with a smile. "She's dying to see you. Hasn't been able to stop talking about you since she knew you were back. Some of those letters and packages you never responded to were from her."

Jesse remembered she'd covered her letters and packages with drawings of bugs and plants—she definitely had her father's love of science. Her letters had been filled with questions and goofy stories about trying out for the cheerleading squad and not getting in.

"I wrote her once," he said, and from Mac's shocked expression he realized that little note had been a secret between his niece and him.

He could not, for the life of him, figure out why he had written her back and told her the cheerleaders missed out on all the fun during the games anyway.

"I don't feel guilty, Mac, if that's what you are trying to do."

Mac stared at him a long time, that weighted assessment that used to torture Jesse when he was a kid. One of those looks from Mac and he'd confess everything.

But Jesse wasn't a kid, and all of his confessions were his own.

"Jesse," Mac said with a slight smile that didn't reach his eyes, "you're carrying so much guilt it's amazing you can even stand up."

Jesse studied the play of sunlight through the poplar out front.

"Well, you've got plenty of food in those bags," Mac said, breaking the thick silence between them. "Rachel's worried about you. Said you looked like a stray dog."

Mac looked him over and Jesse knew what he saw, the scars and the lopsided collarbone, the ribs that were all too visible, the muscles that were wiry and tough.

"That doesn't look healed," he murmured, pointing to Jesse's damaged collarbone.

"It was a bad set." Jesse touched the slight bend. "They wanted to rebreak it and try again, but I thought it gave me some character." He tried to make a joke to ease the unbearable pressure between them. His body was witness to how close he'd come to dying and Mac was taking it all in.

"Does it hurt?"

Jesse shook his head.

"God. We're just so glad you're alive, Jess," Mac whispered and a muscle in his jaw clenched. It seemed as though Mac was going to grab him in one of those bear hugs again and Jesse's body tensed in fight-or-flight mode. Instead Mac tucked the hand he had raised into his pocket.

Jesse looked away. Too many emotions. *Why the hell did you think this would be easy?* His plans to come home and sell the house didn't include encounters with Rachel and Mac. Which was stupid, really, because if there were one thing Jesse knew in this world, it was that he could always count on Mac.

"Well." Mac heaved a huge breath. "I gotta get back to the farm. We're harvesting." Suddenly, Mac threw his head back and laughed his big loud bark that filled the room. In the corner, Wainwright woke up with a start and a growl.

You're too late, Wain.

"Remember when I hired you for harvest and you were what…sixteen?"

Jesse focused his eyes out the window, watched a cloud inch its way over the sun and fought to find that place in himself that was removed from the past, Mac, his sister. He needed to be far away from all of it, back in the desert.

"I needed you to drive the tractor from—"

"I remember," Jesse murmured. "Ancient history, Mac. I'm trying—"

"And you couldn't figure out how to put it in Park—"

"I remember," he said, his voice louder and colder.

"The thing rolled down Main Street and Sheriff McNeil tried to give you a ticket until I—"

"Damn it, Mac!" he yelled, breathing hard. "I remember."

The room was silent and Jesse immediately regretted his crack. Things were building in him, pushing against his bones and his skin, clawing through his efforts to remain detached.

"I don't think you do, Jess." Mac's eyes turned solemn, sad. "Rachel and I have written you every week for the past three years, because *we* remember." He looked out the window to where his daughter sat in the truck. "My daughter wrote you. She got classmates to write you and, man, if you had seen her four years ago you wouldn't have thought it was possible for her to care about someone else."

Jesse saw so much in Mac's eyes. He saw every late night Mac had bailed him out of jail because Mitch had grabbed some woman's purse, or he and Mitch had tipped over the pop machines at the high school. Every twenty bucks Mac had loaned him when times got hard. Jesse saw the pride Mac had felt when he'd gone off to basic training. He saw the calm and strong way Mac had constantly stood by him when Rachel had deserted them both.

"I'm glad things worked out for you, Mac. I really

am. You loved Rachel for a long time." Jesse struggled to keep his voice steady. "But I am not here to mend bridges with my sister. I don't know her and I don't want to know her. There's no point in it."

"Well, that's too bad because she's a heck of a person." Mac turned to leave. "I'll come by and see you tomorrow."

"There's no point, Mac. I'm getting rid of this house. Even if I have to tear it down with my own hands."

Mac laughed. "Well, it's a good thing you started with the roof. It needs a new one."

The closing door sounded loud as it shut behind Mac. Jesse watched as Mac appeared from the side of the house and climbed into the truck. He drove off with a honk of his horn as though they were a normal family who got along and Amanda lifted her arm out the window in farewell.

Such simple gestures. But the expectations behind them weighed Jesse down. He had to get out of here fast. Otherwise affection and caring would lock him in the prison of this town.

"HE DOESN'T SEEM DIFFERENT than he did three years ago. Is he? I mean, he just looks skinnier," Amanda said, unable to look away from the guy standing in the broken window. Three years ago at Eva's funeral, he'd looked mean. He didn't look like a cold-blooded killer now. Not that she knew what that kind of person looked like, but still, it was hard to imagine that guy killing his best friend, the way the whole town was saying he had.

She tilted her head to stare at his shrinking figure in

the rearview mirror. He looked like the dog she and her dad had found by the highway last year. Cold, angry and flea-bitten.

She smiled at the idea.

Gotta write that one down.

The article she was trying to write on Uncle Jesse for her English assignment was going pretty slow, no thanks to Dad making her sit in the car like a baby. Her teacher had already warned her twice that the project was worth thirty percent of her final grade.

When she brought home a C in that class it was going to be all Dad's fault.

They turned toward Main Street, making Jesse and the house out of sight. Amanda faced her dad, who looked as though he'd seen a ghost. A skinny, lopsided ghost.

"Whoa, Dad. Are you okay?"

He nodded. He wiped a hand over his face and sat back against the truck seats with a shaky sigh.

"Tell you the truth, Amanda, I don't know who that guy was." He shook his head.

An illicit thrill shot through her. "Did he, like, pull a gun or something?"

"No." Dad looked at her askance, as if she'd asked if Jesse wore human skulls around his neck. Which, frankly, she thought he might do when no one was looking. The way everybody talked about this long-lost uncle of hers, she figured the guy was half wolf or something. A wild animal trying to readjust to society.

"Was he wearing clothes?" The scary thought just occurred to her.

"Of course, Amanda. Don't be silly."

"If you'd let me meet him, I wouldn't have all these silly questions."

Dad groaned. "We've been over this a million times, Amanda. I know you want to meet him, and you will—"

"When?"

"Soon. We've got to give the guy time. He's been through a lot and he needs space to be comfortable and get to know us."

"It's not like we're going to get to know each other if I have to stay in the truck all the time. I'm sixteen, Dad. I'm not a kid," she grumbled, crossing her arms across her chest.

Really, Dad was getting a little lame in his old age.

"You wanted to come and I told you that was the deal."

"You and Mom act like he's crazy—like he'd attack me." Oh, God, that would get her an A in English for sure. "Do you think he'd attack me?"

"You've got more imagination than this whole town put together." Dad didn't sound as though that was a good thing.

"Well, the whole town thinks he's going to kill all of us in our sleep or something."

"You know that's not true."

"Clara at the grocery store said that Jesse had been trying to kill Mitch Adams since they were kids. It just took him a few years to get the job done. But Rita says that's not true, that it was the other way around."

"Why are you talking to Clara and Rita about this?"

"Everybody is talking about it. Uncle Jesse coming

back is, like, the biggest thing since the football team won conference."

"What else is everyone saying?"

"That Jesse killed Mitch and three other guys."

"It was an accident."

"I also heard that he went to jail for beating a kid up to get his tennis shoes in high school. I heard he beat the kid so bad he had to have total reconstructive surgery. "

"That's completely exaggerated."

"I heard he got three girls pregnant."

Dad finally turned to her, furious. "That's not true!"

"I'm just telling you what I hear." Amanda held up her hands like the innocent messenger she was.

"Jesse was a tough kid in high school and he did some things that I'm sure he regrets. But he's not half as bad as what—"

"Then why can't I meet him?"

Her father swallowed. She knew what he would say. Something lame about her being too young and Jesse being too unpredictable and how he'd hurt Mom for years and how Dad didn't want Amanda's feelings to get hurt.

"He will meet you when he's ready. When he's... better. Okay?"

Amanda didn't want to wait until Jesse was better. She wanted to know him now. She wanted to find out if he really did all those things. If he was as bad as people said he was.

Well, that was part of it.

The other part of it had to do with knowing exactly how it felt to be tired, cold and flea-bitten.

"Amanda?" They were stopped at a light and Dad was staring at her in that old way of his. It had been four years since she ran away, four years since she finally told the truth and Dad still sometimes looked at her as though he didn't know what she was going to do next.

"I'm serious. Leave Jesse alone until your mom or I say it's okay. Don't go over there by yourself."

"Fine." She huffed like she was angry with this decision of his.

But Thursday after school, she'd skip cross-country practice and do some investigative journalism.

She turned her head so Dad couldn't see her grin. What if Jesse did pull a gun on her? She felt giddy with possibility.

This story was going to be awesome!

CHAPTER SIX

THURSDAY MORNING, the college application papers were propped up against the plate sitting in what had quickly become "her spot."

Julia was happy to have a spot. Any spot. At anyone's table. But those application forms sent a jittery blast of anxiety right through her. She didn't want to have to disappoint Agnes so soon, but college wasn't in the cards for her.

"I hope you don't mind," Agnes said, standing in the doorway to the kitchen. "I just thought—" She shrugged. "I just want to help."

She looked so nervous, so unsure of herself, standing there in the sunlight, that Julia smiled to put her at ease. Agnes took that as the invitation she needed.

"You can get your degree in just about anything. Dental hygienist, legal secretary, teacher's aide. Anything."

All of those things sounded terrible. Dental hygienist? Julia would rather go back to waiting tables.

"Look, Agnes, I'm not sure—"

"You don't have to pick your courses right now. Just fill out the early application form and then you can take your time looking at the pamphlet. That way you can get acceptance out of the way and later talk to some counselors to help you make a decision."

"But—" This wasn't what she wanted. Her future was a murky at best, but she knew it didn't include school. "I know Mitch told you I wanted to get a degree, but I am a terrible student—"

"Well, who isn't as a kid? Mitch was such a poor student, if it hadn't been for sports I don't know that he would have even graduated."

"Up!" Instinctively Julia bent in answer to her son's cry, but he wasn't standing in front of her with his arms up demanding to be held. He stood in front of Agnes.

"Up, Nana."

"Well, good morning, little boy," Agnes cooed and lifted the heavy baby into her arms. "Are you hungry?" she asked and when Ben nodded, she smiled. "Of course you are. Let's go see what Nana's got to eat." Ben patted Agnes's face.

"Morning, Nana," he said and Agnes turned to kiss his hand. Ben's hair stood up in an airy blond cloud and his grandmother slowly patted it down, stroking his head and face as she did it.

Finally she turned to Julia. "Just fill out the application. You still have plenty of time to make the decision. It would mean a lot to us to be able to help you get your degree."

Julia nodded, words deserting her.

What would it hurt? she thought and tried to swallow the sickly sweet taste of gratitude and obligation from the back of her throat. She'd come to New Springs to give Ben a family and for the love that Agnes gave Ben, so Julia would fill out a million applications.

She uncapped the pen that had been left beside the papers and sat to fill out the paperwork for another dream that wasn't hers.

AFTER A BREAKFAST of yogurt and fruit, Julia loaded her son into the old stroller. He had to practically kiss his knees to sit in it he was so big, but she didn't have the money for a new one, yet. She prayed the screws, worn out wheels and cheap fabric would hold out just a little bit more.

"You gonna do some sight-seeing?" Ron asked, lowering the newspaper from in front of his face. The envelope with her completed application stuck out of his shirt pocket. He'd insisted on delivering it himself, as if it would change the inevitable outcome. Even if accepted, she had little intention of attending. But she'd cross that bridge when she got to it.

"I'm going to look for a job."

"What?" Agnes asked, her voice and eyes sharp. "Why?"

Julia was taken aback by Agnes's sudden tone.

"You've been so generous, but Ben and I have to make some effort to be independent." She tried to make it a joke but Ron and Agnes didn't laugh. "I'd feel better if I was working at least part-time. Saving up some money so we could get our own place."

"Why?" Agnes asked. "Why do you want to leave?"

Clearly the woman took this personally, something Julia had not expected at all. She'd expected some halfhearted protestations and reassurances that they were welcome to stay as long as they liked, but the deeply wounded look on Agnes's weathered face surprised the heck out of her.

"It's not that I want to leave—"

"Then why do it? You and Ben can stay here. We're happy to help you out in any way. Besides with you going to school what would be the point?"

Julia looked between the two, but they shared the same stern expression. It was as if her not wanting to be a burden was an insult to them, as if she were throwing their hospitality in their face. She hadn't anticipated the costs of being a family with the Adamses.

Julia sighed, defeated by their questions and their expectations.

God, you're spineless, Mitch's voice chimed in.

"We're just going to go check things out. I need to get some kind of job, I can't live off your goodwill forever. We should contribute something to the household."

The older couple looked at each other in silence and Julia felt as if she'd been tricked. What happened to the happy welcoming people she'd met a few days ago?

It's my life, she thought with a surge of rebellion. She had every right to want her independence.

"Well, at least you've got good daycare," Ron finally said with a wink.

Julia heaved a sigh of relief, unsure of what she'd have done if they'd continued to object.

Ben waved goodbye and she maneuvered the stroller

out the door and down the slate path to the sidewalk. She took the long way, down two blocks, deliberately walking past Jesse's house. It looked even prettier in the sunlight. The red geraniums bobbed in the breeze like rubied sock puppets. The ladder still leaned against the house and her eyes, despite her best intentions, searched for Jesse.

He was on the roof, his back to her, naked under the sun. Jeans clung to lean hips as he stood from his crouch, his long, tough body unfurling so he could toss an armful of shingles into the side yard. He tugged on the wrists of his gloves and twisted at the waist as if getting rid of a kink.

He shouldn't be working so hard so soon.

The sunshine and sweat of his labor made the red color of his scars against his pale skin even more alarming. More shocking. He was all bone and muscle and scar tissue. But even the crooked collarbone and the ribs that pushed at his skin didn't detract from his breathtaking beauty.

His arms, belly and back still rippled with muscles, exuding the sort of power that seemed only slightly diminished from when she'd seen him in Germany.

His black hair had gone shaggy over the months in the hospital and now covered his ears and flirted with his eyes. He brushed it out of the way, looking right at her in the process. His dark eyes cut through her like a flashlight in a dark room. She felt like a thief, caught touching something forbidden.

His eyes didn't move, they stayed locked on her and

everything in her started a slow burn. Blood pooled between her legs, in flesh so forgotten it hurt. Her skin ignited under his hot gaze, her mouth fell open, suddenly parched for air. Dying for something she didn't have. This was the connection she'd been missing; this is what it was supposed to be between men and women. Surely, Jesse hadn't meant it when he told her to stay away. How could he deny— Just as she was about to step forward, get closer to him, Jesse bent down to his work.

He tore up shingles as though she weren't even there.

"Mama?" Ben asked. "Let's walk."

The blood rushed from her breasts to her face.

"Right, Ben. Let's get walking."

She jerked Ben's stroller and stalked away from Jesse Filmore as if the hounds of hell were after her.

JESSE HAD TO GET OFF the roof; his hands shook so much it wasn't safe. As soon as he was sure she was long gone, he climbed down the ladder and went inside.

Jesus, that woman had the power to kill him. He went to the sink, tore off his gloves and splashed cold water over his face, sluicing it down his chest and over his back, trying to cool his damn body.

He had to get out of town. If he could keep going with the roof at this rate he might be able to get it done in a week—two at the most.

He nearly groaned. Two weeks of pretending she wasn't a hundred meters away? He shook his head, spraying the room with water droplets. He had to find a real estate agent. And screw him doing the roof on his own, he needed professionals. Guys who could get it done in a few days.

He went into the living room to the small telephone table where for years the yellow pages had sat collecting dust. But, of course, the table was bare. He banged his way through the cupboards under the TV stand and the end table, but they were all bare, too.

"Damnit!"

"Uncle Jesse?"

Everything in him went cold. Then hot. He turned to the doorway to see the blond teenager who had stared at him through the hole in the picture window.

"I'm not your uncle," he said. Stupidly, faced with Amanda's brilliant blue eyes, that's the best he could come up with. *You're really doing a great job here, handling all these women. She's, like, sixteen—surely you can scare her away.*

"Well, not by blood. But marriage counts." She shrugged her thin shoulder and the sun hit the fall of white-blond hair along her narrow face.

"Can I come in?" she asked, with a half grin.

Man, she looks like Mac.

"Will you leave if I say no?"

She pretended to think it over and finally shook her head, that grin turning into a beatific smile. "Probably not."

"What do you want?" he asked.

"My final project for English class is due in a few weeks and I was hoping…" She poked her pinky finger through the metal spiral at the end of the notebook she held in her hand. "I was hoping I could interview you."

"No." He walked away from the window toward the kitchen, hoping she'd get the hint, but worried that the glint in her eye suggested she didn't take no for an answer.

"You shouldn't leave your door unlocked," she said as she walked in. "Anyone could just come in."

"I'm serious, kid—"

"Amanda." Her chin came up like a boxer going into the ring and those eyes of hers, God, were they familiar. It wasn't just their likeness to Mac's; it was also the knowledge in their blue depths. She looked like his soldiers had after their first missions into Kabul. A surprising steadiness lived in her eyes, a fearlessness that told him she'd seen everything that could possibly scare her and lived through it.

Mac said something had happened to her four years ago. Something bad.

It made him sick thinking about whatever she'd seen to give her that terrible adult knowledge. One of his barricades, which stood so tall around any emotion he might feel or share, trembled.

"My name is Amanda. I'm your niece. I wrote you a hundred and four letters last year and I sent you two pictures and fourteen bags of gummy worms because Mom said that's what you used to like best." She stood, all elbows and knees, but he could already see the promise in her—she was going to be a knockout. A loudmouthed knockout.

"For all that work you sent me one letter. One dumb letter about cheerleading."

"Not much of a writer," he mumbled and dug into the

refrigerator for something to do since it didn't seem as if the kid was going anywhere. Could he kick her out? Physically grab her and throw her out the door? Probably not. Mac would come down off his mountain like a nightmare if Jesse did.

"So can I interview you?" she asked, practically bouncing on her toes. "I want to be a journalist so this would be, like, the best—"

"No interviews," he interrupted. He'd given one statement to the press after the accident: *All of his soldiers acted with valor and courage. It was an honor to serve alongside of them.* That was all anyone needed to know.

Amanda's face fell and, for some reason, that disappointment pricked him like a knife.

"Mom said you could be stubborn," she muttered.

"Mom?" He'd thought Amanda's mother had died— that Rachel had married Mac.

"Your sister. Rachel. She's my mom."

Jesse whistled through his teeth in surprise and Amanda's blue eyes turned stormy. "Don't be mean about Rachel, she's awesome."

Jesse shrugged, not about to burst that particular bubble. Amanda just stared at him with that strange forthright manner.

What the hell am I supposed to do with a teenager who's broken in and refuses to leave?

"Aren't you supposed to be in school?"

"We got out early," she told him. "Teachers' conference."

He remembered the thrill of half days, leaving school

with most of the day ahead of him for whatever he and Mitch wanted. It would never have occurred to him to work on an English paper.

"You want something to eat?" he finally asked.

"Do you actually have food in there?" She tried to peer around the open fridge door.

"Here." He took out one of the many plastic containers Mac had included with the groceries the day before.

"You didn't even try one of those?" she asked, taking one of the peanut butter cookies. "These took me, like, all Saturday afternoon to make."

She was already pissed off at him and he'd just met her. "I didn't ask you to," he told her, his hackles raising.

"That makes it nicer," she said slowly, as though he might be stupid. "Makes it a gift."

He couldn't help it, didn't even know he was about to do it until the laugh had clawed its way out of his ruined throat. It was one bad-sounding laugh, like a rusty door slamming, and it hurt like hell but he couldn't stop.

"You've spent too much time with my sister," he told the girl and watched her smile.

"There are worse things," she said. He could feel their shared knowledge of those *worse things* fill the room.

The girl had ghosts. Must be the only reason he hadn't gotten rid of her yet.

"So, you want to tell me about the war?"

"You want to tell me what happened to you four years ago?"

"No," she said fast and sure.

Jesse almost smiled at her. Poor kid. "Okay," he said.

He turned away from her and his knee twinged. He'd need another painkiller tonight at the rate he was going. If he could keep them to every other day and still get the roof done, he'd be in good shape.

"Where you going?" she asked. "Aren't we going to talk—"

"Hell, no."

There was a pregnant pause. "You shouldn't swear in front of your kid niece."

He eyed her over his shoulder and she grinned like the Cheshire cat, the way Mac said Jesse used to, as if everything was going according to plan. He almost laughed again.

"You shouldn't break into people's houses. Now, you can either go or you can give me a hand out back." He hit the aluminum door and stepped out into the bright sunlight.

Just go, he thought. *Just head on back to Mac and Rachel and leave me alone.*

But the girl was right behind him, talking about slave labor and minimum wage. He couldn't deny it—part of him was more than a little happy.

ADMITTEDLY, Julia's plan to find work had not been carefully thought out. It was day three of her job search. The first day she'd walked down Main Street looking for Help Wanted signs in the business windows. There weren't any so she'd grabbed New Springs' weekly newspaper and yesterday she'd filled out applications at the hair salon and movie theater.

But today she had a new idea. Instead of getting whatever job was available she was going to find the job she wanted.

She had an idea of what that job was. She'd carried the fledgling dream around from base to base since she was a little girl. But how to take that idea and turn it into a career—well, she was more than a little clueless.

"Hi," she murmured aloud. "I'd like a job planting flowers. Oh, and can you pay me lots of money for that? Oh, and did I mention I don't have a college degree and I barely passed the GED?"

"Mama?" Ben tried to turn around in his stroller, no doubt trying to see whom his crazy mother was talking to.

"Boo!" she said with a big smile and that started him on a long laughing, babbling monologue.

First, she would try the grocery store, to see if they had a horticulture department. If that didn't work, she could expand her search.

The sun warmed the top of her head, and her legs stretched and ate up the concrete. It felt good to move, to be going somewhere with, if not a plan, at least an idea.

And the yards in this neighborhood were fantastic, like works of art! These people had some cash and didn't mind spending it on plants and flowers. Purple and gold and pink lupine was everywhere, as was the ubiquitous eucalyptus. She stopped and stroked the silvery leaf of a plant she didn't know and accidentally kicked over a small lawn sign. She righted it, sticking its metal poles back beside the hosta and the mystery plant.

Holmes Landscaping, it read.

Julia had that breathless, shaky feeling that accompanied her belief in anything Mitch said was too good to be true.

Don't count your chickens, she warned herself.

But she picked up the pace to the grocery store. Once there she skipped the bulletin board and went right to the white pages attached to the pay phone out front.

Holmes Landscaping was located on the highway, close to the Motel 6 where she'd stayed in for all of five hours.

She bought her son some grapes and a bottle of water and thanked her lucky stars that she'd put on her walking shoes this morning.

She headed out toward the highway with her hopes high. She'd love to work with plants all day. Maybe once she'd brushed up on her knowledge she could help customers design their flowerbeds. She had a little artistic flair and getting to use it in her job seemed like a dream.

But her hopes and dreams were smashed under the heavy work boots of Virginia Holmes.

"We're not hiring," Virginia, the sixty-year-old owner who sported glasses and spinach in her teeth, growled at her. The faded green shirt stretched across her broad back and shoulders as she picked up a bag of topsoil from the skid as if it were a bag of feathers and added it to the stack under the sale sign.

Julia shaded her eyes from the bright sun.

"I understand, but—"

"Well, clearly you don't—" Virginia turned, the sun

hitting the edge of her glasses giving her glum expression a wicked glare "—or else you'd be leaving me alone, so I could get my work done."

"I understand you're not hiring for a cashier position, but I don't want a cashier position."

"Well, you look too white and too small for anything else."

Julia had no idea what to say. Was that a racist comment? Did the woman hire only Mexicans? Virginia Holmes was not the kindly, benevolent job-giver Julia had been expecting on the long walk out here.

"You're white," she ended up saying.

Nice one. She mentally hit herself in the head.

"Not like you." Virginia heaved another bag of soil from the flat to the pile on sale. "You're white like you've never worked a day in your life. And trust me—" she laughed a big, loud trucker kind of laugh that made Julia feel about two inches tall "—that's not a nice white."

Well, you're not a nice woman. She almost said it, but Virginia Holmes or not, Julia wanted a job. And she wanted a job here, amongst the bags of dirt and flats of jade plants, the blossoming dogwoods and cherry trees. She wanted to water the pine trees with their burlap-covered root balls and the rose bushes in their black planters that lined the asphalt.

She wanted to take care of the damn plants.

"Mama?" Ben asked from where she'd parked him about five feet away next to the hose equipment.

"And another thing—" Virginia jerked her gloves

higher on her wrists and then plunked her hands on her thick waist "—who brings their son to get a job?"

"A woman who doesn't know any better!" Julia finally said between clenched teeth. "A woman doing the best she can. And I wouldn't mind doing the best I could for you, but if you want to be a racist jerk, that's fine. I don't need this job." She stiffened her sagging spine and stopped her runaway mouth. Her fingers tingled from the adrenaline that flooded her system. *That's a first.* She took a deep breath and shook out her hands. She almost laughed—the first time in her life she actually stands up to someone and the woman clearly couldn't care less.

"Thanks for your time," Julia managed to say politely.

She turned away, hoping that Vons had a flower department and that the manager didn't care how small she was. She and Ben were halfway past the annuals when Virginia's rusty bark called out after her.

"Fill out an application and leave it with my daughter, Sue, at the cash. We're not hiring right now, but you never know."

Julia turned to thank her, but the cantankerous old woman had already moved on.

"Great," she muttered.

"Great!" Ben echoed, clapping his hands and the poor sweet boy really meant it.

CHAPTER SEVEN

BEN KNOCKED THE TOWER of blocks Julia had built to the ground. The clatter and minor destruction startled then thrilled him. He clapped, laughing and looking to her to join in the fun.

She applauded and started to rebuild, but her heart was a million miles away.

It was Wednesday morning and a week had gone by since she'd started her job search. She'd applied to five jobs and so far, nothing.

Things were not going as planned. She'd used up much of her savings to get here and the check from the army wouldn't come until the end of the month. There would be an insurance settlement, but she didn't know how much or when it might arrive. All the paperwork she received made vague promises about "settling in full after the inquiry." The thought of receiving money for Mitch's death made bile rise up in her throat which meant that money would be for Ben, for college. It was only right.

Agnes's open hospitality had evolved into a hovering kind of tyranny. Every decision Julia made—whether to give Ben applesauce or yogurt, to let him have juice or water—had become a platform for Agnes's opinion on what was bad for her grandson.

Every time Julia left for a walk, or returned minutes later than she'd said she would, Agnes expressed her disapproval in the icy turn of her shoulder, the superior lift of her nose.

Julia couldn't win with Agnes and she didn't know if the change in treatment was the result of something she'd done or if it was simply just the way Agnes acted. Certainly Julia's previous experiences with Agnes would support the latter. But as long as Julia was dependent on the Adamses' hospitality, she was forced to be polite.

That pressure fueled her desire for a job, a place of her own. Food she'd bought and provided for her son. She needed to stop feeling like a guest in her own life.

Her train of thought was interrupted by the phone ringing in the other room. Her cell phone number was long distance so she'd given all the prospective employers the Adamses' number. Her heart jumped into her throat— maybe this was the call she'd been waiting for. It was stupid and foolish but the prayer was there just the same.

Please be Holmes Landscaping. Please be Holmes Landscaping.

Someone picked up the phone midring. Moments later Julia heard footsteps and then the soft swish of the door opening.

"Julia?" Agnes said. "Phone's for you."

"Thank you," Julia said past dry lips. She reached for the extension beside the couch.

"Hello?"

"Julia? This is Lisa down at Hair Expressions."

"Hi, Lisa," Julia said into the phone, her stomach in minor knots. They'd been looking for an afternoon receptionist with experience. Julia had lied about the experience.

"I just wanted to let you know that our usual summer receptionist decided not to go away to band camp this year, so we aren't considering anyone's applications."

Band camp? Every job she'd applied for had been filled by one of the two hundred high school students starting summer vacation in a week.

It was disheartening to be turned down in favor of a band camp dropout. Not the most disheartening thing in her life, but quickly climbing the charts.

"No problem, Lisa, thanks for giving me a call."

"Hey, are you really Mitch Adams's widow?"

"I am."

"I went to prom with Mitch," she said and Julia sighed. Everybody had a Mitch story. "He was a great guy, I'm sorry for your loss."

Everybody in this town loved him, but no one really knew him.

Jesse's words echoed around her.

"Thanks," she murmured, the words sticky in her throat.

"They're looking for servers out at the Petro by the highway," Lisa's voice wasn't patronizing, just helpful. "You might try there."

"I will," Julia said, swallowing. "Thanks."

She hung up, all too aware that Agnes had stood

behind her during the conversation, listening to her further failure.

"Honey, I don't know why you're so set on getting a job." Agnes sat in the stiff wing chair to Julia's left. "There's no need for you to do that."

Julia bit her lip to stop the fast and ugly retort that expressed all the frustration she felt.

"I stayed home with Mitch. That's what mothers do," Agnes said.

That's what good mothers do, was what she meant.

The words hung in the air solid and tangible.

Good mothers, the kind you clearly are not.

"I would feel better," Julia said, slowly turning a yellow block in circles on the faded flowered rug she and Ben sat on, "if Ben and I could support ourselves."

"What about the money from the army?" Agnes asked the personal question as though she had the right and Julia burned a little hotter inside. "I'm sure Mitch made provisions for his son."

Julia faced Agnes, incredulous. Surely the woman had to be joking. This whole town and their hero worship had to be joking!

"Mitch left debt for his son." The words came out before she could stop them. She'd never intended to tell Agnes this.

Agnes's gray eyebrows clapped together. "What debt?"

Julia debated her response for a split second. The truth would only hurt Agnes—no mother wanted to hear about her son's mistakes.

"Mitch wasn't that kind of man."

Agnes had no *clue* what kind of man her son had been, and Julia felt a small amount of pleasure enlightening her.

"He made two bad investments while in California before the war and…" Agnes blanched and Julia swallowed, suddenly uncomfortable with her vindictiveness. "He gambled. Not a lot, but…enough."

Enough that she'd had to max out her credit card with cash advances to pay just half of his outstanding losses. A significant portion of her monthly check from the army went directly into a bank account set up to pay back Mitch's "buddies" in the army.

"Don't be ridiculous." Agnes laughed, but there was no humor in it, only sharp anger aimed at Julia. "Mitch was never a gambler."

"Maybe not when he was eighteen but he sure was the last few years."

Agnes stood, bristling with anger. This was the woman Julia had met when she and Mitch had gotten married. This judgmental woman glaring down her nose was the woman who'd called her a gold digger.

"Perhaps he needed a diversion out there in that desert. Maybe he needed to be distracted from the fact that he was so far away from his family. Maybe he was under too much pressure having to support a wife he hadn't planned on."

Julia could only blink at the venom in Agnes's voice. There was no way Julia could battle a mother's untarnished image of her dead perfect son.

"Perhaps, you're right," she lied in a vain attempt to

restore the peace. She bent to the task of rebuilding unstable towers for her son.

Agnes left the room, slamming the door behind her. Julia shut her eyes as the vacancy surrounded her. It seemed as though Agnes had sucked all the vitality from the room with her blind defense of a man who didn't deserve it. Julia's heart felt too heavy to be borne.

The one person who would understand the burden of Mitch's memory, the man who she longed to talk to, refused to see her.

AMANDA CAME BY Jesse's house on Wednesday afternoon. Again. It had been a little more than a week of Amanda stopping in after church and after school. She was like lice. Lice that never shut up.

Oddly enough, when she wasn't there, however, he missed her.

"So, Uncle Jesse?"

"Yes, Niece Amanda?"

They were in his backyard cleaning up the last of the old roof. He'd stripped it of the ruined shingles and it was now ready for new ones. He'd worked himself raw getting to this point and still managed to take the pain-killers only every other night.

"Considering I've been working my butt off for a week now and not getting paid…" she said.

He smiled.

"I think it's time we start talking about how exactly you are going to reimburse me for my efforts."

"No interview, Amanda."

"Okay, we can talk about something else."

He looked at her over his shoulder. "No more stories about your friends' love lives. I can't take any more."

"Fine." She arched one eyebrow and picked up a shingle. "But there have been some very interesting developments between Christie and—"

"Enough!" he cried.

"How about you tell me about your love life."

He shook his head.

"Well, I heard that when you were in high school—"

"I already told you I never got anyone pregnant in high school and I never beat anyone up for their shoes and I never sent anyone to the hospital."

"Fine." She harrumphed and silence filled the lawn. He waited patiently for her next effort to get him to talk about the war. Fending off her clever and wily attempts to engage him in conversation.

"Let's talk about your dad."

Jesse paused for a moment, stunned. *Never expected that one.*

Wain barked at his ankles and Jesse took the opportunity to stall as he winged the board in his hand toward the garage. Wain, old but still game, trotted after it.

Jesse's father, the memories of him, no longer hurt—those scars were old and faded. But the times with dear old Dad were not things he ever talked about.

"Why would you want to talk about him?"

"He's, like, my stepgrandpa."

"He's dead." Jesse pointed out the obvious.

"Would he have liked me? Eva liked me a lot."

Jesse almost choked on the sudden wave of emotion. Of course Eva had liked Amanda. *He'd* been trying hard to not like Amanda and had failed pretty miserably.

But his father would have been a different story.

"Dad didn't like much of anything." That was a ludicrous understatement.

"Mom said he drank a lot."

Jesse nodded.

"She said he was mean."

"I can't really argue with that," he muttered, grabbing shingles from the grass with a bit more speed than he had before.

"She said he hit you two."

"I think I'd rather talk about your love life some more." He tried to joke, but she didn't laugh. And he didn't, either.

"My mom was mean, too," she said. "Not Rachel, but my birth mom."

Jesse realized again with a sudden pang that despite her bold words and bravado, she was still young and, therefore, frail, this niece of his. He hated the idea of her being hurt by a callous parent. He knew first hand how painful that could be.

"She didn't hit me or anything, but she wasn't very nice."

"I'm sorry," he said lamely. He didn't look away from her eyes, and she didn't flinch from his. In the midst of this intense honesty she wormed her way deeper into his heart.

"Yeah, it sucked."

The air in the backyard felt heavy.

"Hey." He tried again to joke the soberness away. "Is this your way of softening me up for your article or—"

"I told you because I wanted to. Because you're my uncle and I like you. You can tell me what happened in the war and I won't write the article if you don't want me to. We could just…talk, you know?"

He didn't. He had no clue. But he nodded anyway.

Wain trotted back from the garage with the board in his mouth and dropped it at Amanda's feet. She grabbed it and tossed it toward the garage. Jesse returned to picking up shingles and the moment passed as though it hadn't happened. Except that he felt a little lighter or cleaner or something. He felt closer to his effervescent niece and that, in turn, made him feel good.

They worked their way around the corner of the house, past the giant trumpet plant, picking up shingles and tossing the stick for Wain, who fetched with less and less speed until he finally collapsed in a patch of sunlight to gnaw on the stick.

In front of the porch, Jesse finally straightened, ready to call it a day. Maybe he could convince his niece to run down to the Dairy Dream and bring back a pint of rocky road ice cream. He turned, ready to make his pitch to Amanda, and saw Julia Adams on the opposite corner wrestling her screaming son out of a stroller that listed precariously to one side.

His body turned to stone, while his heart ran to liquid, the way it always did when he saw her.

At the sound of the boy's cries Amanda dropped her

garbage bag and ran past him toward the corner, ready to offer her assistance.

"You gonna come help her?" she paused to ask.

Julia had walked past his house twice a day for days. Every time he could feel her eyes on his back, on his legs, on his chest like a caress. But when he turned to face her she'd stare straight ahead, pretending the air between them wasn't on fire with her desire—that same desire that filled him and spurred dreams of her. And when he wasn't dreaming of her, he dreamed about the crash. The situation would be laughable if it wasn't such agony. And now he was supposed to play knight in shining armor?

"No." He leaned down to grab another armful of torn shingles. The rough asphalt bit into his arms and hands and he pressed his flesh against the pain as hard as he could. It reminded him he was here only to finish this house, not to spin wonderful dreams about his best friends wife and her son.

"Mom was right. You can be such a jerk, Uncle Jesse," Amanda said, without much heat.

The words still stung even after she went running across the lawn towards Julia. Jesse dumped the shingles in the bag and continued working.

You don't know the half of it, kid.

JULIA MANAGED to get Ben, screaming as if he'd been attacked by bees, out of the collapsed stroller. The screw holding the two crossbars in place had vanished and the whole damn thing had given up the ghost.

Ben had one long scrape across his shin, but most of

the commotion was because the poor kid had been startled out of a sound nap.

"Sh, sh, sweetheart. It's okay." She murmured nonsense into his ear until the screaming faded to whimpers.

She wished she could scream. Just lie down on the ground and have at it until all her stress, worry and frustration were gone, or until someone picked her up, comforted her and whispered soothing nonsense into her ear.

But she knew better than anyone that that didn't happen in real life. Not for her.

Standing on the sidewalk with her sniffling baby in her arms and his stroller in ruins at her feet, she had to wonder the same thing Agnes had been insinuating for days. What the hell was she trying to do?

Tears burned behind her eyes. She couldn't go back to that house right now. She was so raw, so…lost that she just couldn't take Agnes's censure and pity.

What made you think this was going to be easy? The voice in her head was her husband's again and she wished that her memory of his voice had faded as much as her memory of his handsome face.

"Ouch, mama," Ben whined. "It hurts."

"I know, sweetheart." She lifted his little calf to see the blood beading up from his scrape. "Let's go home and get that cleaned up."

Home was still a couple of blocks away. She took a step forward but the stroller wouldn't roll properly and she had to drag it. She took three awkward steps then bowed her head, defeated by the stroller, her empty bank account, the ghost of her dead husband and his living family.

Oh, please God, help me. I don't think I can do this.

"Are you okay?"

Julia whirled toward the voice to find a pretty teenager, her blond hair scraped away from her thin face, standing there with a world of sympathy in her eyes.

"We're okay, thanks," she lied with a smile and tried to lift the stroller so it wouldn't drag, but she accidentally rubbed Ben's scrape and he lost it right in her ear.

"Here, come on," the stranger said. "Let me help you get this—"

She tried to take the stroller from Julia, but just as she grabbed it the right front wheel, already cockeyed, fell off and bounced down the street.

She and the girl watched it go and finally, Julia realized there was nothing left to do but laugh.

At first it was only a weary chuckle. But when the teenager joined in and then Ben, they all laughed until things didn't seem so bad.

"Are you okay?"

He was behind her.

Her lungs went tight and face got hot. She could smell him—sun and sweat and something else, something dark and moody that crept into her head and made it swim. Jesse's gravelly voice scraped down her spine into her belly.

"We're fine," she said, pleased her voice didn't tremble or waver or give away any of her discomfort. She turned to face him, but she couldn't look at him, and she guessed that gave away everything her steady voice did not.

"I'm Amanda," the girl said into the thick hot silence that surrounded Jesse and Julia. "Do you want to come over and clean up a little?"

"That'd be great," Julia answered quickly, trying to pretend the side of her neck, where she could feel him staring, wasn't on fire. "Do you live—"

"Uncle Jesse?" Amanda asked, her voice and eyes held a note of steel and accusation. "Would that be all right?"

"Oh, don't worry. We can make it home." Julia quickly backpedaled. She'd rather deal with Agnes than her own fiery reaction to Jesse's icy dismissal. "We're only a few houses down."

"It's not a problem," Jesse said, and finally she had to look at him. Thank God he was wearing a shirt. But the faded black T-shirt was threadbare, damp with sweat and clung to his chest and arms in a far more provocative way than the sunshine and air had.

"Do you two, like, know each other?" Amanda asked, her eager eyes darting between them.

"No," she said, just as Jesse said, "Yeah."

"Whoa. Cool," Amanda said, but Julia was barely listening.

"No, really, I'd much rather—"

"Deal with Agnes?" he interjected and Julia's gaze flew to his. "I doubt that."

"She's been great to us," she said, feeling stiff and prickly even though he'd somehow read her mind.

"I'm sure she has. You can use my bathroom or not.

Your choice." His black eyes seemed to understand that she dreaded going back to that house with a crying baby and a broken stroller. She couldn't take any more of those sideways looks and barbed words that accused her of not being the best mother to her son.

Jesse's eyes seemed to see right through to her worry that the Agnes was right. Good mothers didn't drag their sons all around the world in a broken stroller looking for jobs they weren't qualified for.

"Thanks," she murmured.

He turned and walked away.

"Come on," Amanda said, "he's a jerk but he's harmless."

"Maybe to you," Julia muttered. She felt in dire peril every time she was near him.

"I'll grab this and we'll see if Uncle Jesse can get his head out of his butt long enough to fix it." Amanda grabbed the stroller and headed toward the house.

Julia knew she had every chance to decide otherwise, to take her chances with the devil she knew at the Adamses rather than the one that lurked in Jesse's eyes, but she picked up the stroller wheel and followed Amanda anyway.

"I DON'T HAVE ANY BANDAGES. Just soap and water," Jesse told them as soon as they walked in. He had braced himself in the far corner of the kitchen between the two counters, like a hunted animal about to strike back.

He took a swig of the beer he'd grabbed the moment

he walked in—as if he needed further proof of how shaken he was, how weak and close to utter ruin.

He rarely drank, but every time he did he felt as though he was his father.

"Thank you, Jesse, we won't take long," Julia said, her eyes clinging to his for a moment too long.

God, did she have to be so naked? Did she have to be so damn obvious in her feelings for him? It made the air so thick he couldn't breathe.

"Bathroom's through there." He pointed down the dark hallway.

"Uncle Jesse, do you think you could fix this thing?" Amanda asked, swinging the stroller beside her as she walked in.

"Sure." He grabbed it midswing and she let go. She looked down the hallway to make sure Julia was out of earshot and then leaned toward him, her eyes wide and bright.

"Wow," Amanda said. "She's so pretty. Do you think she's married? 'Cause, she's totally into you. So, you shouldn't—"

"Call your folks to come pick you up," he told her. "I don't need your help around here anymore."

His too-wise niece eyed him with skeptical disbelief, and he watched her right back until she finally looked away, clearly disappointed in him. He took a long swallow of the beer that slid down his throat like ice after a trip through the desert.

"Fine," she said, then grabbed her school bag from

the kitchen table and dug out her cell phone. "I'll tell them you're mean and a jerk and—"

Jesse walked out, cutting off her tirade with the slam of the screen door.

He'd let that girl hang around and it had gotten into his head, made him forget who he was and what he was here to do. And now, thanks to her, he had Julia and her boy in his house, using his sink, his towels, filling the rooms with her smell.

Things had gone too far.

Well, he knew how to fix that.

He headed to the garage and the tools he'd spent sleepless nights cleaning up. He rattled all the jam jars filled with screws until he found one that might work. He had to bend the metal crossbar to its original shape. Even with the new screw and a little grease, the stroller maybe had a week left.

"Do you need this?"

Julia stood in the doorway of the dark garage, sunlight streaming in around her, turning the dust in the air to glitter.

"What?" Her beauty physically punched him.

"The wheel." She smiled, shy and careful like the beautiful woman/girl he remembered in Germany.

He grabbed the beat-up wheel from her and bent over the stroller.

"Thank you for doing this." She stepped closer and Jesse fought the urge to step away, to keep the distance between them tolerable.

"It's not going to do much good. This is a piece of crap."

He saw her shrug from the corner of his eye. "Well, it's all the crap I've got at the moment."

"Where is the boy?" he asked, glancing around her feet for the boy with Mitch's hair.

"Amanda and Wain are playing with him." She fiddled with the clamp attached to the old workbench. "She seems like a very nice girl."

Jesse searched through the jar at his elbow for a screw that would work with the wheel.

Cheap plastic things. What was she thinking hauling her baby around in this?

"You never mentioned a niece that night in Germany," she said in the way of a woman who wanted to play with fire. He didn't answer her.

He twisted the screw in and spun the wheel once. It wobbled, but it worked.

"I don't understand you, Jesse. This isn't what you were like in Germany." She reached out a hand to his shoulder and he dodged it. He ignored the foolish bravery and determination she seemed compelled to display and concentrated on chasing her out of his life.

"Well, it's what I'm like now."

"Is it because of Mitch? I'm not married anymore," she finally whispered, like some sort of invitation to his worst impulses. "He's not between us."

Mitch would always be between them. Every time Jesse looked at her, he saw Mitch in that burning helicopter. Every time he thought of her he was reminded of all the reasons he couldn't have her. And having her so close and still so far out of reach hurt worse than any of his injuries.

And he just couldn't take it.

"We need to get something straight." He propped himself against the bench because his knee seemed suddenly weak. "Whatever you think happened, whatever you think it meant—" he leaned forward and spoke real slow just so she got the point "—it didn't."

Her pale skin glowed red at her cheeks.

"We won't be friends," he continued.

"But—"

He stepped in closer.

"Ever."

Stepping closer was a mistake. The atmosphere between them sizzled and glowed with electricity. She breathed hard, her mouth parted and her eyes fell to his lips. He could feel every cell of her body reaching toward him because every cell in his body was doing the same.

Good God! How much did a man have to take?

"We're both alone in this town. I thought—"

"I'm going to say this one more time. Real slow. 'Cause you don't seem to be getting it. I do not want a friend and I don't want anything else you're offering me."

"I'm not…"

He smiled, mirroring all the slick men he'd known who'd hurt countless women. "Yes, sweetheart, you are. And I don't want it."

He stared into the endless blue of her eyes, willing her to accept what she could not change and get the hell out of his garage before he fell apart in front of her.

SHE BURNED. She burned with her shame and desire. She couldn't breathe for the pain of wanting him and hating him. She reached for the stroller and fought tears.

"Thank you," she whispered and pulled the stroller from his hands. For a moment, a mere second, he didn't let go. Her gaze crept to his. For the briefest flash the look in his eyes was the very same look he'd given her that morning in Germany.

She wasn't the only one who burned with want.

He let go of the stroller and turned away from her, his broad back looking so strong yet so terribly wounded in the half light.

A wild current traveled over her skin.

She could leave. She could continue doing the things people told her to do. She could fill out a million applications. She could marry another man who was completely wrong for her. She could live with her mother or, worse, remain in the charity of her in-laws. She could walk out of this garage and avoid Jesse until he left, or she did.

She could do all of that.

It was what she was good at—what she'd done her whole life. Allowed other people's wants and expectations to dictate her life.

And where has it gotten you? she wondered, bitterness sliding through her blood like anger.

To this moment. This moment when she could change everything.

"You're lying." The strength of her voice surprised her, jolted her shoulders back and her head up. "You don't want me to leave."

"This isn't a game, Julia." He didn't face her, and her sudden knowledge of him, her ability to see through his sharp armor, filled her with a power she'd never dreamed of possessing.

"I know that, Jesse."

She took a step closer and finally he turned. She took a deep breath, relieved to see that all of his put-on anger, his cruelty and indifference, were gone.

This was the man she'd known in Germany.

"I killed your husband." His voice seemed dredged from the depths of his throat.

She gasped, horrified that he felt that way, that he should carry that guilt.

"That's not true." She believed it to her bones. Mitch had been on his own path to destruction for too long to need someone else to take him there.

His nostrils flared and his lips went white and thin. "It doesn't matter what you think. Your husband's dead and it's my fault." He shook his head. "Your stroller's fixed, now just go."

He moved to her right as if to walk past her. Emboldened by her own actions and on fire to touch him in some way, she put out her arm to stop him. Her hand curled around the inside of his elbow where the skin was smooth and warm. She could feel his pulse under his skin. Her fingers slid under the sleeve of his shirt and her lungs clogged and shrank.

He moaned. Whether from her touch or her newfound stubbornness she didn't know, but her body stirred at the rough sound. She turned toward him, yearning for the kiss that lingered in the air around them.

He grabbed her hand and pulled it, yanking her off balance, sending her into a light-headed and lustful collision with his body.

"I have nothing to offer you." His gaze roved over her face, lingering on her lips. "If you want to be my friend, if you have any feeling for me at all, you'll leave me the hell alone."

His grip squeezed the bones of her hand together but she was so wrapped up in the misery she could see in his eyes, that her own pain barely registered. Finally, he dropped her hand and took a step away. "Please," he growled.

He opened his mouth as if to say something else, but in the end he just walked away, limping back to the house.

CHAPTER EIGHT

THIS WAS NOT going to be pretty.

Amanda sat at the kitchen table while Dad and Mom paced around her in an imitation of the Spanish Inquisition. Dad worked the area in front of the fireplace and Mom was behind her at the french doors.

"Nothing happened," Amanda said, taking the first shot into the still, tense air.

Dad's back went straight and Amanda cringed.

Should have kept quiet.

"You know that's not what this is about. We asked you to not go over there. We asked you to leave him alone." Dad put his hands in his pockets and rocked on his toes, which she'd come to learn—the hard way—meant he was trying not to lose his temper.

"I don't think he wants to be alone." Amanda shrugged. "I mean, I think he says that but I don't think he means it."

"Amanda, there are things going on that Rachel and I don't understand—"

"Well, did you ask him? He's not the total freak everyone thinks he is. He's just grumpy.... I think if we kept asking him…"

Mom turned, tears standing out in her green eyes. "Amanda, this isn't a game. It's not some fight between you and Christie. It's not a chance for you to get an A on your English paper."

Amanda immediately felt about two inches tall. "I'm sorry," she said, staring at the flaking pink nail polish on her thumb. "It's not just about the paper. I mean it sort of was at first but...I wanted to get to know him. And I really think he liked having me there. But today when Julia showed up—"

"Julia?" Mom's eyes cleared and went sharp. "Who is Julia?"

Amanda looked between her parents and the tension in the air changed. "I—I don't know."

"A journalist?" Mom asked.

"No...I mean, I don't think so. I think they knew each other."

Mom scowled, and Amanda rushed in to defend the pretty woman who'd seemed so lost with her baby and the broken stroller.

"She's was totally cool. Not mean or anything. I think she was into him."

"What do you mean, *into him?*" Mom asked.

Amanda rolled her eyes, but Mom wasn't looking. She and Dad were sharing a surprised look.

See, she thought smugly, *a little investigative journalism is just what the sit—*

"Amanda, I need you to go up to your room," Mom said, her eyes still on Dad's.

Amanda scoffed. "Up to my room?" *What am I, nine?*

Dad turned his I-mean-business look on her and she jumped up from her chair and headed for the stairs. It'd been four years since Rachel had walked into their lives and made everything a million times better. It'd been that long since Amanda had been sent to her room.

And it'd been just as long since she'd eavesdropped. In fact, the last time she'd tried she heard them making out, which had pretty much scarred her for life and ruined her taste for spying. But something was up right now and a little spying was clearly in order.

As if she'd sit in her room while they talked about Uncle Jesse who, she wished she could point out, had actually let her hang out for over a week. He even joked around with her.

Amanda stomped up the stairs and made sure she hit all the squeaky floorboards in the hallway before slamming her door hard. Then she pivoted on her toe, flattened herself along the wall and eased back toward the edge of the hallway. She got just close enough that she could hear their hushed voices.

"Do you know who this Julia is?" Rachel asked.

There was a silence and Amanda guessed Dad was shaking his head. "I don't quite understand what's upsetting you so much about her."

"Everything about this situation is upsetting me." Mom was sounding desperate.

"I can see that, sweetheart. But you're the one who wanted to give him space."

"I thought that's what he needed." Mom sighed and

Amanda could hear that she was crying. "What if I'm wrong? What if he leaves before we can talk?"

"Then let's not keep our distance. It's been killing me watching him fix that roof on his own."

Boris, the dumb dog they'd saved from the highway, caught sight of Amanda from her parents' open bedroom door.

Crap!

He stood from his spot on their bed, shook himself all over and then seemed to grin at her.

She held her finger up to her mouth but it didn't do any good. He barked cheerfully at her anyway.

"Why did you think this Julia woman is a journalist?" Dad asked. "And not just an interested single mom?"

"I got a phone call the other day from the hospital. Caleb Gomez is conscious."

Caleb Gomez was one of the guys in the helicopter crash. The only one besides Uncle Jesse that lived. *Something is up!* Amanda's inner reporter perked up. *Oh, something is definitely up.*

"That's great." Dad sounded totally relieved. "He's recovering."

"He's asking to talk to Jesse."

Boris jumped down from the bed and walked into the hallway, his collar jangling. Because he was a dog and dumb to boot, he managed to step on all the squeaky floorboards.

"Well, I'd imagine he would. The guy's alive because of Jesse," Dad said.

"The guy is a reporter. What if Julia has something do with that? Or if she's from the—"

"Relax, Rachel. Just relax. I think it would be a good thing for Caleb to get in touch with Jesse. Let him see that he did some good in Iraq."

"You think Caleb could do that?" Rachel asked. "I think he just wants to capitalize on the accident for a story—"

Dad sighed long and hard. "You can't protect him forever. Jesse can take care of himself."

"I know, but I just want to help. I just…he's so stubborn and I hurt him so much."

"Okay, we'll change tactics. We'll stop giving him distance and we'll start treating him like family."

"That should be interesting," Mom grumbled and then came the creepy sound of more kissing.

Amanda made a face at Boris who sat panting on her feet and patted his scruffy head.

I wish I could make all of this better. For Mom, for Jesse, even a little for Julia. But how?

Boris twitched and leaned against her leg.

Maybe it wasn't how. It was *who*.

Maybe it was Caleb Gomez.

"HOW ARE YOU DOING, sweetheart?" Beth asked and Julia sank onto the steps of the Adams' back porch with relief. Her mother's voice, beamed across the world by satellites and distorted by static, was so welcome over the cell phone she almost laughed with the joy of it.

"I've been better, Mom." She cupped her forehead in her hand and studied the dirty toe of her tennis shoe.

"What's wrong?" she asked.

What isn't?

"Julia?" Agnes stood at the screen door, backlit by the yellow kitchen light, holding Ben.

"I'm here," Julia said. "I'm just talking to my mom."

"I didn't know where you'd gone to," Agnes said in her light, friendly way that made Julia's hackles rise. "Benny was looking for you." She jostled Ben in her arms. "Weren't you, Benny?"

"Hi, Mama," he said and pressed his hand against the screen.

"Hi, sweetie." She smiled back and bit her lip. Agnes did this sort of thing all the time, used Ben as a way to make Julia feel bad or to check up on her. "I'll be in when I'm done."

Agnes left and Julia sighed hard.

"Things aren't quite what you hoped for, are they?" her mother asked.

"Not at all." Julia stood and walked into the yard just in case Agnes lingered by the door to hear her conversation. Even though she knew she was being paranoid, it wasn't a maneuver she'd put past Agnes.

"Tell me," Beth said, and Julia let it all spill out.

"I came here looking to give Ben some permanence and, at first, everything seemed so good. The Adamses treated us like family and…" *Jesse's here. He's actually here but he pushes me away with both hands.*

She almost brought up Jesse, but she was still too raw

and her mother's advice, she knew, would be to not go rushing into anything. Too late for that.

She was up to her neck in murky feelings. Julia remembered the harrowed expression on Jesse's face in the garage. The haunted eyes filled with appeal. *Please,* he'd begged, and she'd walked away.

But she also remembered the heat of his eyes. The way he'd groaned when she touched him. The way he'd touched her in Germany, like a thirsty man in front of water.

Which was true? False? He'd rejected her twice, how much was she supposed to push?

"And now?" her mother asked, pulling Julia back into the conversation about the Adamses.

"They're so stifling."

"You've been on your own a long time," Beth said and Julia nodded, though she couldn't be seen. "It's hard to give up your independence that way."

"I didn't think I was!" Julia nearly cried. "I thought I was getting a support system, not a mother hen."

"Family isn't all it's cracked up to be sometimes."

"That's not very helpful, Mom."

She laughed. "No, it isn't. But I'll tell you something, sweetheart. Sometimes you have to make your own family. It's why your father and I were in the military and it's why we stayed. We found friends who felt more like brothers and sisters than our own ever did. And each of us had mentors that felt like parents."

"Mom," she sighed. "I hated the military life."

"I know, sweetheart, and I'm so sorry for that. But

sometimes you have to create what you need out of what you get. It's not easy. It's hard work but you have to keep at it."

"Nothing seems easy right now."

"It takes courage to get what you want," Beth said. "Courage and patience. Which you have or you'd never have gone out there in the first place."

"That wasn't courage, Mom." Julia laughed. "That was desperation."

"You've always sold yourself short, Julia. You're much stronger than you think you are."

"And you've always seen things in me that aren't there. I'm not strong, Mom."

"You left home at eighteen. You made that disastrous marriage work. You've raised that darling boy all on your own."

Julia laughed. "You're right. I'm the strongest woman on earth."

"Don't be flip, Julia. It's long been time for you to decide your worth. You've let other people do it for you for too long."

Julia sucked in a deep breath, tasting the truth on the air. Her worth? It was true. She'd let Mitch convince her she was worthless and now Agnes was doing the same. And Jesse—he'd told her she deserved more but then he walked away from her.

What did she think?

What did she determine her worth to be?

She was certainly worth more than the way Jesse had treated her yesterday, that was for sure.

Maybe it was time to listen to her mother. More importantly it was time to listen to herself.

"Thanks, Mom," she whispered. "That's what I needed to hear."

"I love you," Beth said.

"I love you, too." Julia sighed, feeling her mother's absence like a thorn under her skin.

They hung up and Julia stared at the sky and tried to find her courage. Her worth.

What an idiot I am for listening to Jesse.

She should have stayed, forced him to be truthful about his feelings for her. Instead she'd run.

Courage, she told herself and thought of his haunted face. She smiled, thinking of his groan at the mere touch of her hand.

I'll just have to try again.

JESSE POURED the other five beers down the drain. He couldn't look at them anymore, couldn't pretend they weren't in the fridge offering him some drunken oblivion. Some solace from his demons.

He tossed the last bottle in the garbage and circled the kitchen again. His knee felt okay, so he couldn't pretend to need the painkillers. It was just him and the demons, trapped in the cramped kitchen.

He checked his watch.

8:00 p.m.

It had only been hours since Julia had been here. Hours that seemed like years.

Suddenly the walls were too close. The air too stale.

"Wain!" he cried and heard the dog's collar jangle as he stood up from his spot on the couch in the other room. He appeared, yawning in the doorway.

"Watch the place," Jesse ordered. Wain barked once in response—the canine equivalent of a good loud "Sir, yes, sir!"

He picked up the keys from the kitchen table and headed out toward his Jeep and whatever salvation he could find in the night. He wanted noise and people and there was plenty of that to be had at Billy's.

The place was comfortably full of folks in various stages of drunkenness and desperation. People all concentrating so hard on their own problems or good times that they barely noticed him walking in. He eased onto a stool at the bar.

"Well," Billy said, approaching him with a cardboard coaster. "Tell me you're in here tonight to do it right."

Jesse looked at all the gleaming bottles. The rack of taps offering him a dozen different beers and one surefire way to forget his troubles.

He could get drunk. Hammered. He could storm home and tear that house down, drink away his dreams of Julia. Of Mitch. Of the rest of the men.

In the end he couldn't do it. Memories of dear old dad kept him sober and on a short fuse.

"I'll have a coffee," he said. "Black."

Billy shook his head and Jesse ignored him.

"On the house." Billy slid a white mug with cold coffee in front of Jesse and walked away, finally showing the good sense a bartender ought to have.

The back of Jesse's neck prickled and he knew he'd finally attracted someone's attention. He looked through the bottles of cheap liquor on the bar to the mirror behind them.

A girl in a turquoise halter top watched him from the safety of a booth in the corner crowded with her girlfriends.

He braced himself and within moments she'd left the table and approached him, her muddy brown eyes locked on his in the mirror.

"Hi," she said, curling her short thick body onto a bar stool. Her hair fell over her bare shoulder in a move so practiced he nearly laughed. "I've never seen you in here before." She smiled at him.

She was pretty in a slightly tawdry sort of way, and her smile was a sweet curve just beginning to grow jaded at the corners. "I'm Samantha," she said and held out her hand. Her eyes darted with laser intensity over his shoulder toward the pool tables to the left of him for an instant. Three men wearing baseball caps and flannel shirts played pool.

He could feel their eyes watching this little scene between him and Sam with typical male propriety. One of them, a small guy, patted the big guy's shoulder.

"Let it go, Mike," he said, and reluctantly big Mike, looking murderous and hard done by, bent back to their game and beer.

A reckless anger churned through Jesse's bloodstream. He couldn't win against Julia. He couldn't fight

Mitch. And that's what he wanted. He wanted to beat Mitch into the ground for the way he'd treated Julia.

His fists clenched, his lungs heaved hard. Adrenaline and the battle readiness he'd lived with for so long steeled him, seeped into his bones, through his nerves. He wanted to hit something, hurt something, be hurt in return. He wanted everything but survival to be obliterated. Destroyed. He wanted to live one breath at a time the way he had during the war.

Instead of sending young Samantha on her way, telling her to get out of this town before it used her up, he decided to let her stay.

Samantha with her sweet smile and old eyes didn't have what he needed. But those three men, drinking hard and talking too loudly, held the salvation he was looking for.

Those three men he could fight.

It wasn't good or decent of him. But nothing in him felt that way.

"Hi, Sam." He smiled at her and shook her hand. "I'm Jesse."

He ordered beers for the two of them and waited.

IT TOOK A LITTLE LONGER than Jesse expected. Sam had four beers while he nursed his one, but eventually the confrontation he'd been praying for did happen.

"What the hell do you think you're doing, Sam?" an angry voice asked from Jesse's left.

"Whatever I want, Mike," Sam answered, hot and fast. Her eyes were heavy-lidded with alcohol but were still shooting out sparks. She'd clearly been waiting for this as long as he'd been. Jesse felt a sudden kinship with her.

"We broke up, remember?" she sneered.

Jesse turned to see the biggest of the three men, Mike, flanked by the smaller ones, not two feet from him.

Perfect.

"Why don't you just leave me and Sammy alone," Jesse asked, throwing gasoline on what was smoldering in the air. Mike went red then purple under his collar.

"Why don't you mind your own business?" one of the sidekicks asked around his toothpick. Jesse wanted to warn him about that toothpick, how dangerous it could be to get in a fight with a weapon sticking out of his mouth.

But that would have been at cross-purposes. He intended to cause some damage with that sharp wood.

"Well." Jesse pushed himself up and away from the stool. He smiled at the men, needling their pride, wanting to get this show on the road. "I figure tonight, for the next few hours anyway, Sammy is my business."

"Holy shit, I know that guy," the other sidekick said, his blue eyes rimmed red. "He's that soldier who survived the helicopter crash that killed Mitch Adams."

And there it was. What Jesse never could outrun or outfight.

"Don't forget Artie and Dave," he muttered.

He stumbled, his knee stiff from the hours of sitting, and Sammy stood up next to him, a restraining hand on his elbow. "Jesse, let's just go. You can come back to my place…."

Ah, she thought he was a cripple. Pitiful. Unable to

stand up to a bunch of fat bullies. Even Mike took a step back and the air cooled a few degrees.

"He's not going home with you, Sam," Mike said, weary rather than angry.

"Well, you're not coming home with me, that's for sure," she retorted.

"Sam, stop playing games."

Well. Damn. Things were getting way out of control. He'd sat with her all damn night waiting for this moment and the big guy was getting distracted. That wouldn't do. To remind Mike why he'd walked all the way across the bar with his buddies beside him, Jesse gave him a solid right hook across the jaw and felt the crunch of bone and teeth.

That seemed to jog Mikey's memory.

Mike roared and grabbed Jesse by his collar.

"Outside, Mike!" Billy yelled, from behind the bar. "You take this shit outside!"

"Gladly," Mike said, spitting blood and saliva onto the floor. His eyes were hot and electric with rage. "You're a dead man, asshole," he growled and pushed Jesse toward the door.

That's the idea, my friend. That's the right idea.

CHAPTER NINE

THREE AGAINST ONE were not his kind of odds, so to make things fair, he didn't fight back for the first few punches. The shot to his face, badly timed and way off target, merely skittered across his cheek.

"Come on, boys. You've got to focus," he told them. "Here, I'll stand real still." He locked his knees and stuck out his chin, taunting them.

The sidekick spit out his toothpick and landed a solid punch to Jesse's gut that radiated down his legs and shook his bowels.

Good one. Better.

The men were mad and Jesse wasn't stopping them so fists landed where they'd been aimed.

Any minute now he was going to fight back. He was going to lay them all out with busted wrists and sprained ankles and noses so broken they'd need surgery. That was what he was going to do. It had been his intention all along. He was going to punish these men for all the things he couldn't have.

But they backed him up against a truck and the blows came hard and fast. His lip split and his eye got hot and swollen. There was a punch, a sharp pop and a crunch, then blood flooded his throat from his broken nose.

Soon, the pain of his body matched the pain he carried in his head and gut and the equilibrium was blissful.

I deserve this.

These men weren't strangers. They were Mitch and Dave and Artie. They were the families he'd ruined. They were the lives he'd destroyed.

If I'd only agreed with Mitch, just one last time…

"Hey, asshole!" Mike thrust his sweaty red face against Jesse's. He grabbed the collar of Jesse's shirt and yanked him around like a rag doll. "Where's your smart mouth now, huh?"

Jesse didn't want to talk, he wanted the beating to keep going. So he smiled, blood filled his mouth and he spit it in Mike's face.

Mike growled, wiped the blood and spittle from his face with his shoulder and threw Jesse back against the truck. His head cracked on the metal and the pain skittered through his brain and he embraced it, wrapped his whole body around it and smiled. He sagged against the vehicle, his body suddenly heavy.

Mike wrapped his thick fingers around Jesse's neck and squeezed, blocking off the blood in his carotid artery.

Good. Yes.

Mike's big, hammy fist went back and Jesse knew this would end things. If he woke up from this punch, he'd be surprised. He lifted his chin just to improve the odds.

But before Mike could get his whole weight behind his fist a truck pulled into the gravel lot, headlights slicing the night to ribbons. Mike dropped Jesse's neck and stepped back, shielding his eyes from the bright lights trained on them.

Jesse sagged.

"Come on, Mike. Let's get out of here," one of Mike's friends said and they were already sliding backward into the shadows past the light.

"We're not done," Mike growled at him.

"Yes, we are," Jesse muttered and spit blood.

Mike stepped close, as if he might finish that punch after all, but whoever was in the truck got out and slammed his driver side door shut.

It was Mac. Of course.

"Get home, Mike. Before the police get here," Mac said and Mike, after one last shove, finally stalked off to his friends.

Jesse didn't turn, he stayed leaning against the truck while his savior walked toward him, his boots crunching on the gravel.

"What the hell are you doing here, Mac?" Jesse asked past the burn of blood in his throat.

"Bailing you out," Mac said, finally stepping into the light. "Again."

"How'd you know I was here?"

"Billy called us, said you were getting your ass kicked."

"I don't need your help."

"Then why weren't you fighting back?" Mac asked.

Jesse spit into the gravel again but didn't say anything.

The answer was as clear as the blood running down his face, and they both knew it.

"Let me get you home. You're in no shape to drive," Mac said, standing beside Jesse like a patient watchdog. A guard.

The death wish was gone, vanished under the lights of Mac's truck. So Jesse nodded and pushed himself toward the passenger side of Mac's truck.

Jesse rolled his head against the headrest and stared out the window at the night sky.

He was going to be sick tomorrow. Hurt and bruised and battered, but for right now, the fight had freed him from his place on this earth.

He didn't recognize himself, as if he'd traveled all this way to finally slip his own skin.

"You gonna be sick?" Mac asked.

Jesse shook his head.

"Unroll the window just in case."

"I'm not going to puke."

"You always used to say that right before you puked."

Jesse smiled and cringed at the pull of the cut on his lip.

"I'm not drunk," he said and could feel Mac's surprised gaze on the side of his face. "I had a half a beer."

"What were you doing back there, Jess?" Mac finally asked, plucking the question from the thousand unasked ones that filled the cab like spiderwebs.

"I think I was trying to get the shit kicked out of myself."

"But why?"

Jesse sighed and shut his eyes. The bump and sway

of the truck over the old asphalt of New Springs lulled him, not to sleep, but to ambivalence. Peaceful uncaring.

"Julia. Mitch. Lots of reasons."

Mac took a right turn and Jesse's head swayed against the window. They hit a big bump, the driveway and then pulled to a stop.

Mac turned off the engine and Jesse could feel him turn to look at him.

"The men in the helicopter?"

Jesse nodded, kept his eyes shut, because that just felt better than seeing himself, this house, his old friend.

"It was an accident, Jess. That's what the army said."

"There are no such things as accidents," Jesse muttered. "There are mistakes. Someone makes a mistake. Friendly fire, ambushes, bad machinery—those aren't accidents, they're mistakes. We tell ourselves that these things happen in war so we don't all go nuts."

I'm going nuts. The thought was as clear as a bell, like a voice in his head. *I am losing my mind.*

"What happened?" Mac asked, his voice as soft and light as shadow, as starlight. "With Mitch and the helicopter?" Jesse's skin crawled from the sympathy, from the tone of Mac's voice, from the words he knew would come next—*it's not your fault.*

He fumbled with the handle, finally found it and yanked the door open. He overbalanced and nearly toppled onto his driveway, but he caught himself on his weaker leg and the pain spread like wildfire up his battered body.

"Jesse," Mac said, urgent and worried. "Man, let me help you. Let me—"

Jesse shook his head and held up his hand. "Go home, Mac. You've done your good deed. You've saved me again. Go home."

Mac sighed, clearly wanting to do more, wanting to fix what could never be fixed. Jesse stumbled away, but Mac was soon right beside him. "Who is Julia?"

Jesse's head shot up. His eyelids flinched and his hands fisted as all that useless frustration bobbed and jerked in him again.

"Amanda came home talking about her. She thought you guys knew each other."

"She's Mitch's widow," Jesse said and swallowed the words, dusty in his throat.

"Oh, Jesus," Mac swore. "What a mess. Amanda said—"

"The roof will be done in another week. Then I'm selling the house and leaving."

Mac breathed hard through his nose. "But—"

Jesse lurched away.

"Jesse." Mac caught up with him again. "Let me look at your nose and that eye—"

"Leave me alone!" Jesse finally roared. "Jesus! How many times do I have to say it?" He got in Mac's face. "Leave me alone!"

"You think you're the only one who's mad?" Mac shouted back. "You think you're the only one hurt by what's happened? Screw you, Jesse. We're hurt, too. All of us! Your whole family hurts with you. But you're too stubborn to see it."

Jesse's rage, boiling over for hours, finally

evaporated into mist. Spent. He was an empty sack of broken bones and scar tissue. His anger had burned everything in its path and now he had nothing left.

He shook his head and stepped backward onto the broken and cracked driveway. "I don't want to fight anymore."

Tears burned in his eyes and he smiled sadly at his old friend, begging him silently to understand that there was nothing Mac could do for him. Jesse was past help—a lost cause, a survivor who'd actually died in the crash, his body just didn't know it yet. "I'm tired." He sighed. "I'm just…tired. Okay?"

Mac nodded, his eyes glowing in the darkness like beacons in the night.

Jesse turned away from the safe harbor and staggered into the dark haunted house of his youth, where he'd never been safe.

Mac followed and Jesse didn't have the strength to fight or care. He lay still on the couch while Mac cleaned his cuts and put ice on his fat lip.

He smiled when Mac called him a headstrong son of a bitch.

He let Mac throw the blanket over his worn-out body and even pretended to snore just to get Mac out of the house.

As soon as he heard Mac's truck drive away, his eyes opened and he stared at the ceiling until he felt Wain's soft nose under his hand.

"Hey, Wain," he murmured, giving the dumb dog a

scratch under the collar. Wain liked that and climbed up on the couch with a sigh.

Jesse let the old boy walk up his legs to curl his old crippled body into Jesse's lap.

Jesse stroked the velvet of Wain's ears, the short fine hairs across his nose and down his graying muzzle.

"I'm sorry, boy," he whispered. "You should be with Artie."

The dog licked his hand in quick absolution.

The earth spun inordinately fast on its axis tonight, no doubt due to the solid shots to the head he'd taken. Jesse dropped one foot to the floor to steady himself so he wouldn't get spun off this twirling ball of rock up into the stars.

"Sorry, Mitch," he whispered. "Sorry about not listening to you and for getting mad. I'm sorry I didn't save you. I'm sorry about Julia." He sighed. He'd made this very same speech so often he had it memorized. Every breath, every blink of his eye was an apology. A plea for forgiveness he'd never receive.

Sorry, Artie.

Sorry, Dave.

Sorry, Mitch.

He closed his eyes, feeling sick, and it wasn't from his ribs and broken nose. He'd carried this sick feeling for months, wore it like a hair shirt. It was guilt laced with something else. Resentment. Resentment that he continued to eat shit for his old friend. That his whole life seemed dictated by Mitch, alive or dead. Married. Cheating. Drinking. Gambling. And he was sorry?

"I'm not sorry about Julia," he said. His eyes popped open.

Wain scrambled off his legs and curled up between his arm and chest, against the couch. Jesse hissed as the old dog pressed against his ribs, but he didn't push him off. "You never deserved her, man. Never."

And you do?

Jesse crossed his arms behind his head and decided tonight he wouldn't answer his own question. Tonight he was going to let the possibility linger. Morning would come soon enough and reality could strip all possibilities away then.

But tonight he was going to pretend that he did deserve Julia. That he still had it in him to create happiness for her.

He imagined her lithe, strong body crossing the moonlit-splashed room toward him. He imagined her hands, warm and sure and small. So small—delicate, like birds. He imagined their touch, their strokes and heat danced across his skin.

He imagined her skin, white and clean and pure. He imagined her naked, pressed against his body, wrapping her arms around him, close enough that he could absorb her if they both tried hard enough.

He imagined telling her, in breaths, in kisses and in long slow strokes of his body, that he loved her. That he'd loved her since she'd opened the door that day in Germany.

He imagined her lips, pink and lush, opening and he imagined her voice, a sweet whisper, a soft sigh saying *I love you, too.*

CHAPTER TEN

THE NEXT MORNING Julia got a job waiting tables at the Petro Truck Stop. It wasn't great, but it was money and it was work she knew she could do. Truckers, chicken-fried steak and bottomless cups of strong coffee—she felt as if she'd been there before. She walked back to the house with her shoulders back and her head held high.

She had a job, her first in years. Even though it was a crappy one, she could feel her self-worth inflate. Grow with every step.

She would start on Saturday, which gave her a few days to get up the courage to tell Agnes. Oh, she wasn't going to like Mitch's widow serving truckers out by the highway.

Julia picked up her son and headed out to the bulletin board at the grocery store.

The first thing on her list was to find some other daycare. She couldn't, and frankly didn't want to, rely on Agnes for every moment of childcare.

Childcare.

Apartment.

Car.

Hopefully the tips out at Petro came in solid gold.

Julia moved the flyers for lost dogs and found cats on the Vons bulletin board, searching for the flyers with the phone numbers on the bottom she could tear off.

There were no used cars, no apartments for rent and only one babysitting flyer, but all the tear-off strips were missing.

"Well, there you go." Her hands fell to her side and she tried to be philosophical about the whole thing. "That's just the way it is."

"Mama." Ben patted her leg and handed her his train and one slimy raisin as consolation. "'Ere you go." He smiled as if he'd known all along what she'd been going through and she swooped him up in her arms.

"Thank you, buddy." She pressed big wet kisses to his neck and he wiggled and squealed. "But you know what Mama really needs?"

He shook his head and shrugged with the beautiful exaggeration of a two-year-old.

"Mama needs chocolate, Benny boy. Lots and lots of chocolate."

She put Ben down on the ground and he ran over to the black pad that controlled the automatic door. He jumped on it with both feet causing the door to open and clapped his hands at the small consistent miracles in his world. She followed her son, pushing the repaired stroller into the air-conditioned store.

It wasn't just chocolate she needed. She needed the heavy-duty, the sugar and fat equivalent to being hugged by her mother. She needed a brownie with walnuts and about an inch of chocolate frosting.

"This way, bud," she called out to her son, who'd been distracted by the cereal display, and they took off for the bakery counter.

She got a brownie for her and a small peanut butter cookie for her son, just so he wouldn't beg for bites of her treat, and joined the express line.

A pretty brunette stood in front of her, buying milk and a big bag of oranges.

"Hi, Rita," she said to the cashier with a merry smile.

"Good morning, Rachel."

"What's new?"

"No, Ben," Julia said, stopping her son from putting all the candy bars in the display on the floor, while Rita told Rachel all about her niece's third birthday.

"How are things at the high school?" Rita asked.

"Busy." Rachel smiled. "I thought I was run ragged working for the county, but being a guidance counselor is keeping me on my toes."

Julia knew she shouldn't listen in, but there was something in the easy back and forth of the conversation that lulled her in.

Imagine living in a town where even the cashier at the grocery store was your friend.

She got chills just thinking about it.

Maybe her mom was right. She could create what she wanted out of what she'd been given. She was in New Springs, for better or worse, and it was time to make the most of it. Create her own support system.

"How's your brother this morning?" Rita asked, with a sympathetic wince.

Rachel paused as she pulled out the cash from her billfold. "You heard about the fight?"

"Clara came in early to buy doughnuts and told me how Mike McGuire and his friends put him in the hospital last night."

"He's not in the hospital, Mac took him home."

Rita clucked her tongue and took Rachel's hand.

"Poor guy, he's had a tough go of it."

Rachel laughed and Julia wondered if she should go to the other express aisle…this one was pretty slow.

"You must be just about the only person in town who thinks that," Rachel said with a laugh that was slightly more acidic.

"I never thought he was as bad as this town thought he was. He and Mitch were allowed to run wild was all. Jesse just needed a firm hand. All that old gossip…" Rita kept talking but Julia no longer registered the words.

Jesse had been in a fight last night.

Her ears burned and her heart fell to her stomach.

"Mac and I are trying to get him to stay, at least for a while," Rachel said and Julia guessed this was Jesse's long lost sister.

"Good luck, sweetheart."

Finally, Rachel walked away with her bags and Julia put two bucks on the conveyor belt for their treats, grabbed her son and the stroller and didn't wait for her change.

"Excuse me," she cried, through the slowly closing mechanical doors. But Rachel did not slow down.

"Excuse me," she yelled louder, racing through the

door. Ben ran beside her, laughing, but still the woman's long strides didn't stop.

"Hey!" Julia screamed. "Rachel! Please stop!"

The woman finally whirled, strands of hair caught in her eyelashes. "I'm sorry, I didn't realize you were yelling for me."

"Hello." Julia halted in front of the woman. Ben banged into the back of her legs. "Hi, I just—" She heaved a big breath, feeling scattered with worry about Jesse. "Is your brother Jesse Filmore?"

"Yes. What about it?" The woman's friendly smile turned guarded.

"Is Jesse okay?" Julia's pulse seemed as if it would pound out of her skin. "I mean, the fight—is he all right?"

"Who are you?" Rachel asked. "Not to sound rude, but it's a small town and I know just—"

"I'm Julia. Mitch Adams's widow." Julia swallowed and watched the woman's eyes go wide with surprised speculation before her reserve fell off her like old skin.

"Oh, no," she sighed, "I'm—I'm so sorry. Mitch—"

"It's okay." Julia managed a smile, something lukewarm that she intended to curtail any sympathetic stories Rachel might have and feel compelled to share.

"I'm Rachel, Jesse's sister." Rachel shifted a bag into her other arm and held out her hand to shake. He smile was bright and welcoming. "You actually met my daughter the other day."

"Your daughter?" Julia hadn't met a lot of kids. Ben tugged on her hand, impatient, reminding her that a few kids would come in handy for poor Ben, who'd been spending far too much time with adults.

"Amanda. She said she met you on the street in front of Jesse's."

"Amanda's your daughter?" The woman in front of her hardly looked old enough to have a sixteen-year-old daughter.

"Yep. Well, by marriage. It's a bit of a story."

Julia laughed. "Isn't everything?" Rachel laughed, too, and Julia felt that sudden pull of kinship.

Wow, I really need a friend. She felt like the new kid at school again, sitting down at a table in the lunchroom filled with girls she'd die to talk to.

I'm too old to be this pathetic.

A car honked and Julia realized they were standing in the middle of the laneway.

"Mama!" Ben hollered and dragged her toward the curb.

"Oops." Rachel moved with them.

"About what Rita said…is Jesse okay?"

"He's pretty banged up." Julia could tell that Rachel was putting a brave face on things, but she wasn't fooled. "I just don't know what he was thinking last night. My husband found him in the parking lot of a bar getting the snot beat out of him and he wasn't even trying to defend himself." Rachel laughed incredulously. "Jesse was in Special Ops. Mike McGuire and his friends shouldn't have had a chance." Her sigh trembled and she looked down at her hands for a second as if she expected them to be able to do something. "I'm just worried about his state of mind. He's—"

"I know," Julia cut in, worried about the same thing. "He blames himself for the accident."

"Do you?" Rachel asked.

"No!" Julia cried, appalled at the idea. "Not at all. It was an accident and a war and Mitch…" She shook her head. "There was no way anyone could blame Jesse for what happened."

"Except Jesse," Rachel sighed and her lips tightened. "We've been trying to hang back and be patient and wait for him, but my husband has decided enough is enough and that we should just treat him like family."

"I don't really know what that means," Julia said, with a rueful laugh. "How does family treat each other?"

"I'm pretty rusty myself." Rachel smiled. "But I think we're going to get in his face a little bit more. Amanda's been doing it for a week and she said it was working, that Jesse was even beginning to joke around with her."

"Your daughter is a great kid."

"Well, she couldn't stop talking about you. She said, and I quote, 'she's totally cool.'"

"That's the best compliment I've gotten in a long time."

"Mama!" Ben pulled with all his weight against her hand and she leaned toward him.

"Amanda couldn't stop talking about your son, either." Rachel smiled and crouched down. "Hi, Ben," she said.

He waved, shy suddenly.

"I'm Rachel." Rachel held out her hand and Ben stared at it suspiciously until Julia nudged him with her leg.

"Hi," he said, putting his sticky hand in Rachel's. "I'm two." He held up five fingers.

"He's adorable." Rachel stood up. "You need a ride or…?"

"We're okay," Julia said.

"Here," Rachel said digging through her handbag. She pulled her receipt from her pocket and a pen from her bag. "There's my home phone." She scribbled and handed the paper over with a smile that was somehow both familiar and reserved. Respectful. "I know you're staying at the Adamses—"

"You do?" Julia asked. She'd never said anything about that.

"It's a small town, Julia. Word travels fast. But if you ever need a change of scenery for dinner or something, please give me a call. I grew up here, but… Well, it would be great to have another woman to talk to besides Rita."

"I…" Julia was literally speechless. She cupped the paper in her hand and pressed it into the breast pocket of her T-shirt. "Thanks. Really. I will. Call, I mean."

"Well, it was very good to meet you, Julia."

"Likewise."

They smiled at each other, Julia so full of an awkward gladness, she felt young.

"Call me." Rachel pointed at her and looked serious.

"I will," Julia assured her, patting her pocket. "Trust me." She laughed, thinking of the never-ending nights of Mitch worship she'd been going through at the Adamses. Last night, after her phone call with her mother, she'd been given a two-hour tour of Mitch's high school football scrapbook.

She'd been nailed to that couch by Agnes's painful grief, and her even more painful desire to keep the good memory of her son alive.

Julia had decided that it couldn't hurt to let the woman have her illusions. But suffering through those illusions night after night was another thing entirely.

Rachel climbed into her car and drove off with a honk and a wave. Julia put her son in the stroller, took her courage in hand and headed for Jesse's house.

CHAPTER ELEVEN

JESSE EXAMINED the damage he'd done to himself last night in the bathroom mirror. He had a black eye and a puffy split lip. His nose felt huge and the bridge was soft, like tapioca pudding. But it could have been worse. He was lucky Mac had shown up when he did.

Jesse bent his head to gingerly splash water on his face.

Last night's suicide mission had been stupid. He had to repair the roof. Fix it, sell this place and get the hell out of town. And he'd just set himself back a day, maybe two.

He'd been in constant motion since being released from the hospital. He'd visited all the families of the guys who had died in the crash. He'd contacted Chris. He'd made plans as though his life depended on it, barely slept and now… He shook his head. He stared at his reflection and barely recognized himself. He'd planned on spending a day, a week at most, in New Springs to get rid of the house and never look back.

But here he was, a week and a half later, stranded like a Jeep caught in quicksand. Every move he made sunk him deeper despite what he wanted. What he planned and needed.

"Get your shit together, soldier."

He stepped out of the tiny bathroom into the hallway and then out into the sunny living room.

Where Julia stood with her son, stock-still, like a deer in the wild.

For a split second, dream and reality converged and his body sparked to life. He could feel her skin again, hear her sweet sigh against his face.

"Scary," the boy said and buried his face in his mother's legs.

"Doesn't anyone knock?" Jesse muttered. "Everyone feels like they can just waltz in here."

He collapsed into his father's old easy chair ignoring, the tearing sound of the old blue brocade and the squeak of the springs.

"I'm sorry," she murmured, looking at Jesse through her eyelashes. He wanted to tell her to stop looking so provocative, so damn appealing, but the words started and died in his throat.

He was hurt and wounded and confused enough that he wanted her to look provocative. He wanted her to come over and sit on his lap, wipe the wet hair from his face and set about kissing all of his minor and major pains away.

"You scared him," Julia explained needlessly.

"Great." He rested his head against the back of the chair. "I've always wanted a career in the circus, frightening kids."

"You're…you're bleeding," Julia said and, slowly, so as to keep his brain from sliding out his mouth, Jesse

KIMANI
ROMANCE

An Important Message from the Publisher

Dear Reader,

If you'd enjoy reading contemporary African-American love stories filled with drama and passion, then let us send you two free Kimani Romance™ novels. These books will keep it real with true-to-life African-American characters that turn up the heat and sizzle with passion.

By the way, you'll also get two surprise gifts with your two free books! Please enjoy the free books and gifts with our compliments...

Linda Gill

Publisher, Kimani Press

Peel off Seal and Place Inside...

PUBLISHERS
FREE GIFT
SEAL
THANK YOU

THE EDITOR'S "THANK YOU" FREE GIFTS INCLUDE:

▶ Two NEW Kimani Romance™ Novels

▶ Two exciting surprise gifts

YES! I have placed my Editor's "thank you" Free Gifts seal in the space provided at right. Please send me 2 FREE books, and my 2 FREE Mystery Gifts. I understand that I am under no obligation to purchase anything further, as explained on the back of this card.

PLACE
FREE GIFTS
SEAL
HERE

▶ DETACH AND MAIL CARD TODAY! ▶

168 XDL EF2K   368 XDL EF2V

FIRST NAME	LAST NAME

ADDRESS

APT.#	CITY

STATE/PROV.	ZIP/POSTAL CODE

Thank You!

The Reader Service — Here's How It Works:

If offer card is missing write to: The Reader Service, 3010 Walden Ave., P.O. Box 1867, Buffalo, NY 14240-1867

BUSINESS REPLY MAIL

FIRST-CLASS MAIL   PERMIT NO. 717-003   BUFFALO, NY

POSTAGE WILL BE PAID BY ADDRESSEE

THE READER SERVICE
3010 WALDEN AVE
PO BOX 1867
BUFFALO NY 14240-9952

NO POSTAGE
NECESSARY
IF MAILED
IN THE
UNITED STATES

lifted his head. "Your nose." She pointed uselessly at her own lovely nose.

He touched the back of his hand to his pained nostrils and his hand came away red and wet.

"Here." A handful of tissue appeared under his chin. "I've got a diaper, too, if that—"

He snatched the tissues, careful to not touch her with his messy hands. "Thanks," he muttered. "Hopefully the Huggies won't be necessary." His lip curved at that ridiculous image. He'd really look scary with a diaper stuck to his nose. He heard her soft chuckle and his body went tense, hard. He'd tasted her last night in that terrible, wonderful dream and that taste, salty and hot, tipped his tongue and filled his fuzzy brain with a biting want. He did what he could to clean himself up with the tissues.

He heard the rattle of a toy and Julia whispered, "Here you go, buddy. It's yummy."

Julia gave her son a small pinch of a brownie. Soon, frosting covered the boy's face and hands, but his smile was wide. Jesse felt himself smile back.

"He looks like Mitch," he said stupidly, and the happy little scene in front of him shattered as though he'd taken a sledgehammer to it.

"That's what everyone says." Julia's own smile disappeared. She stood and Ben sat on the floor, playing with a toy train and licking frosting off his cheeks. "I think he looks like himself."

She tilted her head as if testing her assessment and then she looked up at Jesse, skewering him with her blue, blue eyes.

That look—that level gaze that somehow saw all the cheap things he'd ever done and then forgave him for them in the same instant—reduced him to something so elemental, so simple, so *forgotten,* he didn't know how to handle it.

He looked down at his bloodied hands, at the ruined tissues.

"Here," she murmured. Laughter like sugar dusted her voice. "You missed some."

Before he could stop her, before he even knew what she intended, she stood beside his chair and licked her thumb and used it to clean a spot on his chin and neck.

"You should go to the hospital, or something."

He didn't answer, just stared, like some kind of green boy in front of his first woman, at the soft sweet swell of her breasts against her pink T-shirt. Her fingers brushed his flesh, grazed the corner of his lips, his whiskers, the erotically sensitive skin of his neck.

He went hard in a painful heartbeat.

"Thanks." He stood, brushing away her hand. "Uh…what are you doing here?"

She swallowed, looking uncomfortable, and if there were ever a moment to rid himself of her, this was it. He could turn her kindness to ice in one moment. One terrible word aimed right at her tender heart. He looked at Julia's bowed head and the boy playing at her feet and knew he didn't have any more pretending left. He wasn't going to kick her out. He wanted her here.

The quicksand was rising and if she pushed the slightest bit, looked too long, stood too close, what would happen? Where would his weakness lead him? He didn't care anymore.

Before his eyes, she squared her shoulders and looked him straight on. She seemed to grow taller. The air changed and Jesse's sense of danger went on high alert.

Julia was here on a mission. And he feared that mission was him.

"There are some things I'd like to talk to you about," she said.

"I said everything I needed to say yesterday," he told her, using the last of his bravado.

"Good." She grinned. "Then you won't interrupt while I talk."

This was it. The moment he'd been running from since she'd shown up on his porch. Well, he was just too damn tired to fight it.

His stomach growled, reminding him he hadn't had solid food in far too many hours.

"Can we do this in the kitchen?" he asked, wanting to have something to do during this conversation. A distraction from his desire.

"Suit yourself," she said and followed him into the kitchen.

"I heard you were hurt and I wanted to make sure you were okay," Julia said, resting against the doorframe.

"I'm okay," he lied, because it was second nature. He pulled out some ham and cheese and looked for the bread he figured should be around here somewhere. He was shaken, off-kilter, not just from the fight, not just from the dream last night or her presence here this morning. He was wrecked by how badly he wanted her here, how badly he wanted to talk to her and touch her.

He picked up a knife and she stepped forward.

"Let me make you a sandwich." She pointed at the knife held in his shaking fingers. "You'll kill yourself the rate you're going."

He put the knife down on the counter next to the loaf of bread that had apparently been there all along.

He stepped out of the way and dropped into a kitchen chair. If she was making the sandwich, she wouldn't be touching him.

"So what happened last night?" she asked, peeling thin slices of pink ham from the package.

"Ran into a door."

She looked over at him with raised eyebrows. "Big door."

"Three big doors."

She smiled and put two pieces of cheese on the meat—just the way he liked it. "Why'd you do it?"

Because you touched me. Because you won't leave me alone. Because it hurts so bad.

"Seemed like a good idea at the time." He took the sandwich she offered, but instead of stopping there, she opened his fridge and took out an apple and the rotting grapes he hadn't touched since Mac dumped the groceries on him. He watched her rinse them, weed out the soft and brown ones, slice up the apple, remove the core.

He wanted to block it out, wanted to cover his ears to stop the sound of Ben singing to himself in the other room.

"You need to eat," she said as a plate clattered in

front of him. "You don't look like you've had a good meal in months."

He nodded, took a big bite of the sandwich.

"I want to clear something up," she said and the tone of her voice made his eyes dart to hers. Her shoulders were back, her small breasts pressed against her T-shirt in such a way that he had to concentrate on peeling the cheese from the top of his mouth or fall on his knees begging for her touch.

"That morning in Germany—" she inhaled through her nose like a bull about to charge "—that was you. You touched me. You came to me. I never once asked for it, or gave you the impression that it was okay for you to do that."

Oh, sweet Jesus. What he wouldn't give to be anywhere in the world but at this table. He chewed carefully and swallowed. She was mad, and he'd never seen this woman in a temper. It made his wounded head spin.

She was pretty when she was angry.

"I know," he muttered.

He'd sat on that couch watching her with her son and he'd battled every impulse he'd had to grab her and take her away from Mitch, the tiny house and the sad life she'd been living.

In the end he'd found a nasty compromise. He'd told her she deserved better. Should have kept his mouth shut.

"But you did it." She put her hands on her hips. "And I don't think you understand what you did to me that morning."

"I know, I understand."

"No, you don't." His one good eye opened wide at the tone of her voice. "You don't know what it was like thinking that I deserved Mitch. That…" She swallowed hard. "The things he did were my just rewards for being young and stupid and getting pregnant."

He knew all too well what it was like to be caught in Mitch's web. To believe you weren't good enough to be stuck anywhere else. It was Mitch's personal form of abuse. And it was effective.

"I'm twenty-four and I love my baby. I am grateful to Mitch for that. But you waltzed into that kitchen and you ruined my life. You tore down all my lies and my illusions and you made me think that…maybe I did deserve more."

"You did," he said. "You do."

"Then what the hell is wrong with you?" she shrieked and Jesse winced. "God, it feels…" She clenched her hands in her short hair. "You're here. I'm here. And I want you. It seems like I've wanted you forever. And you push me away but you look at me like you're starving and I'm a ham sandwich. I'm not such a fool that I don't understand that."

He swallowed and felt himself hit the bottom of that pit of quicksand. He nodded. He let go of the charade and breathed deep, a full breath. His first in months. "You're right," he said.

"Then why won't you let me—" She reached out to touch him and he grabbed her hands, stared right into her eyes. "Mitch is dead," she whispered. "He isn't between us anymore."

"He'll always be between us."

"But—"

"You married him, Julia."

She nodded.

"And I killed him."

She shook her head. "I don't believe you."

He stood, the chair screeching across the linoleum. "What the hell is wrong with you?" he asked. "You know, go ask anyone in this town whose fault that accident was. Go ask Agnes, she'll tell you."

She put her hands on his arms, his chest. She stepped closer, like some new version of Julia, someone brave and daring.

"I don't care what anyone else says."

He pushed at her arms, angry with her foolishness. Her recklessness.

"Mitch knew how I felt about you," he told her, and watched her eyes go wide with surprise. That he should admit his feelings for her this way seemed wrong. But he could tell it didn't matter to her. And he wanted to touch her, taste her, claim her.

But he had no right.

"He told me I shouldn't sniff after married women. I shouldn't sniff after his woman."

She opened her mouth to say something.

"How do you know that I didn't let him burn in that helicopter so that I could have you? So that you would be free of him?"

There it was. There was the truth, the dark cancer that ate at him in the dark hours.

"You don't believe that," she said. "You're not that kind of man."

"How the hell would you know what kind of man I am?" he yelled.

"I knew you the moment I met you. You're good, you wouldn't let anyone die if you could help it. My God, Jesse, look at what you did for Caleb Gomez—"

"Right. I put him in a coma. I'm a real hero."

"You are, Jesse. Even if you don't see it. Even if this town doesn't see it. I see it. I know it." Her voice shook, but her eyes were steady, those blue eyes that seemed to know even before he opened his mouth. "Why don't you let someone else be the judge?"

She stroked his hair back from his forehead the way he'd seen her do with Ben and in that gesture, that sweet touch, he was lost.

He resisted for a moment. A second of telling himself that her foolish hopes held no sway over him, that her romantic vision of what and who he was were her problem and he'd best just stay clear. And then all his restraint snapped and he leaned down and did what he'd wanted to do since Germany. He pressed his split, sinner's lips to hers.

She sighed, and he could taste her breath, sweeter and hotter than anything he'd ever known.

He cupped her face with his rough hands, slid the tips of his fingers into her short, silky hair and memorized her, one sense at a time. Her small body trembled and her hands gripped his shirt as if at any moment he might push her away again. So he pulled her closer until her breasts touched his shirt and he could feel the bones of her hips against his thighs.

They were suspended, hung in amber, in the bright sunlight streaming through the kitchen windows.

Slowly her mouth opened and her tongue licked his lips, an unholy, earthly benediction against his wounds and his lies.

He groaned, a lost man, and his hand cupped her head. He opened his mouth and the innocence of their first kiss burned in the heat of the second, the fourth, the tenth. Unending, until she was on her toes and he had gripped her hips and pushed her backward against the counter. His hands slid up her rib cage to the warm curve of her breasts.

She hiked herself up onto the counter, curled her legs around his hips and his erection pressed tightly into her.

"Yes," she hissed, when he raked her neck with his teeth. She sighed and groaned and pulled at the back of his shirt until he felt her hands, her short nails against his skin.

"Anyone home?"

She jerked away and stared at him in stunned, panicked silence.

"Hello?" the voice said again and this time there were footsteps heading from the front door to the kitchen.

"Shit!" Jesse muttered. He stepped away and he and Julia tried frantically, uselessly to put themselves right.

He watched her smooth her hair and wipe her mouth, but her lips were still swollen and her nipples were hard under her shirt.

"This is why I don't want you around," he told her.

She smiled at him the way Eve must have when she had that apple in her hands. For a minute he didn't recognize Julia as Julia. The quiet, shy woman whose smile was like summer and whose eyes forgave every stupid thing he'd ever done had disappeared. She was someone else, someone else with secrets and hidden depths. A woman with a plan, an agenda of her own.

She scared the bejesus out of him.

"You're such a coward," she murmured moments before his sister and niece barged in.

CHAPTER TWELVE

JULIA WAS TREMBLING. Shaking from a giddy combination of adrenaline and desire. Had she done that? Was that her saying those things? Good gravy, she felt... great. Liberated.

Oddly enough, she felt taller.

Did I just call Jesse a coward? She nearly laughed.

"Well, well." To Julia's horror, Rachel, Jesse's sister, walked into the kitchen and suddenly she didn't feel quite so bold. Instead, she felt like a teenager caught with her pants down. "Good to see you again, Julia."

She could hear Amanda in the front room talking to Ben. Rachel stepped deeper into the room and leaned against a kitchen chair. She crossed her arms over her chest and smiled as though she knew exactly where Jesse's hand had been just moments ago. There wasn't any anger in that look, just a feminine understanding, but it still made Julia uncomfortable.

"I was just...ah..." Julia couldn't look at Jesse and she couldn't get a feasible lie to stumble through her lips.

"She was leaving," Jesse said and Julia's overheated body temperature chilled considerably.

"Right." She turned to Jesse. "Glad to see you're doing…okay." She nodded once, briskly. And walked past Rachel.

Ben heard her coming and greeted her as though she'd been gone for months. "Mama!" he cried.

"Hi, Julia." Amanda pushed herself up on her elbow from where she'd been lying on the floor beside Ben. "Ben was just telling me about his train."

"He loves his train," Julia said stupidly. She could feel Rachel's and Jesse's eyes on her back and she wanted out of there immediately.

This is what happens to bravery, she thought. *It turns into foolishness real fast.* "Let's go, Ben."

"I'll walk with you," Amanda said, standing with Ben.

"No, it's—" But Ben clapped, clearly besotted with Amanda.

"Thanks," she muttered, feeling caught.

She didn't turn back around, she didn't wave or say goodbye, but she was barely out the front door before a rough touch on her hand stopped her.

"Thank you," Jesse said, his eyes sincere and warm. "Thanks for stopping by."

"You're welcome," she whispered, hope and her heart lodged in her throat.

He squeezed her hand before dropping it and she, in her short years of marriage, had never felt something so tender. So important to her bruised and battered spirit.

Ben and Amanda skipped on ahead and Julia followed with a foreign lightness in her own step.

And just like that, foolishness pays off, she thought with a smile.

"Hey, Julia?" Amanda turned around and walked backward.

"Yes, Amanda."

"You know, if you ever need a…like, a babysitter or something. You could call me." Amanda smiled and tripped a little, ruining her sales pitch.

"I could?" She smiled at the girl. God, could it be this easy? A great girl whom she trusted and liked ready to babysit?

"For sure," she said emphatically. "I babysit all the time and this summer I'm going to be doing an internship at the paper, so I'll be, like, totally broke."

"Sadly, Amanda, I know that feeling very well."

"Well, you should know—I am very affordable."

Julia laughed, feeling free and easy in a way she couldn't remember feeling. Jesse's kiss still burned her lips, his touch still burned her hand and her heart floated someplace above her head, in the low-lying clouds that filled the California sky.

"That's good to know. I just got a job and I am going to need someone to take care of Ben while I'm working in the mornings."

"Really?" Amanda's face lit up. "I could totally do that. I mean, I could do it at your house or—"

"Hey, this is me," Julia said pointing at the Adamses' house. They'd done some work on the lawn and it no longer looked like a neglected eyesore. She knew she'd done that. Well, she and Ben. They'd given

Agnes and Ron the emotional boost they'd needed to rejoin their life.

She was glad she'd been able to do something, besides fill out applications and listen to Mitch stories.

"I totally forgot," Amanda said, the smile and color leeching from her face. "You live with the Adamses."

"Yeah, I'm Mitch's widow." Julia watched her, puzzled by Amanda's suddenly nervous and worried demeanor as she walked Ben back to Julia.

"I won't be able to babysit here. I'm sorry, I should get going—"

"Julia!" The front door opened and Agnes, animated and clutching a letter, stepped out onto the cracked sidewalk. "You're never going to guess—"

"I really need to go," Amanda whispered and she took off running back to Jesse's house.

"What was she doing here?" Agnes asked, her eyes following Amanda as she ran. "What were you doing with her?"

Julia forced herself not to roll her eyes like the kid Agnes seemed to think she was. "I met her the other day, she offered to babysit Ben if I needed her to."

Agnes's mouth fell open. "Absolutely not."

Julia blinked, at a loss for words. "Agnes, what—"

"She's completely inappropriate to take care of Ben."

"I think I can judge the appropriateness of who takes care of Ben."

Agnes's eyes turned to hard stones. "All right, but that girl was arrested a few years ago. Did you know that?"

Julia swallowed. "No, I didn't. But I'm sure there's—"

"She burned down a farm." Agnes crossed her arms over her chest, looking as smug and mean as possible. "Nearly killed a man. And now, thanks to her father marrying Rachel Filmore, she's related to—" Agnes's face turned hard, as though her anger turned her into a statue "—Jesse Filmore. Who, I don't have to tell you, shouldn't even be allowed to breathe the same air as Mitch's little boy."

Julia reeled, silent. There were so many things wrong with Agnes's assumptions and prejudices that she felt paralyzed. "Amanda has been nothing but kind to me and Ben," she said, lamely. "And Jesse—"

"I can't expect you to understand in a few short weeks what that girl is like." Agnes patted her arm in a patronizing way. "You just have to trust me on this. That family is trash."

Julia pulled away, determined to defend Jesse. "Agnes, that's not fair. And it's untrue. I know what everyone in town is saying about Jesse. But they're wrong. Jesse didn't kill Mitch. They were friends. Mitch's death is tearing Jesse apart."

For a second Julia thought Agnes was going to slap her. Or have a heart attack. Her nose flared and the letter she carried crumpled in her fist. Her skin went pale and sweat beaded her lip. She even seemed to sway.

"Agnes…?"

"Do not mention that man's name again." She bit the words out.

"Jesse?"

"He should have burned in that accident. He should be dead, not Mitch." Her eyes dilated, her eyelids fluttered. "Not Mitch."

Julia did not know how to handle this malice, this violent hatred for Jesse. She wanted to run far away from this venomous woman, yet, at the same time, she worried that Agnes would collapse right there in front of her.

"Let's go inside, Agnes. You should lie down."

"I just want the best for you," she whispered. "The best for Ben."

"I know. I know." Julia put her arm around Agnes's soft, round shoulders. "Ben, go on inside, let's find out what Ron is doing." Ben skipped ahead and Julia took one of Agnes's fists in her hand—the fist holding the letter.

Agnes looked down at it as if she'd forgotten it.

"It's for you," she finally said. Color was coming back into her face. "It's from Lawshaw." She put the letter into Julia's hand and smiled, big and warm and friendly. Julia could only gape at the change from the hateful person she'd been just moments before. "You've been accepted." Agnes pulled a stunned Julia into her arms. "I'm so proud of you. Now you can forget about that job and get your degree like Mitch wanted you to."

She read my mail! That was the only thing Julia could think. *She opened my mail!*

"Oh, Ben!" Agnes yelled, her attention inside the house. "You do not put that in your mouth. I better go get him his lunch. He always comes home so hungry when he's been walking with you."

With that unsubtle jab, Agnes hurried into the house.

Julia stayed in the front yard. The words of the letter—*Dear Mrs. Adams, it is our pleasure to inform you that you've been accepted*—blurring in front of her eyes.

What have I done? What am I in the middle of?

And how do I get out of it?

"I'M SORRY, JESSE," Rachel said. "I didn't mean to interrupt—"

"You didn't," he said. He tore his eyes away from Julia's back as she crossed the street with her boy and his niece. "You didn't interrupt anything."

"That's not what it looked like." Rachel laughed and Jesse wanted to put his hand through the wall. He stomped past her to the kitchen. He took all the plates and dumped them in the sink, where one of them broke.

"Jesse, I'm sorry." She put her hand on his shoulder and he jerked away. "I didn't mean to make a joke."

"No, make jokes. It's hilarious. Me and Mitch's widow. It's the funniest damn thing on the planet."

"It's not. It's not funny." Rachel's dark green eyes swept over him. "I can tell it's really important to you."

God, sympathy…understanding even, from his sister of all people. He rubbed his hands over his face and cursed when he bumped his nose and he tasted the copper of blood all over again.

"Here." Rachel emptied her pockets of tissues and held them out to him.

"Thanks," he muttered and snatched them out of her hands.

"Have you known her a long time?" Rachel asked, her voice a soft comforting purr that smoothed all of his ruffled feathers. It was stupid—ludicrous—but he wanted to talk about Julia. He was a mess. He was spinning in circles, paralyzed by his guilt and his want.

"I met her a few weeks before the accident."

"Do you…are you…?" Rachel stalled and he lifted the wad of tissues from his nose.

"In love?" he asked, brutally of himself and her.

She nodded.

So did he and instantly felt better. Better for having admitted it to someone, anyone.

"Wow, Jess, that sucks," she said the words that so perfectly summed up his entire life that he couldn't help but laugh.

"Excellent assessment, counselor," he said and when her eyebrows creased he realized the error he'd made.

"How'd you know I was a counselor?"

"I threw away your letters, not Mom's."

He kicked out a chair and collapsed into it. The easy moment they'd just shared lay gasping between them. "I'm leaving, I'm not joking. The house is yours."

"You should wait until you can see out of that eye." Rachel leaned against the counter, her arms crossed over her chest, and suddenly Jesse was hurled back in time.

He was watching his big sister talk on the phone, the cord wrapped up her arm as she leaned against that counter. She was talking to Mom, leaning against that counter. Fighting with Dad, helping Jesse with his homework.

Being in here with her brought it all back, those things he thought he'd forgotten. The rare good islands in the sea of rot that'd been his childhood.

And now hot memories of Julia were thrown into the mix and he couldn't look over there without thinking of her. Pressed against him, her breast in his palm.

He shut his eyes.

"Mac and I are having a baby."

His eyes flew back open. Something small and weak ignited in his head. "What?"

"We're having a baby." Rachel smiled, though the tears in her green eyes stood out like gems. "In December."

Jesse was speechless. Surprised, actually, that he felt something about this. That he could be moved by this news.

"Mac is at the lumberyard right now, picking out wood. We'd like you to make a cradle."

"I don't do that anymore," he said.

"Well, I know you probably didn't have time in the army, but maybe while you're here. If you stay...we'd like you to stay."

The words weren't out of Rachel's mouth before Amanda came running into the room as if she were on fire. He didn't have a chance to say no, to even shake off the sickening desire he had to do just what his sister wanted.

Something in his gut wanted to sit in this kitchen with the ghosts of his sweet childhood sister and the hot available Julia circling him.

Quicksand.

I am never drinking again, he thought.

"Whoa, Mom, you're never going to guess who I just saw—" Amanda stopped abruptly, her shoes squeaking on the old linoleum. "What's going on?" she asked, warily eyeing him and Rachel.

"I just told your uncle about the good news." Rachel wiped at the tears under her eyes and Jesse held the tissues to his nose.

"Isn't it great!" Amanda cried. "I swear to God, I'm like the only person in the world without a little brother or sister. I mean, Mom always says that having you as a little brother was the coolest thing in the world. That she and Dad used to go camping with you all the time and that you followed them around wherever they went." She shook her head. "I cannot wait!"

There were explosions in his brain. Memories long suppressed. Wood smoke and Mac playing Eagles songs on a beat-up guitar. Jesse falling asleep with his head in Rachel's lap while the fire burned out.

She used to let him sleep in her room.

She used to put him on the handlebars of her bike and ride him to school.

She used to make breakfast when Dad was passed out and Mom was at work.

He moved the tissues and stared down at the blood pooled there. He'd forgotten those things. Her leaving had cut through his life like a wide scythe.

"I have to leave sometime," he said thinking about San Diego and Chris.

"But maybe not for a while," Rachel said. "Not right away."

"You should come for dinner Sunday. Dad's making steaks," Amanda said and licked her lips in exaggerated appreciation of steak.

"We'd love to have you," Rachel said, hope, like mist filling the air.

All the rejection and denial rushed to his lips. *No,* and, *I can't,* and, *get the hell out of my house!* He was silent instead.

To avoid giving an answer he pressed the tissues to his nose again, even though it had stopped bleeding.

"We better get going," Rachel finally said, taking the hint.

"Hey, with that eye and stuff, you're going to need help around here again," his niece said, her eyebrows arched in a purely speculative way. "I don't want to take advantage of a man when he's down, but I'll give you a deal on my salary."

"I never paid you a salary," he said, glad the tissues covered his smile.

"All things we should discuss." She nodded her head, like some old sage. "I better stop by tomorrow."

"Amanda, leave him alone before he decides to strangle you," Rachel called from the other room and Amanda smiled at him as if they were old conspirators. He supposed they were. She whirled, her hair a pretty blond fan behind her, and was gone.

The echo of their voices, the sound of Rachel's truck starting up and leaving, all faded away. Wain emerged from one of the back bedrooms where he'd taken to chewing on the corner of some carpet that had come up and he sat on Jesse's foot.

His warm weight settled, solid and comforting, across Jesse's bare skin.

"Just don't fart," he told the old dog.

Jesse realized that what was happening to him right now was normal. Real life. Nieces and family dinners and stolen kisses with beautiful blondes in kitchens. These things happened every day to humans around the world.

And it felt so good.

CHAPTER THIRTEEN

SHE'D MADE A MISTAKE. That much was clear. Coming to Agnes and Ron had put Julia smack-dab in the middle of a web, sticky and terrible. But she couldn't get out. She had nowhere to go. No car. No money. A job that started in a few days.

"So," Ron said, as he cut his pot roast into small pieces. He watched her over his glasses, those grandfatherly eyes not nearly as kind and welcoming as they'd been three weeks ago. "I hear congrats are in order. Lawshaw is a wonderful community college."

I'm an adult, she told herself. *Time to act like one.*

"I am not going to school," she finally said, sounding like a rebellious teenager. She looked up from the salad she'd been pushing around her plate and set down her fork. "I've gotten a job and I'm going to make some money so Ben and I can move out."

The words fell like bombs in the still air. Ron also set his fork down. Agnes pressed her napkin to lips and made some excuse to go to the kitchen.

"Is this your gratitude?" Ron asked.

"I am grateful, very grateful, Ron. You can't imagine what your hospitality has meant to us—"

"Well, this is a terrible way to show it."

Julia suddenly saw Mitch's childhood played out in front of her. His parents had created a liar—a man who constantly took the path of least resistance to avoid this burden of guilt, this responsibility of pleasing two people with a narrow rigid view of the world. And Agnes and Ron had no idea. They were blind to what they'd done to Mitch, what they'd made of him.

She thought of Ben, sleeping upstairs, and promised never to force her expectations upon him. Mitch's son would have no idea what it was like to be Mitch.

"Ron, my son and I need to get settled. I am a grown woman and I cannot take advantage of your kindness any longer."

What she really wanted to say was "I can't live with your wife's insanity any longer," but that hardly would have served her purpose.

"We don't feel you are taking advantage. We feel that this is an opportunity for us to get to know our grandson."

"I'm not taking him away from you, I'm staying in town. I just need to get an apartment closer to work—"

"What work?" Agnes asked, having returned from the kitchen in time to catch the last of Julia's words.

Julia took a deep breath, steeled herself for the firestorm of disapproval. "Petro."

"The truck stop?" Agnes gasped.

"I'm waiting tables. I got a few morning shifts and—"

"You don't know what you're doing, Julia." Ron's

voice, pitched somewhere between pity and condescension, lit the fuse on her dormant temper.

"I know exactly what I am doing, Ron. I am trying to make a home for my son. I am trying to pay off Mitch's astronomical gambling debts and I am trying to get on with my life."

"You never loved Mitch," Agnes spat. "You never—"

"You're wrong, Agnes. Mitch never loved me," Julia yelled. "Mitch never loved anyone. He didn't have it in him."

"You're lying," Agnes cried.

"How would you know—"

"Calm down, both of you. Before you say something you regret." Ron's voice cut through the haze of anger that surrounded Julia. "You're getting worked up."

Yes, she thought. *Finally, I am getting worked up.* Her hands trembled but she felt so strong. Ready to take on any comers. She felt ready to beat back these false memories of Mitch.

"I think perhaps maybe we'd all better take a breath," Ron said. "We understand your desire to move on. To make a home. We are gratified that you want to do that near us."

It's not like I had much choice, she thought. She could have moved anywhere in the world and been alone, or she could have come here and had some kind of support.

Now she was beginning to wonder if anywhere else in the world might be better than here. But then she would never have seen Jesse.

She was twenty-four years old. She had a son. She'd

lived all around the world and she was just now figuring out what she really wanted. Jesse was a part of that, but he came with a price—her pride.

"Will you take care of my son while I'm working?" she asked. "Just until I have enough—"

"Of course," Ron interrupted. "You don't have to ask."

"I'd also like to discuss private mail," Julia said, still outraged that Agnes had opened that letter.

"Hold on a second, Julia," Ron said, holding up a finger. "The letter was addressed to me. It came with a private note from a friend in admissions at Lawshaw." Again those kind eyes turned cold. "I pulled a lot of strings to get you early acceptance—"

"I didn't ask—"

"You filled out the application, Julia. If you weren't interested you should have said so then."

She felt as though she were a child lacking in common sense. Guilt curved her shoulders and pressed her eyes to her plate. "I'm sorry. I didn't want to upset anyone."

"Well, you've done a terrific job of that," Agnes snapped.

"Agnes," Ron barked, chastising her. Collectively they held their breath, watching each other from the corner of their eyes, waiting to see who would make the first move.

I can leave. I should leave. I should just go.

But where would she go? She had no money for an apartment. She had no friends. She had only Jesse, and she didn't even know what he was.

She felt torn between circumstances and her desires.

"Now, if school is not in the cards for you right now, I think that's fine," Ron said and she waited for the catch. "I understand. You should have some money. But you should consider what a college education can do for you. For Ben."

The guilt choked her so she could barely breathe. All of her strength, anger and righteousness vanished. "I will. Thanks," she managed to say.

"All right." Ron nodded as though everything was settled. "Agnes, a wonderful meal, as usual." He patted his belly. "I'll wash if you dry," he said to his wife, who appeared to feel as small as Julia felt.

"Thanks," Agnes said and turned into the kitchen.

"I'm going for a walk," Julia told Ron's retreating back. She had to get out of here.

"Sounds like a fine idea, take a sweater."

HOW HAD SHE MANAGED to be so bullied? Again? Julia wondered, shutting the oak door behind her. All they had to do was mention Ben and she folded in on herself with guilt. She was a good mother. She had nothing to be ashamed of.

Except for a meager bank account and homelessness.

She'd wanted to hold out for that Holmes Landscaping job, for any job that didn't actually involve polyester uniforms and chicken-fried steak. But a job was a job and she needed one desperately. Especially now with the open hostility in the Adams' house.

Before she'd even realized it, she'd skipped across

the dark lawns and jumped the ditch and stood on the sidewalk beside Jesse's house.

Jesse's house was dark but lights pooled on the grass from his garage. She saw his shadow pass one of the windows and her heart swelled, trembled in recognition.

There was nowhere else she wanted to be but in that garage with him. It was as simple as that. Her body, her heart, everything led her here.

She remembered the squeeze of his hand as she'd left earlier, the unshuttered look in his eyes as he'd thanked her for stopping by as though he'd meant it. As though he'd wanted her there.

The memory of that look was enough to propel one foot in front of the other across the grass in the direction of that old building.

Unsure of her greeting, she knocked tentatively on the splintered gray wood of the garage door.

His head turned toward the doorway and, for a moment, she thought his battered lips might smile. Instead he bent back to the wood he was inspecting.

"Hello," she said.

He grunted in response.

"I saw your light on…."

He was silent.

"Thought I'd come in and say hello."

"Hello," he practically barked.

Tired of being pushed around and playing games, Julia threw her hands in the air. The idiot had been kissing her just a few hours ago.

"You're worse than a sixteen-year-old. Either you

like me or you don't. Whichever it is, stop playing this game with me."

"Sorry," he said, his head stayed bowed. "I'm sorry." His hands flexed on the wood he held and the moment stretched. He breathed and so did she. She blinked. Toyed with the hem of her sweater. "Stay. I'd like you to stay." He watched her over his shoulder and then finally smiled. "I've been a jerk for so long I've forgotten how to be anything else."

The smile, more than anything, gave her pause. Enchanted her, really.

"Okay." She nodded.

"You can sit." Jesse pointed to a wobbly old stool to his right.

"Thanks." She lowered herself onto the stool, hooked the heels of her battered tennis shoes on the rung and tucked her hands under her thighs. "What are you doing?"

"Looking at this oak."

Hmm. This was going well.

"Rachel and Mac are having a baby." He wiped his stubbly chin with his hand. "They want a cradle."

"Are you going to make it?" She didn't know he could do that sort of stuff. But the image of Jesse as a woodworker, covered in sawdust, hammering things, made her warm.

"I don't know." He leaned against the workbench and crossed his arms over his chest. The soft gray flannel of his shirt pulled across his shoulders with the movement.

"They must be so excited." A baby. She remembered that feeling of holding a treasure in her body, a secret that only she knew.

"I think Amanda's more excited than anyone." His smile pulled and stretched his bruised and puffy skin.

"I had a weird moment with Amanda and Agnes today," Julia ventured, stretching out into the unclaimed territory between them. Friends.

"I can imagine. Agnes is a sociopath."

Julia wished part of her didn't agree with him. "Do you know Amanda was arrested? Agnes seems to think Amanda started a fire."

Jesse shrugged. "You can't take anything Agnes says seriously."

"She's beginning to freak me out," Julia admitted. "She's so possessive. I mean, I would understand her feeling that way about Ben, but she actually forbid me from saying your name today."

Jesse laughed.

"That's why I stayed friends with Mitch for so long," he said. "Even though the guy had everything, I felt sorry for him." He picked up another piece of wood.

"I did, too," Julia said, so relieved to be talking about this. "I feel like I had to come all the way out here to finally understand him and—" she blew out a long breath "—forgive him, I guess."

"He doesn't deserve that from you. Not for what he did."

"But who could live with the kind of pressure Agnes and Ron put on him? I used to wonder why he lied so much, about the dumbest things. But it all makes sense once you get to know his parents."

"The first time Mitch did real bad on a test—" he looked over his shoulder at her "—Ron got a copy of the test and made Mitch stay awake studying until he got every question right. Mitch was awake for two days straight."

"That's awful."

"Yeah, it got to the point where the way my own dad dealt with things just made a lot more sense."

"What did he do?" Julia didn't want to ask but had to know.

"He drank mostly. He got pretty violent."

Jesse began piling the wood on the bench under the stronger light that was clamped there.

"I'm sorry," she said stupidly, sensing all the pain under those words.

"Don't be. I'm over it." He shrugged, his shoulders tense despite the casual words.

"I never knew my dad," she said.

"He ran off?"

"He was military. Career."

"Sometimes that can be worse," Jesse said and it was so true there was nothing she could add to it.

Jesse stretched out the measuring tape. He pressed it against the wood, took a pencil from behind his ear and made a small mark on the oak.

A small, beat-up, paint-splattered radio was playing a Johnny Cash tune and Jesse hummed along with it for a moment.

Julia felt aglow, relieved and happy in the way of a person finally setting down a burden. "I got a job."

"Good for you." He obviously meant it. There was no sarcasm in his voice.

"Out at Petro, the truck stop. I start on Saturday."

"I used to dream about their meat loaf."

"You're kidding." Julia laughed.

"God, I wish. The big secret about life in the military is that most of the time all you're doing is dreaming about food. And sex. That's it."

"Did you like it? The military, I mean," Julia asked, wondering at what point all of Jesse's walls would go back up and the relaxed, laughing man in front of her would revert to the cold solider she dreaded.

He selected another piece of wood and measured it. "Some of it. Some of it I loved."

That was all he said. She made a humming noise and let the subject drop.

"What about you?" he asked. "What did you do before you ended up being a helicopter pilot's wife?"

"I moved to the coast, got a job waiting tables. One day I went for a run on the beach and ran into Mitch." She shrugged. "That's my whole life story."

Jesse wiped his hands on a cloth from the bench. "Mitch used to talk about you nonstop. But I could never know what was real and what was bullshit."

"Most of it was lies I bet." She laughed, feeling awkward under his sideways gaze. "I never wanted to go to college and I never wanted to be a dancer—"

"Really?"

She glanced up at him but not for long. "Well, maybe for a second or two out of high school. I took some classes, but nothing serious."

He smiled. "You look like a dancer. You move like one."

Julia blushed like a schoolgirl and loved every minute of it. She felt as though she were being wooed.

"So, what do you want to do now?" he asked. "If not college, if not dancing, then what?"

She bit her tongue against putting her wish into words for fear of jinxing herself. But this was Jesse, the man who'd seen through to the best parts of her from the moment they'd met.

"I want to work with plants," she confessed. "Landscape or horticulture or something." She waved a hand as if to say, "it's no big deal."

"You know Holmes Landscaping—"

"I applied. They're not hiring." She looked away, embarrassed by wanting something she couldn't get.

Worth. She reminded herself. *You are worth more than that job. It's their loss.*

"Mitch never mentioned that," Jesse said.

"He didn't know."

She met his eyes and suddenly him knowing her aspiration was more intimate than then kiss in the kitchen.

"Mitch talked about you all the time, too," she said, changing the subject in a rush. "Same thing, though. Didn't know what was real."

"Well—" he scowled and searched through the

clutter on the bench "—I never went to jail and I never beat up a kid for his shoes and—"

"Until I met you," she interrupted his tirade. "The second you stepped into my house in Germany I felt like I knew what was real and what wasn't."

He stood still, his hands hovering over the work-bench, as though waiting for something.

"I knew you were smart, but didn't do so well in school. I knew you were a good athlete. I knew you liked books and music. I knew you never lied."

"Well, I wouldn't go that far."

"I knew you were one of the good guys, no matter what Mitch said."

Jesse stared at her and somehow she knew he needed to hear this, he needed to be stroked and patted. His ego was as battered as hers, she could see it in his eyes. "I feel like I've known you all my life, Jesse. Doesn't that sound crazy?"

"No," he murmured. "It doesn't sound crazy at all."

He cocked his head and watched her. The air suddenly changed. Became electric, dangerous. The core of Julia's body, simmering for days now, erupted and she felt her face flush.

"What are you doing here, Julia?"

"I…ah…was just out for a walk," she muttered. She was proud of herself for meeting his eyes. For not looking away despite the intensity between them and the lack of oxygen in the room.

"You do a lot of walking." He put the pencil and tape measure down and took a step closer to her. She tilted her head back wondering, thrilled and scared, what he was going to do. "And you always end up at my door."

His thigh butted her knee and she let her legs fall open. Her foot went to the ground and Jesse moved in until she could feel the heat of him between her legs, down the front of her body.

She swallowed audibly. His hand touched her face, skimmed her hair. "You're so beautiful," he whispered, his eyes branding every inch of her face.

"I'm plain," she said and then wished she could just gag herself for the next hour or so.

Jesse just shook his head. "Not to me." His other hand came up and cupped her throat. She swallowed again, her head, so heavy, tilted back at an awkward angle, but she didn't care as long as he kept touching her. "I've thought about you every day since Germany."

I must be dreaming, she thought. *Or I've stumbled down a rabbit hole.*

It was as though this terrible, wonderful moment had been plucked from her dreams.

"I thought of you," she whispered. It was all she allowed herself to admit. She couldn't begin to tell him the hole his brief presence in and subsequent absence from her life had made. And how every day she gazed into that hole and wondered if she'd see him again.

He bent, she stretched and their lips touched. A kiss. Soft, sweet, fleeting and then gone.

Her eyes fluttered open only to see him staring down at her with an expression she couldn't discern.

"What are you thinking?" she asked after the silence had expanded too much and he seemed content to just watch her.

"Dangerous question." He seemed so solemn. Serious. She wondered what he saw when he looked at her that made him so sad.

His hands touched her face one more time and her eyelids fluttered shut. His fingertips skimmed her eyelashes, her cheekbones, her earlobes. He touched her lips and they parted on a gasp. She felt alive, electric, in every sense. Every cell and fiber of her body was trained on him. Focused with a sexual intensity she'd never known existed. She was so attuned to him, she hurt. She ached where his hands didn't touch her. She burned where his breath didn't reach.

And then suddenly he was gone.

Her eyes flew open and that, too, hurt.

He put up a hand as if warding her off. "That kiss was for me. Something I've wanted for years, but we need to talk. Not about Mitch or meat loaf but about—" he waved a hand between them "—this."

"Okay." She shook her head. "We can talk."

"I'm not staying here," he said and the words barely made a dent in her desire. "I'm leaving soon."

"How soon?"

"A week, two at the most." The solemnity in his eyes drilled through her. "I want you. That's not a secret anymore."

She stood. "I want you, too, Jesse."

"But I'm leaving. I can't stay and anything…" He

paused, took a deep breath. "Anything between us—anything sexual—would just complicate things."

"When have things ever been easy?" she asked and stepped toward him.

"Probably never, since you seem bent on pushing the issue," he snapped. He took a step back. "I already feel responsible for you being here, for Mitch."

"Don't," she said firmly.

He blew out a big breath. "I wish you saying that could change it, but it doesn't. Nothing can happen between us. This is the right thing to do."

"Nothing? How can that be right?" *How can that be right when I am burning alive?*

He grabbed her arms when she was within reach and held her away from him. "You wanted friendship. We can be friends, but that's all. That's it. I can't deal with any more."

"You just kissed me," she reminded him, exasperated.

"I know. And it won't happen again." He licked his lips. "I didn't want you here. I didn't want this house. My sister, this wood, I didn't want any of it and suddenly I can't get rid of you. You're Mitch's widow. You're living with his parents. You have his son. You're putting down roots here and I am leaving. You said you were trying to move on and trust me, falling into bed with Mitch's best friend is not moving on. For either of us. I can't stay and I don't want to."

Well, she thought, removing herself from his hands, *when you say it that way...*

Silence filled the room like cotton bunting. She

brushed back her hair and looked at him, ready to take him at his word. He was right. She was trying to get her life on track and so was he. Anything between them would put them off course.

"I just can't be responsible for everything." He sighed.

"I never asked you to."

He ignored her. Grabbed a tape measure and put a pencil between his teeth, as if she'd never spoken. How could she convince him that she didn't blame him for anything? He'd never listen. Not now.

Not yet, but maybe he eventually would if they really were friends. Maybe in time, she could convince him that Mitch was no longer between them.

"Friends?" she asked, skeptical. "For real? You're not going to go all freaky on me next time I come over."

He watched her, removed the pencil. "You're not the same woman I met in Germany."

"You're right." She grinned. "I am different."

"The woman you are now would have scared the hell out of Mitch."

"And you," she said, narrowing her eyes at him. "Clearly I scare the hell out of you, too."

"You don't know that half of it." He turned to his wood and his shoulders slumped with a sigh. "I'm terrified."

This wasn't what she wanted, or what she expected. But it was good to stand in this room with his chuckle echoing around the battered walls. She was working in small degrees of better. She was the merchant in the smallest amounts possible of happiness and satisfaction. She added another kernel to her meager stockpile.

"You want some help?"

"Sure. Hold this."

He gave her the end of a tape measure.

She nodded, though it hurt, but something was better than nothing. "Okay."

CHAPTER FOURTEEN

AMANDA RACED to the phone when it rang.

"Got it!" she yelled so no one would interrupt and hear her talking to Caleb Gomez. Oh, man. That would be bad. She'd called the San Diego Naval Hospital two days ago, leaving a message for him to call back today. Right now.

She wanted to talk to Caleb Gomez for two reasons. One, her mother refused to, thinking that Caleb only wanted to write a story about what happened. But what if Caleb wanted to thank Jesse for saving his life? Wouldn't that help him? Wouldn't that make him feel better?

Two...well, was her English paper. It was already too late, school got out three days ago and she'd turned in that stupid essay on government spending for social work. But she still wanted to write an article about her uncle, and maybe Caleb, for her summer internship at the newspaper.

She grabbed the receiver in the kitchen and quickly snuck into the crawl space under the stairs. All the buttons glowed green in the darkness. She hit the talk button.

"Hello," she whispered and then realizing she'd whispered she practically yelled, "Hello."

This is not the way a journalist works. Even a teenage one.

"I'm looking for Amanda Edwards." The guy on the other end of the phone had a slight Hispanic accent and Amanda's eyes shut in relief.

Jackpot!

"This is her. She. Her." *Oh, brother.* "You're talking to her."

Caleb Gomez's laugh was deep and kind of nice. "Hi, Amanda. I understand you have some information about Jesse Filmore."

"Maybe." She'd thought about this part. She wasn't going to blow this. "But before I tell you anything I have a few questions for you."

There was a long pause. "How old are you?"

"Seventeen." Almost.

"Well, you're either thinking about a career in journalism, politics or extortion."

"What's extortion?"

"Good for you, kid, ask me your questions."

"First, are you planning on writing a story on my... on Jesse Filmore."

"Yes."

Her lips twisted. "Hmm." Not the best answer. She didn't want to see Jesse hurt any more and she just knew a news story would kill him.

"I think my readers would be interested in how Jesse did everything, including risk his own life, in order to save me."

That was better. Much better. Points to Caleb.

"Do you think he caused that crash? I mean, do you think he killed all those guys?"

Caleb sighed. "I know it's hard to believe otherwise when it's been speculated about all over the news."

"Tell me about it," she groused.

"But I have some information and I think it's important I talk to Jesse before I write about it. I'll be able to sit in a car in a few days and I want to see him."

"You know how the crash happened?"

"Amanda, let me give you a lesson in journalism. A journalist never tells anyone what he does or doesn't have in terms of information."

"Makes sense," she said, though she wasn't entirely sure what it meant.

"All right, Caleb Gomez. I do have some information for you." She gave him Jesse's address and cell phone number.

"Wait," Caleb said when they were about to hang up. "How is he? Jesse? Is he okay?"

She thought of his wrecked face and his bloody nose and the dead look in his eyes and the way he couldn't even be in the same room as Julia.

"Caleb. I think the sooner you get here, the better."

"I SHOULD BE BACK BY NOON," Julia said for the third time. It was Saturday, her first morning of work and her first morning of Agnes Adams's daycare, which made Julia feel a little twitchy. She kept remembering the story Jesse had told her about Mitch and the test and being kept awake for two days. And the stories he'd told her in the days since then.

She didn't want Agnes to have that kind of influence over Ben, to harm him in the million ways she'd hurt Mitch.

Julia looked at her sweet little boy, who was covered in Cheerios and sliced bananas.

"Of course, it's fine." Agnes's voice was cold but the hand that stroked Ben's head was tender and the glances she saved for Ben were as sweet and grandmotherly as Julia could ever dream. "I am his grandmother after all."

As long as she only hates me, she thought, tucking her uniform apron into her purse. *As long as she never takes it out on Ben.* "All right then." She looked around to see if she was missing anything and, of course, wasn't, since she didn't have anything. "I'll see you in five hours."

She kissed her son, thought for a second of saying something that would kill the tension between her and Agnes, but in the end stayed silent. She always bent. She always gave in, took the high road. She wasn't going to do it anymore.

She put her hand to the door and was nearly out it, before Agnes stopped her.

"Julia?"

"Yes." She paused.

"I'm sorry," Agnes said and Julia turned. "I am sorry for the things I said the other day."

Julia nodded, stunned. "Me, too."

She stepped out into the cool California morning and shut the door behind her.

She wanted to believe that Agnes was sincere, that she was truly regretful for the spiteful things she'd said, but Julia didn't believe it for a minute.

The apology had seemed mechanical, manipulative, as insincere as Julia's own.

The situation between them never going to get better.

THE WORK WAS PREDICTABLE. Familiar. Lots of coffee. Extra gravy. Seasoned waitresses who took their smoking breaks seriously and loved to talk at the coffee machines. Julia had forgotten how the slow times at restaurants created plenty of room for nearly instant camaraderie. Nothing to do but roll silverware and chat.

It wasn't even an hour into her shift and she knew all about Lynn's youngest son's problems at school. And that Jodi's ex-husband was getting married in a few weeks.

"It's killing me," Jodi whispered, pulling her ponytail tighter. "I dumped him and he's getting remarried before I've even had a steady boyfriend."

"You got to stop acting so desperate when we go out," Nell, another one of the waitresses, said without looking up from her crossword puzzle. "Hey," she said, turning to Julia. "You should come out with us next weekend."

"Ah…" Julia laughed. "I have a baby—"

"Don't we all, sweetie." Nell sighed. "Get yourself a sitter and kick up your heels. You look like you need it."

I do need it.

"Thanks." She smiled at the three women and kept rolling silverware into napkins. "I'll keep it in mind."

"Someone just sat in your section," Lynn said. "And

I tell you what—" she whistled "—if you don't hurry, I'm going to steal that seat. That is one good-looking man sitting there."

All three women stood up on their tiptoes to look over the huge bank of coffee machines. Julia found herself on her toes, joining them.

It was Jesse, sitting with his back to the women. But she'd know him anywhere.

"Well, well. Something tells me this isn't an accident," Nell teased good-naturedly, watching Julia as she blushed.

"That's Jesse Filmore," Jodi said. "You know him?"

Julia nodded, unwilling to go into all the details.

"Oh, man." Jodi sighed. "I had the biggest crush on him in high school. He was so tough, you know, and quiet."

"The strong silent types always get you in trouble," Lynn murmured and bent back to her crossword.

"Amen," Jodi agreed. They all started talking about where they were going to go out next weekend and that was the end of the Jesse conversation.

Julia wondered if the hatred Jesse felt for this town wasn't all in his head.

She touched a nervous hand to her hair and headed out to see what Jesse wanted.

"Hi," she said as she stood at the end of his booth. His shirt was red and his eyes were bright and she wished she could slide into that booth with him.

"Morning," he said with a smile.

"What are you doing here?" she asked as her heart tripped and hammered in her chest. Just the sight of him, the look of him, made her knees weak.

"Craving for meat loaf." He tapped the menu.

"For breakfast?"

"Cravings are cravings, Julia. Why fight it?" He smiled again, but then seemed to realize what he'd said. All the things they were fighting exploded around them.

"I, ah…I knew it was your first day. Thought I'd come in. As a friend," he said, denying her the sweet memory of his heated kisses in his kitchen and the tender press of his lips to hers in his garage.

"Sure," she finally managed to say. "I mean, right. Friends. You want a meat loaf?" She scribbled non-sense on her pad, sure her hair was on fire she was blushing so much.

"That'll be great."

"Potatoes?"

"Mashed. Thanks, Julia."

"Well, it's my job," she said in an attempt to make herself feel better, and less like a fool. She walked away before she did any more damage.

"Ordering," she hollered back to the guys in the kitchen as she put her guest slip on the circular ticket holder in the window between the servers' station and the kitchen.

"Got it!" one of the men back there yelled.

She turned around to see Nell, Jodie and Lynn all grinning at her.

"Now I know why you don't want to go out with us." Jodi laughed. "It's got nothing to do with your baby."

They pressed her for details about Jesse, but she held them off, the whole time secretly pleased that anyone would even care.

The next few days chugged along in a steady rhythm and Julia's confidence slowly grew. Agnes and Ron weren't crowding her and seemed to have come to some kind of understanding about her having a job.

And Jesse. Jesse came by the restaurant regularly for meat loaf. When it was slow she sat down with him and had a cup of tea. It was torture, sitting across from him with her hands clenched against the need to stroke his arms, his lips and eyebrows. It hurt to pretend that her feelings had mellowed into friendship when every moment spent with him only sharpened them. As his defenses dropped and his smiles came with more frequency, she knew deep in her bones that she was falling more in love with him every second.

"I never really liked San Diego," she said one morning when they were talking about the city he planned to move to.

"No? Could you pass me the ketchup?"

She slid the ketchup across the table to him and she made sure their fingers brushed in the exchange. There was a spark and a sudden heat and she blushed and he frowned.

"It's so crowded." She pulled her hand away and spun her mug of tea, hoping her opinions might change his mind. "And expensive. You'll be totally shocked by the cost of rent. You'll be living in some student's closet for about a million dollars a month."

"So where would you go?" he asked. "Of all the places you've lived, where did you like the best?" He took a big bite of meat loaf and Julia considered the question while he ate. He asked a lot of this sort of question, forcing her to think about her life and her wants in a way she never had. With all of her answers she felt as though she gave away pieces of herself to take with him when he left.

"I liked it in Hawaii." She smiled and he returned it, his mouth closed. "But you know—" somehow this feeling had snuck up on her the past few days "—I really like it here."

"New Springs?" He choked and put his fork down. "You're kidding."

"Nope." She shrugged away his horror at the idea. "I like small towns and I like the heat and desert…well, I like the plants."

But it was more than that. This was the first town she'd picked on her own. The first place where she'd started to create what she needed out of what she had and it was working.

"Well, I suppose if you never have to talk to anyone—"

"I really like the people," she interrupted and looked directly at him. She dreamed at night of being able to stop him from moving, of being able to keep him here, but that would never happen if he thought the whole town hated him. "They're not as bad as you think, Jesse. And I don't think people even remember all the stuff you did."

"They remember, trust me." His expression shut down, his shoulders hunched and Julia dropped the subject.

"Jodi, the redhead—" Julia nodded her head toward the bank of coffee machines, where the girls were spying on them "—has a crush on you." He lifted his eyebrows and kept chewing. "She has since high school."

"Get out." He turned again toward the coffee machines and wiggled his eyebrows like a horny Groucho Marx. Julia laughed and their conversation drifted to the trivial as their favorite foods, movie star crushes and the best driving songs.

He avoided touching her and she went out of her way to make sure their fingers brushed. They never talked about Mitch or how they felt, or the desire that breathed like a dragon whenever they were close to each other.

Julia mourned every second that led them nearer to the time he would leave her. But she couldn't ask him to stop visiting her at work. She couldn't turn him away, no matter how hard it was going to be when he left.

"TAKE MY TABLE that just sat down, would you?" Nell asked on Julia's fourth day at work. "If I have to wait on Virginia Holmes one more time I swear I'm gonna dump that pot of tea in her lap."

"Virginia Holmes?" Julia asked, peeking over the coffeepots.

"In the flesh. Good luck." Nell walked off with a tray of oversize sodas for the truckers at the counter.

Julia mustered all of her courage and approached the cantankerous woman who'd inadvertently put her life plan in reverse.

"Good morning, welcome to Petro. Can I get you something to drink?" She tried to look all business with her pen poised over her pad, tried to wipe all recognition from her eyes, but there were Virginia and Sue Holmes staring at her like fish left out of water.

"I thought you'd left town or something." Virginia's white bushy eyebrows met over her eyes. She turned to her daughter. "Didn't you say you called her?"

"I called her three times," Sue said. "I talked to Agnes Adams each time."

The world spun and dipped. "You called me?" she asked Virginia. "Julia Adams?"

"Three times, like I said. We got to talking after you came in with your boy and figured we'd be better hiring someone who'd stick around rather than those high-school kids that flake off at the end of every summer."

"You called to offer me a job?"

Virginia and Sue exchanged looks and then nodded.

"You talked to Agnes?" Julia needed to clarify the situation. Every controlling maneuver, every conversation Agnes had listened to, every unwanted opinion the woman offered had paled in comparison to this crushing betrayal. Julia couldn't breathe past the anger and hurt.

"Left messages to have you call us. Last one was—"

"Last week," Sue supplied.

Last week. Last week when the letter from Lawshaw came through.

"She never gave me the message," Julia whispered, despite the tightness in her lungs. "I never received those messages."

"Apparently," Virginia said.

"Is the job still open?"

"Sure, but we need someone right away. We've sort of waited long—"

Julia bit her lip and looked back at the girls at the coffee station. Jodi wanted more hours so she could pick up Julia's shifts if she quit. Plus a girl had come by yesterday to fill out an application, so the bosses could get someone else in right away.

"I can start on Monday," she said rushing headlong into unknown territory.

"Monday morning would be fine," Virginia said.

"What time?" Julia asked.

"6:00 a.m."

"Wonderful." She reached out to shake Virginia's hand, feeling both giddy and weak. "Thanks." She shook Sue's hand. "Really. I appreciate it."

"Well, if nothing else, it looks like you're going to be entertaining," Virginia said with a smile.

Julia finished her shift early and then resigned with promises that she'd be out to visit.

She left Petro and walked back to the Adams', fanning the fire of her anger the whole way. She'd been duped. Tricked and betrayed and she felt like a sucker for ever giving Agnes the benefit of doubt. She'd let Agnes make her feel guilty, given Agnes far too much authority in her life and the whole time Agnes had been lying.

"Hello?" she called, walking through the front door. "Agnes?"

She heard Ben's squeal from the kitchen and the

clatter of something hitting the floor before he came tearing into the dining room, covered in flour with a dish towel around his neck.

Oh, sweetie, she thought, *how can this be happening to us? I thought I was doing the right thing.*

"Hi, Julia." Agnes followed, wiping her hands on another towel. "You're home early. Is something wrong?"

She had the nerve, the gall to look worried, as if she cared.

"Yeah, I'd say something is wrong," Julia managed to say in normal tones. "I'm going to sit Ben down with the TV for a minute—"

"Oh, Julia, do you have to? We were just having—"

"Yes, Agnes," she snapped. "I have to. Let's go, Ben," she said to her son, whose eyes had gone wide at her tone. "Let's see what we can find on TV."

Ben followed her, subdued. But thanks to the satellite selection she was able to get Ben settled with Dora and that pesky Swiper and all was well in Ben's little world.

She found Agnes in the kitchen, sweeping mounds of flour from the counter into the garbage can.

"Ben and I were making some cookies and he got pretty—"

"I had a conversation with Virginia and Sue Holmes this morning," Julia interrupted. Agnes swallowed but didn't pause, didn't even flinch.

"I don't much care for your tone, Julia."

"Well, that's too damn bad, Agnes. Because I don't much care for your lying to me."

"I never lied." She returned the garbage can to under the sink and began to stack bowls without once looking at Julia.

"They called three times to offer me a job."

"Did they?"

The top of Julia's head just blew right off. She reached out and tugged on Agnes's elbow, forcing her to at least face Julia.

"They left three messages with you."

"Well, I'm sorry I seem to have forgotten." She put a hand to her forehead. "My memory is not—"

"Cut the shit, Agnes," she snapped. "You managed to give me every message for every job that didn't want me."

"Yes, well—" She shrugged.

Standing in her mother-in-law's kitchen, wearing her bad polyester uniform, Julia realized that this wasn't something she could change. She could confront Agnes with all of her anger. All of her rage and disappointment. She could try and try, beating her head against the wall, to get Agnes to admit she'd done something wrong. But it would never happen. And if Agnes did admit it, what would it change? Nothing.

Julia turned for the stairs.

"What are you doing?" Agnes asked.

"Packing," Julia shouted over her shoulder while she stomped up the steps. She pushed open the door to the Mitch Museum she and Ben had been sleeping in.

She pulled her suitcase from under the bed and flopped it open.

"What are you talking about?" Agnes asked from

the doorway. She looked panicked, sincerely worried. Julia steeled her heart.

"I'm taking Ben and we're leaving," she said clearly, so there would be no misunderstanding.

"Where will you go?"

Jesse's. Her heart pinged and popped at the thought. But she couldn't say that, not without starting World War Three. "I've made some friends here, Agnes. I will stay with them."

"What about Ben?" she cried. "You'd just take Ben away from us?"

Julia sighed and braced herself as she wadded up clothes in her suitcase. "Of course not, Agnes. I am not leaving town. I am not running away."

To join the army. Oh, Mitch, it all makes so much sense right now.

"It sure looks like it."

Julia heaved a deep breath. "You lied to me." She looked Agnes right in the eye. "I needed the support and stability of family and you used that need to make me totally dependent on you. You've made me feel guilty and like I'm the worst mother on the planet. I wanted that job at Holmes. I wanted it a lot and you almost cost me that."

"Julia, I just forgot. Surely—"

Julia shook her head. Why did she even try?

"Ben and I are moving out. I will let you know where we are in a few days. Maybe a week. But I need to cool down. You will be allowed to see Ben, just not right now. Not when I am so mad."

Agnes's jaw went tight. "Ron is not going to like this."

Ron can kiss my—

"I don't much like it, either, but you've left me no choice."

Julia grabbed the assortment of toys and sippy cups from the beside table and threw them on top of everything else in the suitcase.

She zipped up the beat-up bag and heaved it off the bed.

"Well, at least wait until he comes home and he can help you—"

"I've had enough of your help." She stood nose-to-nose with Agnes in the doorway. "Let me go, Agnes, before you make things worse."

Agnes didn't move for a long second and Julia wondered if she was just going to have to shove her way out of this house. But finally, eyes on the floor, Agnes stepped back.

"You're breaking our hearts," she whispered and Julia felt herself waver, felt her strong resolve and anger flicker.

"I'm sorry," she said. "I'm so sorry things happened this way. But you are at fault, Agnes. Not me. You should think about that."

She stumbled past Agnes with the diaper bag and her suitcase banging into her legs.

"Ben," she called. She put the bags down by the front door.

"Swiper no swipping!" he called in response. She smiled despite the tension ratcheting up her back.

"Hey, buddy, we're going on a walk."

He ran out of the TV room, his dish towel bib all askew.

"Here, let me help you." Julia reached for the towel and Ben jerked himself out of the way.

Oh no, please, buddy. Please let's just go.

"No walk!" he said, his blue eyes suddenly mutinous.

"He doesn't want to go," Agnes whispered over Julia's shoulder, her voice dripping with criticism and Julia felt her reserves drain. Tears pricked her eyes.

"He's two, Agnes. His mind changes every few minutes," she spat. She crouched in front of Ben and fought tears. "Ben, we have to go," she whispered.

"I don't want to!"

"Me, either, but—"

He stomped his foot. His face twisted and a full-blown tantrum gathered steam. She rubbed her forehead and wished herself a million miles from this place.

"Stay!" he shouted.

She pulled the towel from around his neck and he started to cry. She picked him up, kicking and screaming, and put him in his stroller.

"Julia! Look what you're doing!" Agnes cried. "Look at him—"

"I see him, Agnes," she growled.

She clipped her screaming, writhing son in, threw the diaper bag over her chest and picked up the suitcase. "I'll be in touch," she told Agnes and left.

She knew Agnes would be watching her, so she didn't take the shortcut. She took the long way—even though it meant parading Ben and his tantrum through the neighborhood—hoping Agnes would never dream she'd go to Jesse.

As exits go, it was a disaster. But at least it was an exit. She'd take her points where she could get them.

JESSE SET DOWN the planer and lifted the headboard. He blew off the sawdust and shavings then eyed the line. Straight. *True,* as his grandfather used to say.

His blood stilled, his ears pricked as a shoe hit gravel outside the door. He could smell her even before he turned.

"Jesse?"

He faced her and saw a different woman, a woman full of anger and hurt, wearing a Petro uniform. Her eyes were watery and her skin flushed an angry deep red. Jesse glanced at Ben, who sported puffy eyes and a blotchy face.

Jesse had the sinking feeling a disaster had just landed at his feet.

"You okay?" he asked.

She told him a story about Holmes Landscaping and Agnes and messages she'd never gotten, but she knew what was really happening. He knew as she took the deep breath what she'd ask.

"Can we stay here, just for a little while?" Her sky-blue eyes tore into him.

His whole body was suffused with heat, and the pins and needles that accompany flesh asleep for too long, finally awakening.

"Sure," he said.

CHAPTER FIFTEEN

JULIA CAME INTO the kitchen from the bedroom where she'd spent the last half hour putting Ben down for a long-overdue nap. She still looked rigid, as if anger had fused her joints.

"Sit down before you fall down," Jesse told her. She eased into the chair. Her hands were fisted in her lap.

It was a physical battle to keep himself from touching her.

Friends, he reminded himself. *Don't be an ass.*

He put an open bottle of water in front of her, thinking she could probably use it. She drank half of it in one long swallow.

He watched her, that shift and play of her throat, and wondered what he was supposed to do. What did friends do right now? If she were Mitch—his only other friend—they'd go get drunk. Or rather, Mitch would get drunk and Jesse would sit and listen to Mitch's bullshit until he ran out of it.

"I don't think you realized what you agreed to when you said we could stay." She set the water down. "We're sort of a logistical nightmare."

He nodded and pushed himself up to sit on the counter—the same spot where she'd sat the other day. He walked a dangerous line having her here, when every moment with her was like brushing against a live wire. And he found that the very time when he needed to be an asshole to preserve himself, he didn't have anything left.

Go figure.

"I have to ask Amanda to babysit, but since I don't have a car, I can't get Ben up to her house. Would it be all right if she—"

"Yes." He nodded and he could practically see the weight of responsibility coming off her in big chunks, her body loosening.

"Jesse," she whispered in the manner of someone who's been saved from going underwater. "I can't—"

"It's no problem," he said. "I'm serious."

She was going to say something else and he couldn't bear it. Couldn't bear to see her so grateful for these meager things.

"I've got some work to do," he told her. "You can use that bedroom and make yourself at home." He knew it was cowardly, but he walked away from her. Headed out to the garage.

There was only so much he could do. Only so much of her presence he could take before his good intentions deserted him.

HOURS LATER dusk turned to night and he was almost satisfied with the curve of the cradle's rocker. He rolled it once more along the flat surface of the workbench. No wobbles.

The oak was good and the old tools still had some magic left in them. And he...well, he remembered how much he loved this work to begin with.

He'd made serious progress today. It was nearing completion even though he'd only started it a few days ago. He glanced down at the parts stacked carefully against the wall. Pieces of oak took the form of railings and spindles. The finished headboard and footboard sat to one side.

He couldn't quite figure out how he felt about this project. He'd spent years of his life forgetting Rachel, burning her letters, giving away the food, candy, socks and books she'd sent in her care packages.

He'd see her name on the return address and refused to feel anything. He'd refused to be curious. To care.

And now he was making a cradle for his niece or nephew because Rachel had asked. Because she'd looked at him with tears in her eyes and said, "Please."

Of course, the real reason he'd made so much progress today was that he was scared to go into the house with Julia there. He'd tried three times in the last few hours, but she was still awake and puttering around so he'd turned, tail between his legs, back to the garage.

He wiped sawdust off the bench and smiled ruefully at his own cowardice.

If my men could see me now...

He moved some of the spindles and imagined for a moment the kid in Rachel's belly. Smart probably, blue-eyed, tons of spunk. They'd take the kid to the ocean, watch the waves lap at their toes. And they'd go to the mountains.

He remembered those camping trips Rachel and Mac had taken him on when he was young. They'd be better supplied now, of course. More food, functioning flashlights and perhaps even a tent.

He smiled thinking about those cold nights that he wouldn't have traded for the world.

The bitterness slid in, as it always did, and covered his memories like a veil, changing the way he saw everything.

He wasn't so dumb to believe that Rachel could have taken him with her when she left for school. It was her complete desertion that had turned him from her. She hadn't returned for weekends or holidays. One day she'd been there, screaming at their father, taking Jesse to the rock quarry and the next...gone.

The rug had been pulled out from under his entire childhood. The person who had sheltered him from their father's abuse and their mother's weariness had left him with no idea how to survive. Every idea he'd had about himself and his sister and family had been ripped away from him and he'd had to make new rules.

The person he was now had no connection to that kid who'd idolized his big sister, besides some shared memories. He didn't know how to love anyone the way he'd once loved his sister. He didn't know how to trust anyone the way he'd once trusted her.

That's what he couldn't forgive.

She'd ruined that little boy before he even had a chance.

He sighed, tired of thinking of these things. That was

the trouble with woodworking, With his hands busy there was too much time to think.

He turned off the light over the bench and shut the rickety door behind him.

Julia had to be asleep by now. She'd had a long day. She must be exhausted.

Please let her be exhausted.

The house was dark. He grabbed the jug of orange juice from the fridge, took a good whiff and decided it was still this side of drinkable.

He closed the fridge and for a moment was taken aback by his mother's chili pot sitting on the stove. His mouth watered at the thought of his mother's chili, a recipe she'd stolen from the diner where she worked most of her life.

He lifted the lid, and steam and spice wafted up to brush his face. His stomach growled and he grabbed a bowl.

This was something he could get used to, that's for sure. He lived like a dog when things were left up to him. He set himself up with a spoon and some paper towels and walked through the dark living room.

He tucked the jug of juice under his arm and balanced his bowl so he could hit the latch on the front screen door. He'd dine alfresco tonight on the porch, instead of over the sink.

"Hello, Jesse."

He almost dropped his bowl at the sound of Julia's husky purr coming from the shadows in the corner of the porch.

Her face was lost in the dark, but her bare legs were stretched out, her toes curled over the railing. The street-light hit her skin and those mile-long legs, turning them to gold dust.

"I thought you'd be asleep, I'll go back—" He moved to retreat into the safety of inside, away from those legs and her husky voice.

"Stay." Her soft voice floated from the darkness. "Please."

"Ah." His military mind summed up the dangers in a nanosecond—her legs, the dark, the living breathing heat that existed between them. This was a suicide mission if ever there had been one.

"Please, Jesse. Stay out here with me."

He nodded. "Sure." *I'm a goner.* He balanced the jug and the bowl on the railing next to her delicate toes. He noticed the chipped red nail polish, so girlish and at the same time so womanly that he nearly fell to his knees. "I'll go grab a chair."

He ducked back in the house. "Such an idiot," he muttered the obvious, grabbed a cracked vinyl chair from the kitchen and carried it outside.

Eucalyptus and the trumpet vine growing at the corner of the house turned the air sweet and spicy. He tried not to watch as Julia recrossed her legs at the ankle.

"What are you doing out here?" he asked, settling down with his dinner.

"I couldn't sleep."

Night sounds filled the silence between them—bugs, a far-off screen door slamming, Wain huffing and shifting. Jesse realized the dog was curled up by Julia. Her hand reached out of the darkness that shrouded her body and she absently stroked his ears.

"Don't spoil my guard dog," he said, joking to crack the tension.

"Some guard dog." He heard the affection in her voice and he couldn't help but smile.

"Well, we do what we can."

"I thought you might be hungry…." She pointed at the bowl in his lap. "It's sort of a poor man's chili. You don't have to eat it if you don't like it."

"It's great, trust me. Better than whatever I would have put together." He took a bite and his taste buds applauded.

The rocker creaked under her and neither of them said anything. The awkwardness built and built until he could feel the pressure crowd his ears.

"When I called Amanda I talked to Rachel. She invited me to come to dinner with you tomorrow. She said she's been inviting you every week and you never show."

"I'm busy." The idea of Sunday dinner with Julia and Ben, his sister, Mac and Amanda as if they were a normal family, absolutely robbed him of thought. Made him stupid.

"Sure you are," she scoffed. "Anyway, I'm going. I never turn down a free meal, but I wasn't sure if you could make it."

"Probably not," he said.

"Why are you so angry with your sister?"

"I'm not angry," he said. He drank the last of the juice and set the plastic jug down at his feet.

"She said you were angry."

"Why are you talking to my sister?" he snapped.

"She's nice. Her daughter is babysitting my son, I'm living with her brother." She shrugged. "Seems like I should talk to her."

"Well, there's no reason to talk about me."

"She wants to talk about you," she said softly. "Incessantly."

"That's her problem." He looked up at the roof wishing he could sit with his dinner in silence. "I'm sorry." He sighed.

"Me, too. I don't mean to pry into your business with your sister. She was just asking me so many questions about you."

He laughed humorlessly. "I imagine." He was about to tell her, give her all the maps to traverse the giant rift between him and his sister. Then Julia would see that some things couldn't be fixed or forgiven. Not that she'd understand. She'd forgiven Mitch, for crying out loud, a man who'd cheated and lied. His sister's betrayals seemed minor in comparison. She'd just left him behind when he'd needed her most.

Julia took a sip from a glass he hadn't noticed. The smell of Scotch drowned out the smell of eucalyptus.

"Are you drinking?"

Ice cubes clinked and clattered against glass as she set the tumbler on the armrest of the rocker.

"I found the bottle in the liquor cabinet, covered in an inch of dust. I couldn't sleep." Her voice was huskier, deeper. "Seemed like a good idea."

Jesse caught scent of trouble on the wind and he set his empty bowl on the ground. The shadows, the light on her golden legs, the smell of booze and flowers. He felt doomed, reckless.

"Do you want some?" she asked, gesturing behind her as though the bottle were there somewhere.

"No. I didn't know you drank."

"I don't." She shrugged and sighed. "Tastes terrible."

"Good a reason as any not—"

"I don't think I can sleep here, Jesse."

He took a deep breath. Another. A long steady exhale as though he were going into battle.

Calm your mind. Calm your heart.

"Why not?"

"The bed…the sheets, the pillows, even the towels in the bathroom, it all smells like you."

And there it was. The match touched to the dormant flame. His body went hot, his skin felt too tight, too small to contain all of his impulses. She crossed her legs again and he bit his lip against the urge to run his hands up those smooth thighs, past her shorts…

"It's killing me, Jesse."

Stand up. Go inside. Leave. Walk away.

"It's killing me to be in this house with you and not touch you."

But he sat there, waiting for the inevitable.

She stood. "I'd better go," she whispered.

She stepped in front of him to make her way inside, but he stopped her. He put his rough palm to the satin skin of her knee and she moaned.

All of the large and small reins he'd attached to himself strained. All of the locks he'd used to manage his feelings for Julia bent and twisted under the force of his desire.

"I can't do this if you're going to pull away from me," she said. "It hurts too much."

"I know." He brushed the back of his hands up her lean muscles until his fingers slid under the hem of her shorts. "It hurts me, too."

The locks snapped and he pressed on the backs of her knees with his fingers until she folded across his lap, straddling him. His hands curled around her hips to the flesh he'd admired for so long and he pulled her in closer until their bellies touched.

Her damp lips parted and, before she could say anything, he kissed her.

It was wet, her mouth open and hot and waiting for him. It was like sliding into fire. He went from fighting himself to fighting to get closer in a heartbeat. His hands slid from her hips to her back and pressed her as fully as he could against his chest. She was so small, he could wrap his arms around her twice. His fingertips brushed the soft sweet curve of her breast under her T-shirt and she moaned into his mouth.

She buried her hands into his hair and arched her hips against him. He could feel the heat of her through his jeans.

He wanted to touch her. He wanted her in his arms, naked and wet. For hours. Years. The rest of his life. These tastes, the desperate touches and soft squirms of her body against him, were torture. Torture he couldn't get enough of.

"We have to go inside," he murmured and, before she could shift or pull back, he simply stood. Julia, bless her, curled her legs around his hips so he could carry her.

He nearly pulled the screen door off its hinges with his urgency. He walked through the dark house to the bedroom he'd been using.

He bent, setting her on the rumpled sheets and, as if she'd read his mind, she didn't let go. She pulled him on top of her.

He eased his hand down her shirt, pressing the thin cotton against her body. She was naked underneath, her nipple pebbled under the pink cloth. He leaned down and took it in his mouth through the T-shirt.

She hissed and arched, pushing her sex against his. She pressed kisses wherever they would land—his head, the side of his neck—and he wanted to smile at her clumsy fervor.

He understood it. Something about having her breast in his mouth made him feel like a teenager, untouched and blind with lust.

She pulled his shirt up his back and he lifted away from her enough to let her yank it over his head. He put his hand under the hem of her shirt, rested his palm against the tight trembling muscles of her stomach.

For a second, the magnitude of what was happening here, this leap off a high cliff, hammered home. This was *Julia.* Julia, Mitch's widow. Julia who owned nothing but the shirt on her back. And there was Mitch's son. He had no—

"Hey." She reached up and forced him to meet her eyes. "It's just you and me, Jesse." She smiled, part vixen, part angel. "And I really need you right now." She arched again, pressing the damp heat between her legs against him. The simple movement pushed away all doubt, all regret. He let himself get burned by her fire.

He slowly pulled her shirt off her body. He kissed the tight knob of her belly button as he passed it. He greeted each thin rib. And finally her small breasts, the nipples drawn up hard with obvious want. He licked them in warm welcome, bit down lightly until she gasped. He smiled and kissed his way to her beautiful lips.

She wrapped her arms around his neck and held him so tightly he could barely breathe.

And he was fine with that.

Just once, he thought. *I'll have her just once and then I'll let her go.*

THE PLEASURE WAS THICK, like syrup, filling her body until she felt full, ripe, swollen with need and want and a feminine power she'd never known existed in her.

She stroked his erection between her hands, ran her thumb over the smooth head until he shuddered and jerked away from her.

He'd already ruined her with his mouth and hands. He'd given her all she thought she could take and then coaxed her to the edge one more time. And now suddenly, here she was hungry once again.

"Make love to me, Jesse," she whispered.

He fumbled at the table in his shaving kit and turned back to her with a condom in hand. He smiled at the incredulous face she made.

"Government issue," he said before ripping the package open with his teeth. He slid the sheath on and was again over her. The solid warmth against her breast and between her legs was a drug she couldn't get enough of.

And then he was inside of her, pushing against walls and muscles and nerves that rang like bells through her body and her heart.

She licked sweat from his shoulder and then bit where she licked, he growled and pushed harder, higher inside of her. She had a sudden appetite for more. She arched, lifted her knees. His hand found its way in between them, stroked the hard ridge of her clitoris and somehow not even that was enough.

She pushed against his shoulder, forcing him to his back and she climbed on top of him. She straddled him like some kind of amazon warrior. A woman staking her ground. Claiming what was hers.

She ran her hands up his wounded chest and felt the hard beat of his heart under her hand.

This is where I belong. Where I was meant to be.

CHAPTER SIXTEEN

HE WOKE UP SLOWLY, which was strange. Different. Usually he woke up on the razor's edge ready for battle, but today he rode a sweet updraft toward consciousness.

The air smelled like Julia. Julia and sex and he wanted to linger in the warm sheets, in the memories of last night, in that sweet woman smell.

But someone was singing off-key in the kitchen and the smells of coffee and pancakes beckoned. Those homey scents brought reality crashing in on him, shoving aside all trace of dreams.

The world was up without him and there was no time like the present to see the damage he'd done. He didn't know what to say to Julia, how to correct what he'd done last night.

He pulled on a pair of pants and a T-shirt and padded out into the kitchen where Julia had her son tucked into a high-back chair. Ben wore a dish towel for a bib. She sang something to him about wheels on the bus and he shouted something back at her. She danced and twirled to the stove where she flipped a pancake onto a plate.

It was like walking into a scene from a fairy tale. The Dance of the Pancake Fairy or something.

"Good morning," he said into the happy scene.

"Look, Ben," Julia said with a twinkle in her pretty eyes. "It's a bear!"

Ben, as if cued, did his bear impression and Julia came over and pressed a quick kiss to Jesse's cheek. He put his hands on her delicate waist before she could run off.

"I don't know what I am doing," he whispered to her. "I don't know how to do this."

"It's breakfast, Jesse," she whispered back. "And it's easy."

"Nothing is different. I have to leave."

"Not right now," she said. She kissed his nose and moved away. She slid cut-up pancakes in front of Ben and a cup of coffee with plenty of sugar in front of him.

Jesse sat and leaned back in his chair in an imitation of relaxation. But he wasn't fooled. This wasn't easy. Relaxing in his kitchen with this woman and Mitch's son was the hardest thing he'd ever done.

Yet at some point between his fifth pancake and second cup of coffee, it happened. Slowly, moment by morphine drip moment, he did relax and enjoy the morning. It was so normal, it scared him if he thought about it too long—which he didn't.

After breakfast Ben asked Jesse to read him a story and he found himself with a lapful of toddler who smelled sweet and warm.

"He's friendly," Julia said with a proud smile.

"I noticed," Jesse mumbled. He'd never done this,

had never read a story about talking bears to a kid. But soon he was settled into the recliner with the solid weight of Ben's head against his shoulder, over his heart.

He could feel Julia watching, tears no doubt in her eyes and a foolish hope about substitute father figures in her heart. It was something he shouldn't foster. He should lift Ben off his lap and head out to the garage, out to safety.

"Hey." Ben patted his cheek, an unsubtle reminder that Jesse had a job to do. "Story time."

"Right." Jesse swallowed and opened the book Ben handed him. "Story time."

THAT AFTERNOON, Jesse's cell phone rang and Julia picked it up from the table and answered it on the second ring.

"Is Jesse Filmore there?" a man with a slight Hispanic accent asked.

"Sure, I'll go get him." She grabbed Ben and went out to the garage where Jesse had been busy for the last few hours. She knew he was hiding from her, hiding from what had happened between them three beautiful times during the night. She was ready to give him the space he needed to come to grips with it, but she wasn't going to go away.

She wanted Jesse. And this time she was ready to fight for what she wanted. She could beat back his ghosts. She was sure of it.

"Call for you." She handed Jesse the phone and looked at what he'd been working on. The cradle was partially assembled. She nearly gasped in reverence. It was so beautiful, so carefully and handsomely made.

"There's no one there," Jesse said, his brow furrowed.

"A guy asked for you." Julia shrugged.

"Chris Barnhardt?"

"He didn't say. Maybe the connection went dead."

"Maybe." Jesse picked up the wood glue. "What do you think?" he asked gesturing toward his handiwork.

"I think it's beautiful. Rachel's going to lose her mind." Jesse nodded and squirted glue into a hole and then carefully placed a spindle.

"Are you going to come with me tonight to give it to them?" she asked, wondering if she might be stepping into territory best not stepped in.

"It won't be ready."

"You should come anyway."

"I don't know yet." He took a deep breath. "I haven't decided."

"Well, Ben and I will be leaving at six." She turned to leave him alone with his decision. "Oh, can we get a ride—"

"Of course," he said.

She knew she was pushing him faster than he could take. But she knew she didn't have a lot of time with this man to change his mind about her and about leaving. She leaned up on her toes and pressed a kiss to the soft pillow of his lips. She inhaled the warm spicy smell of him that she knew she'd never forget. No matter how far he ran from her.

"Kiss!" Ben said and pressed a wet smacker to the

underside of Jesse's chin. Jesse gave Ben a big raspberry right on his chubby cheek and Julia's heart swelled to three times its regular size.

Swelled past what was sensible.

The six o'clock departure time rolled around like high noon in the old westerns. She could feel Jesse's agitation build until she thought the roof would pop off the house.

He'd finished the assembly of the cradle and loaded it into the back of the Jeep, packed it with old towels and blankets like precious cargo. She crawled back there with it after buckling Ben up in the front in an old car seat Nell had dropped off for her earlier.

"Off we go!" Ben cried, his hands over his head as though he were about to take that first big hill on a roller coaster.

"Off we go!" she echoed brightly, trying to beat back the tension that rolled off Jesse. The drive up the mountain to Rachel and Mac's farm was painful. Jesse's silence had razor-sharp edges. His jaw was held so tight she could practically hear his teeth breaking. He gripped the steering wheel so hard his knuckles were white.

She hoped for his sake that seeing his sister would bring this tension to a head, would relieve some of what tormented him.

They pulled to a stop in the gravel parking area in front of a low dark house.

Julia crawled out the back and walked around to unbuckle Ben. She took one look at Jesse and left her son buckled in, cheerfully trying to kick open the vents. She approached the driver's side.

"Jesse," she murmured. "Are you okay?"

THERE WAS A CRUSHING PAIN in his chest, a burning in his head.

"I don't want to be here," he said, staring blindly through the windshield.

"You can leave," Julia said. "You don't have to stay."

"She left me." He licked his lips. "She protected me and she just walked away."

"I know." She touched his hand, slid her palm over his white knuckles.

"How am I supposed to forgive her? How am I supposed to give her that cradle and eat dinner at her table and pretend like nothing happened?" he asked on a huge breath.

"You don't have to pretend," Julia said. "No one is saying you have to."

"I don't think I can forgive her."

"Really?" she asked and he turned his stinging eyes to her. "You can't forgive your sister but you can understand the way your dad used to beat you? And you can put your entire life on hold for a dead man who wasn't worth half of you? But you can't forgive your sister for something she's spent years trying to make up for?"

He wiped his forehead but didn't say anything.

"Mama!" Ben screamed, and Julia squeezed Jesse's hand.

"I am going in. You can leave if you want to, but think

about this. Of all the people you've accepted in your life, she deserves it the most."

And then she was gone. She grabbed her son and he was alone with his thoughts and the cradle and the gathering night.

He didn't know how long he sat out there. But in the end, the thing that got him out of the seat, that forced him to put one foot in front of the other, was Julia.

If Julia could find it in herself to forgive her husband all of his crimes, Then Jesse could forgive his sister for those things she'd done when her back was to the wall.

Julia was ruining him. Changing him, his house, his family. He felt caught up in her current. Her giggle and cheer, her fiercely sunny disposition, her belief in the good things that he'd doubted for far too long.

He pulled the cradle from its nest of blankets in the back and walked over gravel and stone to the door of his sister's house.

He put his hand to the door and knew that once he opened it, things with Rachel would be different. He couldn't be the person he'd been for the past few years.

He was going to have to be that boy he'd forgotten and pushed away.

He pushed open the door and stepped into the bright light and laughter of his sister's home.

THEY LOVED THE CRADLE. So much so that Jesse felt a bit embarrassed by the tears, from both Rachel and Mac. He shot Mac a disgruntled look, but Mac only clapped a hand on his shoulder.

"You'll understand when you have one of your own," Mac said. Jesse's gut trembled at just the thought. "Sympathy symptoms."

"He's even having sympathy cravings," Amanda chimed in. "All he wants are French fries! He's worse than Mom."

"That's how much I love my wife." He bussed Rachel on the forehead. "I'll put those steaks on."

Rachel led them out to the patio, where the setting sun blazed across the valley, turning the air into liquid gold.

"It's so pretty." Julia sighed.

"The view is part of the reason why I married Mac," Rachel joked.

"She loves me for my land," Mac said from the grill. "It's a sad marriage."

"Let's have a story, Dad." Amanda sat with her chin in her hand. "Something from when you were a kid."

"You've heard all my stories," Mac said, flipping steaks onto the grill.

"Mom?"

"Don't look at me, all my stories are the same as your Dad's." Rachel set down chips and salsa and Amanda dug in. Julia reached over and grabbed a chip for Ben and no one said anything.

Jesse could feel Rachel's eyes on him, like a motherly hand across his forehead. So he kept his own eyes focused on his plate.

I'm here. That's enough.

But he knew if ever there was a moment to bridge the chasm, this was it. Awkward and painful he stood on the edge of forgiving his sister, a breath away from erasing the past and setting things between them right.

He looked at Julia, trying to gather some strength from her, and found she was staring right at him, as if she could read his mind.

Go on, she seemed to say. *Let it go.*

"I have a story," he said. A pin dropping would have created a cacophony it was so quiet on the deck. Rachel's hand stalled on the way to a chip. This was his olive branch and they all seemed to know it. "I was about eight, which would have made Mac and Rachel about fifteen."

"Oh, this should be good," Amanda cooed and rubbed her hands together.

"Mac found a wallet with five hundred dollars in it in the rock quarry." Jesse studied his hands, the cut on his thumb, as the memory exploded through him

"I thought I found it," Rachel looked perplexed. "Didn't I find it?"

"Nope." Mac shook his head.

"Mac told me he found it on a dead body. He had me looking for a skeleton down there for about three years," Jesse told Amanda.

"I found it," Mac insisted, "but it was only a hundred dollars."

"But Mac—" Jesse said.

"Are you sure?" Rachel interrupted and Jesse felt a smile tug at his lips. "I remember us spending a lot of money. We went to the movies every day for months."

"Of course I'm sure." Mac nodded.

"Whose story is this?" Amanda asked, rolling her eyes. "Let the man tell it."

"It's our story," Jesse said. His eyes darted to Rachel's and he managed to smile in the face of all of her emotion. *You're my sister,* he thought. *You did the best you could and I forgive you.*

"All of ours."

"THANKS AGAIN," Mac said at the door, his hand a firm weight against Jesse's back. "The cradle is beautiful."

"Remember to let the glue set a few more days," Jesse said. "And it will need some finish. I just didn't get that far."

He held open the door for Julia, who carried a sleeping Ben out to the Jeep, and he avoided his sister's eyes. He'd taken a huge stride tonight and didn't think he could handle any more. He could barely breathe as it was.

He'd told the story. Forgiven his sister and survived the dinner. He'd only said about four words and eaten about three bites afterward. But he was here, on the other side of it, a survivor.

"Thank you, Jesse." Rachel sighed, wrapping her arms around his waist. "Thank you for coming."

Jesse looked up at the halogen overhead light and blinked back sudden painful tears.

"Oh," Rachel said, as he was stepping out the door. "Have you heard from Caleb? Or gotten in touch with him?"

"Gomez?" he asked, blindsided by the name.

He hadn't even tried to reach him in the past few

weeks. Shame trickled through him. He'd started living again and forgotten about the dying.

"Coma," he said. "Last I heard about three weeks ago."

Rachel shook her head. "Not anymore. He's called here."

Jesse couldn't contain his surprise. "What did he want?"

"He wanted information on you." Rachel smiled sheepishly. "I didn't give it to him. I thought he might want to write an article."

Jesse swallowed, clenching his fist on the doorknob. "I'll call him."

But that was a lie. He had no intention of revisiting that crash with Gomez.

"Good night," Jesse mumbled. He patted his sister awkwardly and took off into the night, toward the woman and sleeping baby who waited for him.

"That went well," Julia murmured. She leaned forward from the backseat.

He pressed a kiss to her head the way Mac had done to Rachel all night long. Jesse understood that kiss. It wasn't sexual or friendly—it was a silent, reverent thanks. "It was the most painful dinner ever."

Julia laughed. "I thought we did okay. There were a few awkward silences."

He rolled his eyes and pulled onto the road. The wind, scented with lime and lemon, flooded the Jeep and toyed with Julia's blond hair.

"Thank you," he said. He didn't look at her, concentrated instead on shifting gears, getting them off the mountain. He didn't know if he conveyed everything he wanted to with those words. They seemed too weak and feeble to carry everything he meant. But they were all he had.

"You're welcome," she said, softly.

He squeezed her hand where it rested on Ben's knee as a weight blew off him in the breeze up into the night sky.

CHAPTER SEVENTEEN

THE NEXT MORNING, Jesse got up before Julia, put coffee in a mug for her and waited for Amanda, who arrived early looking like a zombie.

"Let me give you a ride," he offered Julia.

"It's okay, I need the walk to calm down a little." She kissed his cheek and skipped out the door like a girl on her first day of school. She had a brown bag lunch and a smile a mile wide.

He felt a little drunk, and a little like none of his bones were doing their job, at the sight of her obvious enthusiasm.

She turned halfway down the block and blew him a kiss. He waved, feeling charmed and smitten from such a simple gesture—that she knew he'd be watching her warmed him. Wain, sitting by his side, barked.

If he'd been told three months ago, hell, three weeks ago, that he'd be grinning idiotically at the knowledge she would be coming home to him, he'd never have believed it.

"The sun's not even up," Amanda groaned, falling sideways on the old couch.

He told Amanda to take a nap until Ben woke up, then he spent a few hours in the garage, cleaning up the last of his work from the cradle and contemplating tackling another project. Did he dare? Would he be here long enough to see it to completion?

The cell phone in his pocket buzzed and he checked the number.

Chris Barnhardt.

His good humor immediately fled. Chris was a sharp reminder that this easy domesticity wasn't his life. His life waited for him in San Diego. Yet he didn't want to think about Chris, the job or the move right now. He considered not answering the call. He pressed the Talk button instead.

"I need more time, Chris," he said right away.

"You're killing me," Chris howled. "I can't keep holding out for you. I've got too much work to get done."

"I know but things have gotten…complicated."

Chris pressed for a reason and Jesse, thinking of Julia and her long legs and her sweet mouth and her soft sigh of pleasure against his chest in the night when he loved her, instead told Chris about the fight.

"It's my eye, I can't see out of it, yet," he lied.

"You got in a fight? And lost?" Chris was clearly incredulous. "That's not the Jesse I went to basic training with."

"You should see the other guys," Jesse smiled. "But I'm going to need more time."

More time with Julia.

Chris sighed, his frustration clearly transmitting over

the line. "All right. Just get here as soon as you can and I'll try to patch something together."

"Thanks, man." He may have stalled Chris, but Jesse knew he couldn't delay much longer. He had to finish up here. He had to end things with Julia and get on with his life, even if his plan no longer held the appeal it once did.

That night, over dinner Julia shared every glowing detail about her day. They put Ben to bed, then made love. Jesse never once mentioned Chris, San Diego or leaving. If he didn't think, if he just let himself feel, then San Diego and Chris didn't even exist.

And he liked—no, needed—it that way.

THE NEXT DAY, Jesse headed to the lumberyard looking for roofing materials. He could get the basic green/gray asphalt tiles for next to nothing, but for some reason he couldn't walk past the cedar shake. It smelled so good on its pallets and he could picture how nice that yellow house would look with the wooden tiles.

Mom would have loved that.

It would take about double the time and work to install the cedar, which was ludicrous considering he needed to get to San Diego. But, he reasoned with himself, the wood roof would net a higher price when he sold the house, so the effort would be worth it.

He'd told Julia he was leaving. Maybe not last night as he'd intended, but she knew that, had known from the beginning. He simply had to get to the leaving part.

Still, Julia didn't have the money for a place of her

own. She seemed so fragile, so…in need despite all the strides to independence she'd taken. His sense of responsibility wouldn't let him walk away from her right now.

Bullshit, the voice of reality said. *You just can't walk away from her. At least have the balls to admit it.*

A teenager with bad skin approached him. "Can I help you?"

"I'll take three flats of the cedar," he said and walked away before he could change his mind.

"Delivered?"

"I can take them today." No time like the present to get started on this folly.

Later that afternoon, Jesse pushed himself off his knees and braced himself against the chimney that wasn't attached to any fireplace. He stretched out some of the kinks in his back and wondered if he should bite the bullet and buy one of those compression hammer guns. It would make his life so damn much easier.

"Excuse me."

Jesse ignored the voice and picked up his hammer, set another row of nails in between his teeth and bent back to work.

"Excuse me! You, up on the roof."

Jesse peered over the eaves to see a guy wearing a suit and tie, standing beside a fancy SUV.

"What?" he asked, spitting the nails back into his hand.

"Are you a roofer?"

Jesse nearly laughed. "Currently."

"Great. Do you have a card or something? A phone

number?" The guy walked into the yard and Jesse heard Wain on the porch start barking. The guy took a quick step back to the sidewalk.

Good dog.

"I'm not in business. I'm just doing my own roof." Jesse shrugged.

"Oh, man. I've got this leak and I can't figure out where it's coming from. Do you think you could take a look?"

Jesse blinked, taken aback by the stranger's boldness.

"I'm over on Cherry Avenue. It wouldn't take five minutes."

"Sure," Jesse finally said, surprised by his capitulation. The guy's face lit up in relief and gratitude and Jesse smiled. "I'll just hop down and wash my hands," he said.

JULIA CHECKED HER WATCH. Again. It was her third day of work and she was going to be late. It was ten minutes before six and still no sign of Amanda. She now realized how stupid it was that her whole schedule hinged on the timeliness of a sixteen-year-old girl. The milky pink light of predawn slid in the windows she checked as she paced.

No truck. Three steps. *No Amanda.* Three steps. *I'm gonna lose this job.* Three steps.

She was exhausted from her late night, from the series of late nights she'd been having. Each night after they put Ben to bed they made love for hours. And they talked about making love. And they laughed about what they talked about and then they made love again.

Her body ached in ways she'd forgotten she could ache.

She smiled despite her stress and her weariness. Changes in her life came like earthquakes. Meeting Mitch, getting pregnant, getting married and moving to Germany. Mitch dying. She moved from one shifting plate to the next and waited for the next disaster to strike.

But this move—across the neighborhood under her own power with nothing but her son and what she could carry—felt different. Hope had settled into this little house. She could see it, feel it, taste it. And she knew Jesse could feel it, too. She saw it in the way he looked at her, watched her, cared for Ben.

Now, if she could only get to work.

"What are you still doing here?" Jesse asked, stepping into the living room.

"Amanda's late." She shrugged.

"Well, go," he said, his forehead furrowed. "I'm here."

"Right, but he'll be up soon and I don't want to impose."

"Impose?" He smiled. "You stole all the covers and snored all night."

"Liar." She laughed. She grabbed her bag from the couch. It was a ten-minute walk and if she left now, she'd make it.

"How'd you know? You were asleep."

She hopped over to him, kissed his cheek. "Thank you," she whispered. *I love you,* her heart sobbed.

JESSE WATCHED JULIA run out of the house.

What am I doing? he wondered. But he knew the answer. He was leading on a good woman. He was pretending. Playing a game he had no business playing.

But maybe it's real, a quiet voice within him said. *Maybe you don't have to pretend.*

He heard a soft thud from the bedroom and braced himself for Ben's arrival. He'd been spending a lot of time with the boy, but never without Julia in the house. Ben came walking out wearing a pair of Spider-Man pajamas that looked like an updated version of a pair Jesse had worn when he was a kid.

"Mama?" He shrugged and looked around.

"She's gone to work," Jesse said and waited for the waterworks.

Ben just yawned and rubbed his eyes. "Hungry," he said.

"Let's see what we've got." Jesse led the boy into the kitchen.

"I like your dog," Ben said as Wain nearly pushed him over with his morning greetings.

"I think he likes you, too."

Ben laughed as Wain licked him. Jesse had to admit he'd never seen anything so sweet.

"After breakfast, let's play fetch in the backyard, what do you say?" Jesse asked and Ben nodded, his curls waving.

Jesse set about gathering a breakfast for both of them.

Ben was an amazing child with all of Julia's good cheer and smiles. Simply looking at him made Jesse feel like laughing. He saw bits of Mitch in him—sudden temper tantrums, a certain look of mischief from the corner of his eye that was all Mitch Adams.

Amanda called when they were part way through

their meal and said she'd be there in a second. She sounded panicked and scared and he told her to relax that everything was fine.

He surprised the hell out of both of them when he told her there was no rush. She could take her time. Sleep a little longer.

"Thanks, Uncle Jesse," she said. "I owe you."

"No problem," he told her. Ben handed him a soggy Cheerio from his bowl.

"Thanks, buddy."

Jesse wondered what would happen to the kid. How he'd grow and change. If he'd keep his generous nature and curiosity.

He wanted to see Ben grow up—the urge surprised him. Ben would surely need a man to teach him how to throw a ball and how to pee standing up. How to fight if he needed to and how to walk away when it was smart. Girls, math class, team tryouts, driving. He'd need help with all of it.

Jesse wanted to be that man.

That quiet voice got louder. *Why couldn't you have this? What's to stop you?*

JULIA NUDGED one of the shrubs into place on the asphalt and directed the shower of water from her hose over the new shipment of roses. The sun was hot on her neck and her shoulders ached but she couldn't remember the last time she felt this…good. This was the best week she could remember having.

She wiped her arm over her forehead and released the trigger on the hose.

"Hey, Julia." Virginia Holmes stood at her elbow, riffling though envelopes.

"Hey, Virginia. The new roses look good."

"Thanks to you."

"Doug's new." Julia stuck up for the young man. He was a nice guy and he knew Virginia was getting tired of his mistakes. "I've just been helping him along. He didn't realize which pesticide he was using."

"Doug's your boss, Julia. And he's been here longer. He's supposed to be correcting your mistakes." Virginia stopped paging through the envelopes and handed her one. "You're doing really good work for us. We're glad you're here."

Stunned, Julia took the white envelope in her gloved hand. "Thanks," she murmured.

"Next week we're sending some staff up to Lawshaw to take a class on herbs. You want to go? We pay."

Julia blinked at both the irony and the offer.

"Of course," she stammered. "That'd be great."

Virginia nodded. "If Doug doesn't shape up here, you'll get promoted," she said, before heading off to deliver the checks to the rest of the employees.

Promoted! She'd been working a week.

All the other guys were taking their checks and finishing up. Julia checked her watch and hustled into action. It was still a long walk to Jesse's house and Amanda was waiting on her.

She rolled up her hose, punched out and grabbed her

uneaten lunch from her cubby in the staff room. She'd been too busy to eat lunch. Again.

She said goodbye to Sue and the other cashiers and walked through the parking lot to the bike path that led into town. She fished an apple out of the bag. Yesterday Jesse had told her that she was wasting away.

Of course, what they'd been doing at the time indicated he didn't much care. She flushed thinking of that man, and his hands and his wicked mouth.

Jesse burned slow, all night, as though he couldn't get enough of her. He watched her, tortured her, stole her breath in ways she'd never thought were possible.

She dodged a pack of kids on bikes and put her apple core back in her bag.

But there was more going on between them than sex. The emotional connection grew with each beautiful meaningful moment they spent together. Every minute with him in that house filled her with secret knowledge. Powerful, intimate knowledge about things such as how he liked his coffee and what he looked like asleep on the couch.

He talked back to the news on his radio in the garage.

He hated onions.

She grew enamored by this knowledge. She studied the airplane posters on his childhood bedroom walls. She touched the small whittling knives lined up like soldiers on his desk. She found the markings on the doorframe that recorded his growth spurts to adulthood. Each memento of his past, each indication of his humanity and his secret heart thrilled her.

She reveled in their domesticity—the shopping lists and dinners, the laundry and cleaning. Each task she performed was a little thing to make up for all that he'd done for her. She liked doing them, liked caring for him.

She liked loving him. While he might be slow in the process, she knew he was coming around. In time he'd realize that something more—something long-term and permanent—could happen between them. He'd understand that Mitch and the army and the accident didn't matter to her. *Jesse* mattered to her. Jesse and his giant heart and his wounded spirit and his battered beautiful body. She wanted *him* and he just needed some time to come to grips with it.

Sometimes when she watched him, she could see him get lost in the past, the accident and Mitch. During those times she held her breath, gathering her courage to encourage him to talk about it. She knew he needed to. But so far she hadn't actually asked him about her past. Couldn't risk what she had with him.

Julia stopped by the bank and deposited her check. She withdrew the hundred dollars that she owed Amanda for babysitting and an additional thirty dollars.

Tonight she was going to take Ben and Jesse out for dinner.

She couldn't be more proud if she'd made a four-course meal.

JESSE STRUGGLED to hear that quiet voice that had been telling him to open his mind and his heart to Julia and Ben. Perhaps he couldn't fully relax and enjoy the first bit of happiness he'd felt in ages, but he could enjoy going out for fried chicken on Friday night with Julia.

Ladd's Chicken was on the main stretch of downtown New Springs and boasted the best fried chicken in all of Southern California. On Friday nights the whole town waited in line to get their fair share.

The whole town that hated him.

What an idiot, he thought, wiping his damp hands on the steering wheel, *going to Ladd's on a Friday night. Why don't I just ask for another fight?*

But Julia had been so excited about celebrating her first paycheck and Ben had caught her enthusiasm. Jesse couldn't look into those bright faces and squash all that hope by refusing to join in.

He guessed the townspeople would do the squashing for him.

"Let's go, Ben!" Julia cried, swinging Ben around as she lifted him from the car seat.

"Let's go!" Ben yelled her words back at her and the both of them turned to look eagerly at Jesse.

"Let's go," he managed to say.

He climbed out carefully and took Ben's tiny hand to cross the street. Julia took Ben's other one completing the image of a family unit that caused Jesse's heart to clench and throb with an emotion so painful he stood paralyzed for a moment.

I want this, he thought. *Why can't I have this?*

Maybe being among the population of New Springs won't be that bad, he hoped. Maybe he'd kept a low enough profile for the past few weeks that everyone would be talking about someone else. Maybe he was old news by now.

But as they approached the lineup, he recognized Patrick standing with his wife and Mr. Murphy, the detention monitor at the high school. They looked at him then turned away to whisper into the ears of the people around them. The sideways glances started and Jesse knew that this was the wake-up call his little fantasy life with Julia needed. He didn't belong here. The people of this town hated him and the feelings were mutual.

He glanced at her, but she smiled and joked with Ben, oblivious to the poison in the air around them. Well, it wouldn't take long for her to realize she'd thrown her lot in with the wrong man.

JULIA FLOATED inches off the ground, she was sure of it. The sun was shining, the air smelled like fried chicken and piña coladas, which wasn't exactly how she imagined her first real date, but at the moment it seemed perfect.

Other people in line glanced at them and Julia blissfully wondered what they saw. A family? A handsome couple?

"You know, Jesse—" She realized Jesse was not with her in this happy place. His jaw was hard and tension rolled off him, strong enough to drop her back to earth.

"Are you okay?" she asked. She touched his arm and his muscle was like steel under his shirt as though he were ready for battle.

"Fine." His eyes scanned the crowd without ever settling on anyone.

Without ever looking at her.

Her hopes for the night plummeted.

"Julia!"

She turned at her name and found Nell with her boyfriend standing at the bar behind them.

"How're you doing?"

"We're good." Julia nearly laughed with the crazy way her emotions were ricocheting off Jesse's tension.

"Hey." Nell's boyfriend, Ed smiled. "Aren't you Jesse Filmore?"

"What about it?" Jesse asked, his eyes hostile, the jut of his jaw a promise of violence.

"I went to school over in Ashland. We played you guys for the conference title in football my senior year."

A slow grin covered Jesse's face. "That was a heck of a game."

"You're only smiling because you won. I was a halfback."

Jesse nodded. "Me, too."

Nell rolled her eyes at Julia as the two men recounted their glory days. Julia wanted to shake him. *See,* she wanted to yell. *It's not as bad as you think. Give this place a chance.*

Finally, their name was called for a table.

"You want to join us?" Julia asked, relieved that Jesse had found if not a friend then at least someone not caught up in the myth of Mitch.

"We already ate," Nell said. "Maybe next weekend?"

"Sounds great," Julia replied with perhaps a bit too much enthusiasm. Jesse cast her a knowing glance from the corner of his eye, as if he suspected she was planning double dates for the next twenty years.

With her son in her arms, her man at her back and her heart in her throat, Julia followed the hostess to their table.

She had not been so happy in years and could only hope that Jesse's prejudice against this place wouldn't destroy her joy.

"Hey!" a man said as they passed his table. Jesse jerked and Julia's back straightened.

Please, please, don't let this be something bad.

The man stood, wiped his shiny fingers on a napkin and held out a hand. "Jesse, good to see you." Jesse shook the man's hand with a one quick pump. "I've been telling some of my neighbors about the help you gave me with my roof and hot water heater. Hoping to drum up some business for you."

"I'm not in business," Jesse said.

"Well, you should be," the man said with a laugh as he sat again. "Enjoy your meal. I had no idea when I moved out here that I'd be getting the best fried chicken on the planet."

"It's good," Jesse said with a taut smile. "Ice-cream shop next door is even better."

Julia sighed with the sudden decompression of tension.

They walked on and she shot Jesse a questioning look but he just shrugged. "Never saw anyone make such a big deal about a leak," he muttered.

"Told you," she said. "Not everyone wants to talk about the past." She wanted to say more, but she bit her tongue rather than add more tension to this outing.

"He's new in town," he muttered. But Julia could see the bright red skin under his collar and the reluctant grin at the corner of his mouth.

The man with the leak had gone a long way toward saving her first date with Jesse.

They settled into the far corner of the restaurant. Ben insisted on sitting beside Jesse.

"I don't know what you've done to Ben, but he's becoming your number-one fan," Julia said and lifted Ben over the table to Jesse, who settled him in the booster seat.

"The feeling is mutual," Jesse said, pushing Ben's curls off his forehead.

Julia lifted her menu to hide the smile she couldn't contain.

It's happening, she thought, giddy with love and success. *It's all coming together. He's going to realize this town isn't as bad as he thought. He'll start his own business here, rather than in San Diego and we'll all—*

"Well, if it isn't the hotshot soldier."

Julia dropped her menu to see a thick, heavy man in a baseball cap come up to Jesse's shoulder. The restaurant quieted, all eyes on them.

"I don't want any trouble," Jesse said quietly. Julia held her breath waiting for the moment to explode.

"That's not what you were saying when we kicked your ass." The guy laughed and a few people around them laughed with him and Julia's heart shattered. This was one of the men Jesse had fought with weeks ago, something she'd managed to forget about, as though it had happened to someone else entirely.

"I'm saying it now. I just want to have dinner." Jesse looked up at the man and Julia felt chilled at his hard cold black eyes.

"We don't see you much over at Billy's anymore."

"I'm not much of a drinker," Jesse said. "Why don't you move along."

The guy leaned down right in Jesse's face. "Why don't you kiss my—"

"Come on, Mike." A brunette in a tight top pulled on the guy's arm. "Let's just go home."

Mike snapped his arm free and straightened, allowing Julia to finally take a breath.

"I'll see you around," he said, dripping with snide disrespect. "You enjoy that dinner."

He left and Julia set down the menu and leaned across the table.

"Jesse?" she whispered, painfully aware that people were staring at them. Jesse didn't answer, he studied his menu as if he were alone. And he was, she realized. In his mind, Jesse was all alone. Always had been and, she feared, always would be.

A waitress appeared. "What do you want?" she asked and Julia flinched at her tone. The girl could have taken everyone's order that way but it felt personal right now. It felt like another attack.

"We'll have two white-meat half dinners," Jesse said. "And a chicken leg for the boy."

She nodded and vanished.

Jesse cast his gaze over those people seated close to them, the ones still watching, and they all turned away.

He smiled at that, as if their actions confirmed that he'd been right all along. She didn't recognize him when he smiled that way.

"Let's just go," she nearly cried. All of the hard work, the inroads to his guilt and unhappiness that she'd made the past week, were crumbling under her feet.

"You wanted to come here," he told her. "So we're going to stay." His eyes glittered. "This is my life in this town, Julia," he said. "This is who I am here."

"No, it's not." She shook her head and reached to grab his hand, but he pulled away.

"I'm not who you think I am, Julia. That man doesn't exist. I've been trying to tell you that for weeks."

Dinner was silent and painful from that point. Ben was fussy and keyed up from the tension between Julia and Jesse. She tried to distract Ben with a few toys and crackers. For herself, she couldn't eat anything and as if to spite her, as if to make sure she wrung every moment of misery from this night, Jesse ate his meal and then hers with excruciating slowness. But finally, they walked out to the sensation of dozens of eyes tracking them.

They exited the building and Julia sighed with relief.

"Thank God, that's over," she muttered.

But just outside the door, in the lineup, a woman stopped them. She was older, gray and hunched over with age, but the hate in her eyes was fresh. Real. Behind her an older man pulled out a cell phone.

Jesse swore under his breath and moved farther away from her.

"You're Mitch's widow, aren't you?" the woman asked, her voice cracking with indignation.

Julia could only nod and hug Ben close.

"And that's his little boy?" she asked.

"Let's go," Julia whispered, ignoring the woman.

"You should be ashamed of yourself. After a good man like Mitch you're going to lie down with this animal?" the woman said and Julia flinched. She turned to Jesse, who stared at the woman, his beautiful lips twisted with ugly, cynical mirth.

"Good to see you, too, Mrs. Alistair," he said with terrible, fake cheer.

"You monster, you have no business—"

"Have a good night," he said. "Give my best to Agnes and Ron."

He curled his hand around Julia's elbow and tugged her away. Julia went, drifting in his wake, moored by his hard grip on her elbow.

She'd stumbled into another earthquake and the fault line ran right between them.

She'd wanted to prove him wrong, show him that he belonged in this place, that the past was the past and the only person still holding him accountable was himself.

It had backfired. And the distance between them seemed insurmountable now.

When we get home, she thought, clinging to hope like a lifeboat in a storm, *we'll sit outside, and watch the stars come out. We'll talk about this. I'll kiss him and tell him I love him. That will fix things. We'll make love and it will be okay.*

CHAPTER EIGHTEEN

BLOOD RAN in Jesse's mouth from the force with which he'd been biting his tongue. He'd wanted to stand up in that place and scream at his accusers. Tell them all of Mitch's sins, every secret he'd ever kept for the man, all of which had ruined his own name.

Jesse wanted a clean slate, a fresh start. But even as the urge filled him, he knew it was fruitless.

His only fresh start would be out of this town. He'd fooled himself long enough. He thought of Rachel, Mac, Amanda and his new niece or nephew and his chest went tight. He ignored it. He could convince Julia to go with him. There was no way she'd want to stay so close to Mitch's folks after all the stunts Agnes had pulled. She'd realize that they had a better chance of making it work if they left New Springs.

Once they got back to the house, Julia took Ben into the bedroom to read to him and put him to bed. Jesse grabbed his cell phone and made the call he should have made long ago.

"Are you postponing this again?" Chris asked as soon as he picked up. "You said a week, two weeks ago."

"No, I am calling to give you a definite date. But it's two weeks from now." Jesse ran his hand through his hair. Cedar shake? Was he nuts? Putting that shit up was like surgery. He should have just tarred it and called it quits. But Julia had come into his life and screwed with his brain, his plan, his whole damn life.

"Jesse, this is getting crazy." Chris laughed. "If you want to stay there, just stay there."

"I don't want to stay here, it's just been tougher leaving than I expected."

"Then don't. Look, man, there will always be a job here for you if you want it. But—"

"I want it."

"The heat is off you. I hired some men so I'm not dying. If you need to stay—"

"Chris." Jesse sighed, rubbed his forehead. "I absolutely promise I will be done here and in San Diego by the end of the month. I swear." His pacing took him to the kitchen window so he turned and saw Julia standing in the door to the kitchen.

"Okay, Jesse. But let me tell you, you sound like a guy stuck between a rock and hard place and I don't want to be the hard place. Take your time, do what you have to do."

"See you in two weeks," Jesse muttered, his eyes still on Julia's.

He hung up and tossed the phone on the table.

JESSE'S WORDS RANG IN Julia's ears. She turned toward the bathroom, desperate to be alone to scream and cry into the pillows that smelled like him.

Oh, God, she'd done it again. She'd done what she always did, letting her foolish heart lead her into dangerous places.

Fool. Fool. Fool.

Tears burned but she blinked them back as she walked past him. She would not cry in front of him. Not now, not after he so easily dismissed her.

She'd almost reached the dark hallway when he grabbed her elbow.

You are stone. You are untouched. He can't hurt you.

"Let me go," she said, aiming for fierce and angry with her tone but landing closer to weepy and vulnerable.

"You knew all along," he whispered.

She nodded and anger chased hurt through her body. "I did. I knew all along. When you were helping me and laughing with me and kissing me and using—"

"Stop it!" He shook her arm. "You know it's not like that."

She wrenched her arm free and stepped close. Anger dried her tears and her vision suddenly cleared. She saw Jesse for what he was—a man caught in the past, lost and blinded by his old wounds.

"You're lying to yourself Jesse. It's exactly like that. You wanted me, you had me and now you're leaving," she spat the truth in his face.

"Julia, I'm sorry," he said the words on a heavy sigh.

"For what?" she cried, her emotions tumbling faster than she could keep up. She was manic—near tears and near murder. "You never lied. You told me this wasn't forever. I've got until the end of the month, right?"

"Julia, I want you and Ben to come with me. Come to San Diego. We'll get a place on the beach. We'll make a fresh start, we'll try for real."

His words spun a web around her, a cocoon of wishful thinking, daydreams and fairy tales. Her heart leaped with the sudden painful force with which she wanted that house and life on a beach with Jesse.

A fresh start.

Another fresh start.

How many more could she take?

How many more times could she move Ben?

How many more men could she follow into the unknown?

She blinked. Shook her head as if to force those negative questions from her mind, but they took root and spread. She didn't want to leave. She wanted the life she was building here.

And he was running from the life he'd built here.

"You're more like your sister than you thought, Jesse," she finally managed to say.

"What do you mean?"

"She ran fifteen years ago. So did you. You ran into the army and you're running now."

Jesse sighed as if weary. "I'm not running. I'm making a choice—a choice for a better life."

"What's better than what you're building here?"

He looked at her aghast. "You were there tonight, Julia. You saw what this town thinks of me."

"I saw one guy with a big mouth. That's all. And that will be forgotten in no time. But I also saw another guy stand up and shake your hand, boasting to his friends about the work you did. I saw Nell and her boyfriend talk to you. I see your niece and your sister and Mac." She swallowed. "I see a life here that I want."

"What are you saying?" he asked.

"I'm saying that I can't go with you. I can't start over again. I'm thinking of myself and Ben. For once."

His jaw turned to stone and his eyes to glass. "So that's it? It's over?"

"You're the one leaving."

"I don't have a choice!" he nearly shouted and she flinched.

"Everyone has a choice, Jesse. You can either choose to stay or to go."

He laughed bitter and angry. "Well, I'm leaving in two weeks. What are you going to do then, Julia? Where will you go? Where will you live? With Agnes and Ron?"

Her heart stopped before resurging. She felt her face go hot. An answering anger built in her.

"It's not your problem. It's not your business."

"It is my business. You're Mitch's widow. You're living in my house."

His words crushed her. That's all she was to him, all she'd ever been. Another one of Mitch's mistakes he had to deal with. Another mess he had to clean up.

"I'm relieving you of it. I'm just another girl you slept with. You are free from worry."

He took a step toward her, his face dark and cloudy with emotion, and she didn't care. She had enough anger for a thousand lovesick and heartbroken women. His self-righteousness didn't stand a chance. "How much money do you have?"

Why did everything in her life come to money? "None of your business."

"You're getting paid minimum wage out there, right?"

"I might get promoted." She sounded indignant, like Amanda, even to her own ears.

"To what, eight bucks an hour?"

"I'm not going to talk—" She turned, ready to walk back to her napping son and the sweet relief of tears, but Jesse slid his hand down her arm, almost like a caress.

"Let me give you some money."

She jerked her elbow out of his grasp. "Not on your life."

"You can stay in this house."

She laughed until she hurt. Was he really that blind to her pride?

"What do you want?" he asked, his face twisted with a pain she recognized.

They'd been ignoring the pink elephant in the room since she'd first stepped onto his porch weeks ago. She'd walked around it, pretending it didn't matter, hoping it might just go away the more time they had together. But their time was up. The accident, Mitch's death and Jesse's survival combined to be the wedge between them. Even if the town had accepted him with open arms tonight, he'd still want to leave. Tonight, two weeks, two months from now, it didn't matter. He would run forever unless he unloaded his burden. This was her last chance to talk about his tangled past and push it out of the way.

"I want you to tell me what happened." She swallowed. "In the desert with Mitch."

He looked at her, incredulous. "What does that have to do with anything?"

"Because that's why you're really leaving me. Whatever happened in the war is what you're really running from and if you don't deal with it, Jesse, it's going to eat you alive."

"What a load of crap."

"Then why haven't you called Caleb? Your sister said he's been trying to get in touch with you. You said you'd call."

"Jesus, why does it matter?"

"You can't," she whispered, "because you're scared."

His eyes flashed to hers but he was silent.

"You're scared because he's going to want to talk about that day. Like I want to talk about it."

"It has nothing to do with us."

"I love you." She finally said the words that had been beating at her lips forever, it seemed. "I've loved you since Germany and the accident is taking you away from me."

"Julia." He sighed. "I can't."

"Tell me, Jesse," she snapped. "I deserve to know what happened. At the very least, I deserve that."

The moment stretched impossibly, to the finest, thinnest wires. She held her breath until she thought her lungs would explode and just when she was ready to give up, Jesse opened his mouth.

"It won't make a difference," he told her. "I'm still leaving."

"It will make a difference to me, because I'm still staying."

It took a few more moments before he spoke again and in that time she gave up the fight against tears. They trickled down her cheeks and over her lips. They tasted salty, like Jesse.

"They were late. Six minutes." He shook his head and shut his eyes. "I sat at the meeting place waiting for Mitch and the crew to fly in the helicopter for six long minutes. Gomez was barely conscious. He was bleeding out, pressure low, heartbeat faint. He had zero time left. Finally they showed up. They'd taken on enemy fire and been hit. They were leaking fuel. Not bad—" he shrugged "—but enough."

"Enough for what?" Julia whispered, worried that too loud a voice would scare him away.

Jesse stumbled back, bumped the table and grabbed the Formica for balance.

"Mitch wanted to head to another base. A smaller one—closer, but with limited medical resources." His laugh was bitter and small. "No medical resources. Gomez would have died."

"So you said no?"

"Uncle Sam couldn't afford to have another dead journalist in the media, mucking up public opinion of the war. So I was supposed to break Gomez out of that prison and Mitch and his men were transport and firepower. Gomez was the mission. I thought Mitch was scared and—" he flexed his hand and squeezed again "—I was pissed. I was pissed because I knew once

Mitch was fired on, he'd fire back. He was late because he'd engaged the enemy when our orders had been not to engage the enemy, under no circumstances."

"That sounds like Mitch."

"I ignored his warnings. He said we were losing too much fuel. That we wouldn't make it."

"But you made it," Julia said stupidly.

"I made it," Jesse growled. "I made it. We crashed and I got Gomez out but I couldn't—" He broke off. "They burned. Artie, Dave, Mitch."

"Jesse, that's all terrible but it's not—"

"If we'd gone to the other base, Mitch would be here. Mitch and Dave and Artie would all be here."

"But Caleb would have died." She realized that was the equation that tore him apart. Three soldiers or one journalist? His best friend and loyal squad mates, or a man he'd never met before?

Mortal men had no business playing with these decisions. The price was high and cut deep through his entire life.

Failure. Death. Either way.

"Jesse," she sobbed. "You did the best you could."

"I chose someone else over Mitch. A stranger. And now Mitch is dead and for what?" he asked, his eyes burning. "To teach Mitch a lesson? Because I was mad?" He pressed the heels of his hands into his eyes and turned away from her, but she didn't let him get away. She slid her hands over his arms, touched as much of him as she could, held him as close as she could while tears ran hot down her face.

"You followed orders," she whispered against his back.

"Good for me. I'm a hell of a soldier." She could hear the sneer in his voice.

"You can't blame yourself for this." She leaned around his shoulder to see his face, stunned that he did blame himself for the accident, for Mitch.

"The blame has to go somewhere and I'm the only one here, Julia. I'm the only one alive."

"Thank God," she said on a choked voice. "Thank God you're here."

He pushed away from her. "This doesn't change anything, Julia."

"What do you mean?" she asked.

"I don't need your forgiveness." He turned to face her, his expression a stone mask she couldn't see behind. "You forgive the unforgivable, that's what you do. It doesn't mean anything."

She stumbled backward, slashed by his words. Her chest hurt so much she could barely breathe.

"It's better this way," he said. "You wanted to move on. You need to move on—"

She whirled on him. All of her grief evaporated in a white flare of rage. "How dare you," she whispered, surprised when fire didn't flare from her lips. "How dare you tell me what I need."

For a second she thought the knocking sound was simply her heart struggling to erupt from her chest, but then she realized the frantic pounding was coming from the door.

She stomped over to the door and threw it open.

Agnes, wild-eyed and trembling, stood in the doorway. Ron was behind her like some sort of guardian over his berserk wife. He put a hand on her shoulder as if reining her in.

Perfect.

"I couldn't believe it when the Alistairs said you were here," Agnes said, her white lips barely moving.

"Well, surprise," Julia snapped.

"You never dreamed she'd be in my house," Jesse said quietly over her shoulder. His acceptance of Ron and Agnes's blame and anger infuriated Julia even more.

"No." Ron wiped the corner of his mouth. "We never thought she'd be living with you."

Suddenly Julia wanted nothing more than to clear the record. To make the Adamses understand what they'd done to Mitch and especially to Jesse with all their blindness and blame. And if Jesse didn't have the guts to do it, she did.

The old Julia, the one who'd arrived in New Springs, wouldn't have been able to stand up for the man she loved against the parents of the man she'd married. She would have tap-danced, made promises, placated and compromised. She would have denied herself, buried her wants deep in places she'd forget about, just to keep the peace.

She wasn't that Julia anymore.

"You mean the man that killed Mitch, don't you?" Julia asked, deliberately goading them. If Jesse wouldn't fight, she would. She would fight for both of them.

Ron shook his head. "I understand war better than my

wife. I know there was no way you could have caused that crash."

"Why so mad then, Ron? Is it because Mitch followed Jesse into the army?" Julia asked. "That he didn't go to school and become a doctor or a lawyer? Was it the trouble they got into high school? Your son was the car thief, not Jesse. He was the one who drank too much—"

"I know what my son was," Ron nearly yelled. "You think I didn't raise that boy and see the trouble in him. But we had it under control. *We* were in control until you came along." He pointed at Jesse. "You came along and helped him, you took the blame and listened to his lies and let it all happen. You let him be the worst of himself and that is how you killed him!"

The ensuing silence was thick. *Ron knew,* was all Julia could think. He knew about Mitch. She turned to face Jesse, who seemed as dumbfounded as she was.

"And you're going to do it all over again with Julia and her boy," Ron said. "She'll never go to school, she'll never want more for herself with you here. You are just like your mother, Jesse. And look what she did to your family."

Anything Julia might have said was crushed under the terrible injustice of what Ron saddled Jesse with. In one fell swoop he'd labeled both of them lost causes.

She opened her mouth, but Jesse, who'd taken all of their abuse, stepped forward in her defense before she could make a single sound.

"I'm leaving, Ron. You don't have to worry." He moved to shut the door in their faces, but Agnes came to life and stepped farther in the doorway.

She held out a shaking hand, a letter clenched in her fist. "Here is your blood money. I am curious to see how much the government thinks Mitch Adams was worth. More than you, you whore. Your husband is dead and you're playing house with the man who killed him!"

Jesse stepped between Julia and Agnes. Her protector and she wanted to weep. Too late, she thought. It's all just too late.

"Your fight is with me, Agnes. Not Julia."

"You." Agnes breathed fire. "You have always wanted what Mitch had. You've always been jealous of my boy." She turned back to Julia. "He doesn't really want you," she snapped. "He just wants you because you were Mitch's."

"That's not true," Jesse whispered. Julia's eyes met his and she could read the truth in them, the utter devastation of his feelings for her. "I've always wanted you for you. Mitch has nothing to do with it."

He touched her cheek and her ebbing confidence flowed back into her, along with the fresh sense of what she was losing in Jesse. Grief sliced through her that Jesse would rather lose her than defend himself.

"He has everything to do with it," she whispered. "You're choosing him over me."

Jesse opened his mouth to deny it, but she couldn't stomach any more denial. She was after the truth now.

Julia stepped around Jesse, hoping to slay one dragon for his sake, and her own. "I've kept my mouth shut for a long time about your son, but I can't do it anymore. Mitch was no saint, Agnes."

"How dare you try—"

"He cheated on me, Agnes. A dozen times. He lied. He drank too much and he gambled. He didn't take care of us. He fed us to the wolves. He did the same thing to Jesse when they were young."

She turned to Jesse for backup. His flesh and body stood there, but he'd already left and suddenly she knew where she went wrong.

He was right, her forgiveness was never going to save him. He didn't need it.

She suddenly felt as though she'd been dipped in ice water. A chill unlike anything she'd ever felt covered her, filled her.

"What do you need, Jesse?" she asked, ignoring Agnes. "Do you need this woman to forgive you?" She pointed at Agnes. "Will that free you? Make you better?"

"I will never forgive you!" Agnes yelled.

Julia shrugged. "Well, there's your answer, Jesse. She's not going to forgive you. So you're just going to have to keep paying for the sin of being Mitch Adams' friend for the rest of your life."

"He killed Mitch. That's his sin."

Julia yanked the envelope from the woman's fist. "Your hothead son engaged the enemy and because of that they crashed."

"I don't believe you," Agnes cried.

"Of course you don't. I'm the lying, cheating whore your son never loved." She took a deep breath and finally got her rampaging emotions under control. "If you ever want to see your grandson again, you'll leave now. Before you do something that I could press charges against."

"You wouldn't."

"Pretty sure I would."

"Agnes, let's go," Ron said, pulling his wife from the doorway. "We don't want to jeopardize our relationship with Ben."

They turned away and Julia slammed the door shut. She faced Jesse, shaking her head.

"I thought I could reach you. But no one can, can they? Even if Mitch came back from the dead, you'd still find a way to be responsible."

"Julia, it's not that simple."

"Of course not." She headed for the kitchen. All her mistakes were so clear now, like footsteps in snow. She'd thought she was taking care of herself, she'd thought she'd managed independence after years of feeling like Mitch's chattel. But she'd relied on Jesse far more than she'd ever relied on Mitch. Jesse took care of her son. He drove them around town. He let them stay in his house. She wasn't taking care of herself, she was falling right into another earthquake. She'd left the Adams nightmare for a worse one with Jesse.

It really was time for her to stand on her own two feet.

She could call a cab and get a hotel room out by the highway until she found an apartment. Then she would be done with Jesse Filmore and his guilt and her terrible need for him that came hand in hand with her love for him.

She grabbed her purse and took out her phone, but

before she could dial he grabbed the phone, gripping her hand, hard.

"Julia, please, I want to talk—"

"Let me go," she said, unable to look him in the eye. This distant battered man could break her heart and that was one thing she didn't need right now. "I need to make a call."

"Who are you calling?"

"A cab."

"Julia, you don't have to leave."

She jerked her hand and cell phone away from him and called information for the number of the only cab company in New Springs.

Twenty minutes. She had twenty minutes to pack, wake her son and rip the skin from her body.

Why did love have to hurt so much?

Jesse stood in the hallway in front of her son's room, his arms across his chest like a sentinel.

"I want to talk to you."

"There's nothing to say," she sighed. "You're leaving."

"But I don't want to end it this way," he said.

"Well, I don't want to end it, so neither of us are happy." She pushed past him and crept into the room. She packed as quietly as she could, hoping to keep Ben asleep.

When she crept back out, Jesse was still there. She walked past him with her packed suitcase and diaper bag.

She resolved at that moment, setting her son's diaper bag on the ground by the door, that her life would no longer be dictated by anyone else. Her life as a leaf in other people's streams was over.

She was here in New Springs and she would stay. Make a life for herself. She had friends. A job she loved. And she would *not* pine after Jesse Filmore. She would not create dreams of what her life might have been if he'd loved her as much as she loved him.

She brushed the hair from her eyes and marveled at how calm she felt. No tears. No hysteria. A bone-deep pain radiated through her body, but she could manage it. She could manage her own pain far more than she could handle Jesse's.

She turned and found him watching her, looking like a man being stretched past endurance.

She smiled tremulously. "Good luck to you, Jesse."

"Julia—" He gasped, reaching for her.

She shook her head and held up her hand to stop him. If he touched her, this equilibrium might rupture like a popped balloon.

"I am so glad that our paths crossed again." She swallowed. "I hope that you find some happiness in San Diego. I hope—" She took a big breath of air, seeing so clearly what Jesse was too pained to see. "I hope you can forgive yourself for those things that happened to you that were out of your control. I hope you can forgive yourself for Mitch and those men in the crash."

"My forgiveness seems pretty irrelevant," he said, his voice low and broken. "Where are you going?"

"I'm not going to tell you that, Jesse." Her brain, ignored for too long in these sorts of decisions, over-ruled her heart. "I won't have you come stumbling back

into my life. I can't take it. My heart is pretty battered."
She tried to smile, but couldn't.

She could see the effect of the accident on his body, on
his entire life, like a bullet wound. It was as clear as all the
mistakes she had made. They were two people crashing
into each other, propelled by human error, bad luck and
disaster. She'd been foolish to think they stood a chance.

Risking terrible trauma, she reached out and stroked
his face one last time, reveling in the rough grosgrain
of his beard. "You deserve better," she whispered, a
terrible echo of his words to her a million years ago. A
car honked outside and she gathered her son, her heart
and every dream she'd ever hung on Jesse Filmore
before setting out to make her own way.

As MUCH AS Julia wished she could reject it, or put it in
the bank and never touch it, the insurance check was a
godsend. A hundred thousand dollars. More money than
she'd ever seen in her life. She was dumbfounded by
that much money. She put most of it in trust for Ben and
his future. With the rest she was going to buy a house.
Something small, maybe a new one out by the rec
center. But she didn't want to rush into anything. So she
spent one night at the Motel 6 and then she moved to a
two-bedroom apartment, close to the nursery, with
south-facing windows and a view of the mountains.

She bought some furniture with Amanda and
Rachel's help. They hung curtains and shelves and told
Mac where to put the new overstuffed chair she loved
along with the rest of the heavy furniture. The entire

time all of them avoided mentioning Jesse's name. But he was there, hovering in the air around them. He was in Rachel's sad eyes, and Mac's slightly bent shoulders. They had all been defeated by the stubborn grip Jesse kept on his pain. They were a survivor's group.

She ordered pizza for everyone as a thank-you and they sat at her new kitchen table and ate off her new-to-her plates.

"Your house rocks, Julia," Amanda said and Julia lifted her glass of Sprite, triumphant.

"I'll drink to that."

Ben, sitting in a booster seat, lifted his hands high over his head, as if his cheerful toddler soul that kept Julia on her feet when she wanted to curl up and die had grown, was in fact growing, filling the room. Their new house.

"Mama!" he shouted.

"Hear, hear," Mac said, his blue eyes sad, and they all raised their glasses and Julia figured, of all her fresh starts and new beginnings, this one, as painful as it was, had to be her favorite.

But that night she dreamed of Jesse. The old dreams, in which he had holes in his chest and his eyes were dead. She woke up with a gasp and painful lurch of heart.

I can't save him, she reminded herself. *He has to do that himself.*

But it didn't stop her loving him and she wondered, staring out her dark window to the mountains, when that would end.

She feared never.

CHAPTER NINETEEN

JESSE WORKED like a man possessed. His body ached and burned with old and new wounds. The first night Julia and Ben were gone, he took some of the pain medication that he had left—pain medication he hadn't touched in weeks because of Julia and Ben. That night his dreams of her, of her body, her kiss, the cool brush of her fingers, were torture, so the next morning he dumped the meds out.

He worked. Four days later the roof was half-finished, but he couldn't sweat or beat out his memories and his quickly gathering regrets.

"Looks good!"

Jesse peered over edge of the roof and saw Mac standing on his lawn, his hands in his pockets.

"Thanks." Jesse stood, braced himself when the blood rushed to his head and then carefully made his way down the ladder. It'd been four days since Julia had left and he wanted to pump Mac for information.

"You've been pretty busy," Mac said, holding the ladder as Jesse stepped off the bottom rung. He wiped his filthy hands on his T-shirt and shook Mac's palm. It was his first contact with another person in four days and he was surprised at how good the solid warm grip of his old friend felt. "You look like shit, though. Do you ever sleep?"

"Not much." Jesse managed to laugh a little. "How is Rachel?"

"Happy. Hungry." Mac shrugged. "Life is good."

Jesse smiled. Gladness, like some kind of seed buried under all his stupid years of pigheadedness, bloomed in his gut.

"Come by for dinner and see for yourself."

"I've got a lot of work to do." Jesse lifted a hand toward the roof. The truth was, stepping inside of his sister's happy house wasn't something he could deal with. His brush with the land of the living had proved disastrous. He was better on the roof. Alone.

"Working yourself to death or making yourself miserable isn't going to change anything, Jesse. Mitch will still be dead."

"I know, Mac. But how am I supposed to live in this town a block away from his parents? How am I supposed to live with his widow? His son? I mean, it's torture."

"More torture than it is living without her?"

His words slid in between Jesse's flesh and bone and settled in his gut like the hard cold weight of truth.

"Where's Julia?" Jesse asked.

"She's got an apartment."

"Where?"

"She asked us not to tell you, Jesse. She's pretty fragile and if you show up on her doorstep—"

"Why the hell does everyone think she's fragile?"

"Because she does." Mac shrugged. "Or used to, anyway."

"Well, she's never been the best judge of character," he muttered. He felt small and evil, as though a black spill of bitterness coated his entire body.

"What would it matter, Jesse?" Mac tilted his head and regarded him carefully. "I mean, even if you did know where she was, what would you do about it?"

"Make sure she's okay."

"She's okay, you can rest easy."

Jesse nearly laughed. *Rest easy.* Right. Not until he was gone from this place. Away from this house and its old memories that had been slicked over by those new ones created by Julia and Ben.

This house was haunted.

He swallowed. "Does she ask about me?" If Mac said yes, he'd run to her. He'd find her no matter what it took.

"No." Mac sighed, as if knowing that was the opposite of what Jesse needed to hear. "She's trying to get over you."

Jesse nodded, eviscerated. "That's for the best."

"Jesse, man, if you love her…" Mac trailed off and Jesse waited, as if maybe Mac would have some kind of answer for him. But he didn't say anything, never finished the thought, and Jesse knew there was no easy answer.

"She's better off without me, Mac. She needs to rebuild her life."

"Why can't you be a part of that?"

"How can I? I'm the past. I'm what she needs to get over. I'm Mitch's best friend."

"She didn't seem to care."

"Well, I do. Maybe I need to get over this. Maybe she's part of the past that I need to forget." He lied, and they both knew it.

"What are you doing here, Mac?" Jesse asked. He turned the old spigot on by the side of the house and splashed lukewarm water over his neck. Anything to cool down.

"We're worried about you," he said. "Rachel asked me to come by."

"Tell Rachel I'm fine. I'm fixing the roof."

"You could tell her yourself on Sunday. Steaks again, maybe some cold beer—"

Jesse shook his head. It wasn't for him. Sunday family dinners. The Filmores didn't have any business even pretending such things.

"No thanks," he said.

"But—"

"I can't, Mac. Just try to understand." He stared Mac in the eye for a long time, willing him to catch on that he just needed to be alone.

The way he should have stayed all along.

Finally Mac nodded. "We're here when you need us, Jesse."

Jesse started up the ladder away from this vicious humanity, but stopped. Compelled by all the changes he'd gone through in the last few months, he turned and grabbed Mac hard in his arms.

"Thank you," he told him. "Thanks for everything you've ever done for me."

Before Mac could say anything, Jesse was back up the ladder to the roof where, as long as he worked until he collapsed, the ghosts never reached him.

IN THE END, Jesse didn't bother trying to fix the lean in the garage. The new owners would probably tear it down—along with his workbench. Tear it down, sod it over. Whatever they wanted.

"The cedar shake was a nice touch, Jesse." JoBeth Miller, a girl he vaguely remembered as "easy" in high school, was now his real estate agent.

She was going over his house—and him—with a mercenary eye. Her skirt was too tight, too short and he wondered if she were still easy. Maybe he could erase the scent of Julia from his mind with another woman. But as soon as he thought it, he rejected it.

"You've increased the value by at least a couple grand. Now if you wanted to replace this floor—"

She seemed prepared to launch into the various monetary benefits to tearing up cracked linoleum, but he stopped her before she could get far. "The kitchen floor is fine. I want the house sold by the end of the week," he said. "At the latest."

"Well, it's a buyer's market in this town. Always has been—no one is really dying to live in New Springs. It might take a bit longer."

"Fine, but I am only here until the end of the week."

She pouted, an immature gesture left over from her adolescent years. "Well, that's too bad, Jesse. We've just gotten reacquainted." She touched his arm and he had to step away or possibly wrench that arm from its socket.

"Sell this house, that's all I want."

She blinked at him, her eyelashes heavy with mascara and he realized he'd never seen Julia wear makeup. Ever.

The thought, like Mike McGuire's fist to his stomach, made him short of breath. For a moment he wished he were the kind of man who stuck around, accompanied her to the big events that required makeup. He imagined her in candlelight, a black dress, red lips.

"Sure, Jesse." JoBeth ripped him from his thoughts. She tugged on her skirt as if suddenly aware of how inappropriate it was. "We'll get it listed tomorrow morning."

He put his hand on the doorknob. "Thanks," he muttered, slightly ashamed of his behavior but not inclined to change it. He swung open the door to let JoBeth out. On the step outside, his hand poised to ring the doorbell, stood Caleb Gomez.

Beside Jesse, JoBeth gasped. Or maybe it was Jesse. He stood, too numb to be sure.

Caleb was a grisly sight, to be sure.

Knotted and twisted red scar tissue licked up Caleb's neck and grazed his right cheek. He was thin, like any man coming home from the hospital would be. He leaned heavily against a cane and his opposite hand was a thick flipper of surgical gauze.

"Jesse Filmore?" the horrific vision asked.

"Yeah," Jesse nodded. JoBeth couldn't run out the door fast enough. As she left, Caleb bowed slightly like a macabre puppet tipping an imaginary hat.

"You need a woman with a bit more stomach than that one." Caleb pivoted and grinned at him. The devil was in Caleb's eyes. Jesse would never forget finding him, tortured, starved and left to die in that Iraqi prison. Jesse had expected to retrieve a shell of a man, but Caleb had turned to him and muttered through cracked, black lips, "You better be John-damn-Wayne with the cavalry."

"A little scar tissue and she was about to puke on me." Caleb smirked.

"I thought—"

"I was dead? In a coma? Yes to both, but I'm tougher than I look." His eyes lost their shine. His wit seemingly deserting him. He gestured into the house with his wounded hand. "Can I come in?"

"Yes, yes." Jesse leaped out of the way. "You want some water?"

"Do you have a beer? Oh, sweet beer." He moaned in dramatic ecstasy.

"Sadly, no." For once Jesse wished he were the kind of man who did keep beer around the house.

"It's just as well."

"The pain meds?" Jesse couldn't help a sympathetic smile.

"I'm all for drug-enhanced good times but the meds with beer give me terrible dreams—"

Jesse nodded. "I know."

"I wouldn't say no to that water." He gestured to the open door behind him. "Never thought I'd end up in a desert again."

Jesse went into the kitchen for the water. By the time he got back to the living room, Caleb was already sprawled across the couch with his shoe off.

"Sorry." He pointed at his foot with the cane. "But the swelling hasn't gone down and those shoes are killing me."

"What are you doing here?" Jesse asked. He lowered himself into his father's old chair, his eyes never leaving Caleb. He felt as though he stood in the presence of a miracle. Some heaven-sent, foul-mouthed apparition. "I mean, weren't you just in a coma?"

He'd been too chickenshit to keep checking up on Caleb. Too scared to see the body count from the accident go up by one more.

"Miracles of modern medicine, Jesse." Caleb drank from the bottle of water, his good cheer contradicting the fine trembling in his hand.

Jesse looked away in empathy. He'd hated the way doctors and nurses stared at him the whole time he was hospitalized, rushing to clean his small spills, to mop his face and the front of his gown as if he were a child, or worse, an old man.

"You're not an easy man to find," Caleb said. "Luckily, your niece was ready to sell your secrets."

"Amanda?"

"I'd watch out for her." Caleb smiled, the scar tissue tightening, gleaming in the late morning sunshine. "She's gonna set the world on fire."

Jesse could only blink. Oddly enough all he felt was admiration for his niece, no resentment at all.

"So, what are you doing here? I mean it's great. I'm glad you're okay, but do you need something?"

Caleb stared at him for a long time and then, finally laughed, a boisterous, loud guffaw completely at odds with the shocking state of his body.

"You saved my life, Jesse Filmore. I would not be alive at this moment if you hadn't pulled me from that prison and then pulled me from that helicopter. Did you honestly think I wasn't going to track you down and offer my pitifully small thanks?"

Jesse stood. "You didn't have to. I was just—"

"So help me, man, if you say you were just doing your job I'll hit you with my cane. You saved my life. My mother is ready to canonize you."

"I don't need your thanks." He meant it. He didn't really want it. He looked at Caleb's injuries and wondered how the man could sit in this house and not blame Jesse for some of what had happened to him.

"Well, I sure as hell need to give it to you." Caleb sat up.

"Okay." Jesse held out his hand, thinking to stop Caleb from getting up but then thought better of it. *Let the guy do what he wants, he's earned it.* "You're welcome."

God, how ridiculous did that sound? How inadequate.

"I'm sorry about your men. I understand the pilot was a friend of yours."

Jesse nodded, his throat too thick for words. For breath.

"My mother lights candles three times a day for those men."

Jesse almost laughed again, caught on some ragged

edge of emotion. Visions of Dave with his attitude and cocky grin, Artie with his terrible sunburns and bad jokes, and Mitch flooded what part of his brain wasn't numbed by Caleb's appearance on his doorstep. "Good," he said. "They need it."

"I understand you've retired, with honors."

Jesse nodded.

"Silver Star and the Purple Heart and—"

"I retired," Jesse managed to say, stopping the list of awards he'd earned because he'd been the only one alive to take them.

"I'd like to do a story."

"On the accident?"

"On the accident." Caleb nodded. "And you." His eyes taunted Jesse and dared him.

"No comment," he growled.

Caleb shook his head. "You rescued me from an Iraqi prison."

"I did my job."

"You pulled me from a burning helicopter."

"No story."

"Well, I don't really need your permission."

Jesse laughed. "Then why bother coming here?"

"Your niece thinks you blame yourself for the accident. And let me tell you, man, that better be the overactive imagination of a sixteen-year-old because I never in my life heard such melodramatic bullshit."

Ice replaced blood in his body. He stood, frozen to the spot. "I appreciate your thanks, but maybe you should go—"

Caleb dug through his back pocket and finally fished out a notebook. He flipped it open and searched through a few pages.

"The helicopter was six minutes late, right?"

Jesse nodded.

"According to Artie, who was trying to keep me alive while you fought with the pilot, they were late because they fired on the enemy."

"I know, they fired back when—"

"No, Jesse. They fired first."

Silence. The beat of his heart, the gasp and wheeze of Wain sleeping in the corner was the soundtrack for the reshuffling of memory and detail that made up that night.

"Artie said that Dave fired on his own. And Mitch circled around to take another pass at the enemy. That's when they got hit. I think Artie called them trigger-happy sons of a bitches, but I can't be sure. Artie was mad, I know that. Artie said if the bird went down it was Mitch and Dave's fault."

A headache blasted between Jesse's eyes and he winced against the light and Caleb's words.

"Mitch took on those risks. I know it doesn't change the outcome. I know how bad it feels to be to be alive when those—"

"You don't," Jesse growled. All of those barriers and walls, the feeble sticks he used to hold himself up, crumbled under Caleb's words. He was the wreck, the wretched jellyfish of a man in need of rescue. It happened so fast, like a tsunami. One minute he was fine, his ghosts managed, his demons caged, and the next he was a boy, defenseless and lost. "You don't know what it's like. To be alive when you shouldn't.'"

"Are you kidding me?" Caleb tilted his head and laughed at the ceiling. "Do you see me here? Do you see my face? I could take off my shirt and show you my chest. Every day I wake up in pain," Caleb said, "like I'm being hit with a sledgehammer all over again. The doctors say it might get better." He shrugged. "Or it might not. Those Iraqis did a lot of damage."

Jesse watched, silent. He'd pulled Caleb out of that rat hole. He knew the damage that had been done to him.

"But every day, before I even open my eyes I think, 'Thank God for Vicodin and Jesse Filmore.'"

Jesse laughed, incredulous. But something weird happened at the end of that laugh. His gut churned and his eyes burned and it felt almost as if he were crying. He lifted his hand to his forehead, at a sudden loss, like he'd been cut adrift.

"How?" he asked.

"Well, clearly you don't love Vicodin as—"

"No," Jesse gasped. "How can you wake up that way? I wake up and all I think about is the damage I've done."

Caleb smiled, sadly. "It's easy. Because I'm alive. Because every day I wake up and get to cause trouble and write about it. I get to eat enchiladas and look at women. They don't look back quite as much as they used to, but I can live with that. Every day is a gift, man. And you gave it to me."

Caleb limped over and clapped him on the back.

"Mitch, Dave, Artie—they were soldiers, not school teachers. They knew the risks."

"It doesn't make it any easier to live with."

"Nope." Caleb nodded. "I don't suppose it does. But at least you get to live with it."

Caleb hobbled over to the couch then eased himself onto it. Jesse's body buzzed with static electricity, like the air before lightning strikes.

"Your niece said you had a girlfriend." Caleb groaned as he lifted his leg up on to the couch. "Julia or something."

"Julia," he murmured. He stared out the window at the street. *Girlfriend?* What a ludicrous word to apply to Julia.

"You've got a girlfriend. Good-looking dog." He yawned. "Crackerjack niece. Nice house in a nice town. Sounds like a good life to me."

It was. It *was* a good life. And it was his. He just needed the balls to go after it. He'd nearly thrown it all away, and why? Because Ron Adams said he didn't deserve it? Because Jesse himself thought he didn't deserve it.

He groaned and stared at the ceiling.

He did deserve it. And more than that—he wanted it.

Finding out that Dave fired first and that Mitch pursued the enemy didn't change anything, but Caleb with his injuries and hope...well, it was inspiring.

"I'll do the story," he said as he turned and caught Caleb with his eyes drifting shut.

"The story?" he said. "Good, because part one comes out tomorrow morning. Front page of the *Los Angeles Times*. Papa wants a new Pulitzer." He rubbed his good hand over his face and through his hair. "Hey, you don't mind if I just take a little nap here do you? My driver isn't coming back until tomorrow morning."

"You need anything?" Jesse asked. He pulled the old green afghan from where it had been folded for decades over the back of the couch. He draped it over Caleb.

"A blind, warm and willing woman?"

Jesse laughed, he really laughed from the gut through his chest. He was oddly humbled by Caleb. Who was he to pity himself so much when Caleb had real gratitude and a sense of humor as sharp as a knife?

He felt ashamed, almost. For the time he'd lost in self-pity.

Julia had been right. She'd been right from day one—you've got to believe in the good things, or what's the point?

"I'll go hit town and see what I can dig up."

Caleb smiled, though his eyes were shut.

"I've gotta take off for a while," Jesse said and Caleb's one eye popped open.

"Bring back some burgers. And fries. God, I'd kill for some grease."

"You got it."

Jesse hit the door running.

RACHEL AND MAC wouldn't give Jesse the time of day when it came to Julia's whereabouts. But Amanda, for the price of an exclusive interview with him and the drugged-up journalist on his couch, ended up giving him Julia's address.

He parked the Jeep on the curb and took the outside

steps up to 3C, two at a time. He'd wasted enough time. He'd caused her enough grief.

He knocked and the minute's wait between his fist on the door and the sound of Julia's footsteps was the longest minute of his life. He died a thousand times, his heart stopped, his vision blurred, he couldn't get his breath.

God, he thought, *love is killing me.*

But when the door opened and Julia stood there with an expression of thrilled joy she couldn't quite contain into something far more mundane, it was all worth it.

He heard Ben in the other room yelling "Swiper no swiping!" Jesse wanted to step into that room, shut the door behind him and hoard this family all to himself. He wanted all their screams, their laughs, their broken strollers and foolish optimism. He wanted their futures, every moment that was going to come their way. He wanted to be there for all of it. The good, bad and boring.

He wanted them to heal each other.

"What are you doing here?" Julia asked. She crossed her arms over her chest and this time her stern expression was believable.

So believable that all the easy words tied themselves in knots and all he managed to say was, "Caleb Gomez is on my couch."

"He is?" Julia asked. "He's okay?"

"He's pretty beat-up and in a lot of pain, but, yeah, I'd say he's good."

"That's great." She stared at him and he stared back for a long breathless moment. He wanted her to understand why he was here.

288   HIS BEST FRIEND'S BABY

"Is that why you're here?" she finally asked.

"No." He nodded. "I mean, sort of, but it's not. No."

She leaned against the doorframe. She clearly wasn't going to ask him in. He hated having this conversation in the hallway, but she wasn't giving him an alternative.

"I want to start over. Brand new. Like you're opening that door in Germany all over again."

She sighed. "Why? What would be the point?"

"We're the point. You and me and Ben. We deserve a new start."

"I've started so many times, Jesse, I can't even keep track anymore. I don't want a new start."

Well, that stopped him in his tracks. "Okay, how about a middle? We deserve a new middle."

"A new middle?" She laughed. "Who are you?" She looked over his shoulder. "Where's the old Jesse?"

He grabbed her hands. "He's gone."

She eyed him carefully, taking her time and he let her right in. He let her look at all the scars, the ugly things he'd kept hidden, even the boy he'd forgotten he still had in him. "I'm sorry I hurt you," he told her.

Finally after a long moment, she bit her lower lip. "I can't let you into my house only to have you decide you can't do this in a few days or weeks."

"I won't." He shook his head.

"How do I know that?"

"Because I love you," he whispered. He pulled on her hands. She resisted briefly and then stepped toward him. "And I love your son. You love my sister and my niece. And you love me." He smiled at her. "We're a family, that's how you know. We're the family you traveled around the world to find. And you're the woman I'll wait for, forever, if I have to."

"But San Diego—"

"I'm here."

"But you don't like this town—"

"It's growing on me." He smiled.

"I'm not joking, Jesse."

"Me, either. I'm staying right here. I've got a journalist on my couch and a garage to rebuild and maybe a business to start. I'm going to help my niece and fix things with my sister. I'm going to help Ben grow up, teach him how to whittle. I'm going to give you more babies and watch you grow old. That's my plan." Tears bloomed on her eyelashes and multiplied until they toppled down her cheeks. "But—" he swallowed "—I know we have to go slow. You need a chance to figure things out on your own. You're just getting your feet under you. Maybe in a week, a month, you'll decide that I'm not right for you. That you don't love me like you thought—"

She threw herself into his arms, stopping his words and his air supply. "Never," she whispered. "Never."

He held her close, hoping he could absorb part of her. Some of her molecules, a bit of her beauty and grace. One of her smiles, so that he could carry her with him all the time.

"So what are we going to do?" she asked.

"Well." He leaned back and brushed some of her blond hair from her forehead. "First I think we'll see if

Amanda can babysit next weekend and I'm going to take you to the movies. Maybe get some fried chicken."

"A date?"

He shrugged with one shoulder. "If you're lucky I'll take you up to the rock quarry and let you make out with me."

"If I'm lucky?" She laughed and it echoed like bells around his whole life. She rained kisses on his face. "I think we're both pretty lucky." She sighed in his ear.

"But I'm serious, Julia. We have to go slow."

"Oh," she said, "we'll go slow."

"Jesse!" He turned to see Ben running across the hardwood floor to latch onto his legs. Jesse pulled him up, held him in his arm so Rachel could pull her son close, too. They made a good circle that way. Strong.

He still saw Mitch when he looked at Ben, but he saw the best of him. All the possibility Mitch had.

"He's a good boy," Jesse whispered.

"The best," Julia cooed, kissing Ben and then kissing Jesse.

"There's going to be a story about the accident tomorrow morning in the *Los Angeles Times*."

Julia looked stunned. "Caleb doesn't waste any time, does he?"

"Apparently not."

Ben patted Jesse's lips. "Kiss," he said. And Jesse gave him a loud wet raspberry on his forehead until Ben squealed with laughter and pushed him away.

"I want to go talk to Agnes and Ron tomorrow."

"Okay." Julia nodded.

"Kiss!" Ben shouted and Jesse leaned down again and raspberried the boy until he screamed.

"I want you to go with me."

Julia took a deep breath. "Of course. We'll do it together."

"Together." Jesse sighed, and he'd never heard a better word.

"Kiss!" Ben yelled and Julia and Jesse leaned through the small space that separated them and kissed each other on the mouth, the first of a million kisses just like it.

EPILOGUE

JESSE HOPPED OUT of the Jeep and checked his watch.

Five minutes late. *Julia is going to have my hide.*

He reached around the back bumper and grabbed the object of mental anguish that had caused his delay.

He was a smart guy, good with his hands, but putting together the blue bike with a red banana seat and silver streamers off the handlebars had him tearing his hair out.

But the finished product was really something to behold. Shiny and new, not a training wheel in sight. Just the sort of thing that would make a five-year-old's birthday.

Ben was going to love it.

He swung the bike clear of the Jeep and jogged across the street toward Ladd's.

Hopefully, Julia would be so high on fried chicken that she wouldn't notice he was five minutes late. Everyone invited to the party knew the only reason it was at Ladd's was because all Julia, six months pregnant, and Rachel, four months pregnant, could think or talk about these days was fried chicken. Luckily, Ben was pretty fond of it, too.

Jesse and Mac, on the other hand, were getting pretty tired of it.

Once inside the dark interior, he headed toward the sound of Ben and Margot—his toddler niece—laughing in the back room. He pushed open the door and nearly ran into Agnes, carrying an empty plastic pitcher.

"Hello, Agnes," he said with a smile. Julia told him he had to smile more with Agnes, make more of an effort at being friendly because the scrooge of his youth was actually scared of him, now.

"Jesse." Her eyes darted to his then away toward the bike. "Oh, he'll love that."

"Let's hope so." He stepped aside so she could get past him.

"Thank you, Jesse. For having us today." She said the same thing at every family function, as if she were out on parole and it could all be taken away from her with one wrong move.

He knew the feeling, had lived with it every day for the first year he and Julia were married. But every day after that, it had gotten easier to believe that what he had was real and his.

"Agnes," he said and could barely believe it as the words came out of his mouth, "you're part of my family now."

He felt Julia looking at him from across the room, could hear Ben laughing. Rachel and Mac stood in the corner, tying a balloon to Margot's pudgy wrist. Nell and her boyfriend were there, too, as well as the other women from Petro and Holmes Landscaping with their kids.

This is my family, he thought, never tired of the realization.

* * * * *

New York Times *bestselling author*
Linda Lael Miller
is back with a new romance
featuring the heartwarming McKettrick family
from Silhouette Special Edition.

SIERRA'S HOMECOMING
by Linda Lael Miller

On sale December 2006,
wherever books are sold.

Turn the page for a sneak preview!

Soft, smoky music poured into the room.

The next thing she knew, Sierra was in Travis's arms, close against that chest she'd admired earlier, and they were slow dancing.

Why didn't she pull away?

"Relax," he said. His breath was warm in her hair.

She giggled, more nervous than amused. What was the matter with her? She was attracted to Travis, had been from the first, and he was clearly attracted to her. They were both adults. Why not enjoy a little slow dancing in a ranch-house kitchen?

Because slow dancing led to other things. She took a step back and felt the counter flush against her lower back. Travis naturally came with her, since they were holding hands and he had one arm around her waist.

Simple physics.

Then he kissed her.

Physics again—this time, not so simple.

"Yikes," she said, when their mouths parted.

He grinned. "Nobody's ever said that after I kissed them."

She felt the heat and substance of his body pressed against hers. "It's going to happen, isn't it?" she heard herself whisper.

"Yep," Travis answered.

"But not tonight," Sierra said on a sigh.

"Probably not," Travis agreed.

"When, then?"

He chuckled, gave her a slow, nibbling kiss. "Tomorrow morning," he said. "After you drop Liam off at school."

"Isn't that…a little…soon?"

"Not soon enough," Travis answered, his voice husky. "Not nearly soon enough."

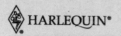

HARLEQUIN®

American ROMANCE®

IS PROUD TO PRESENT

COWBOY VET
by Pamela Britton

Jessie Monroe is the last person on earth
Rand Sheppard wants to rely on, but he needs
a veterinary technician—yesterday—and she's the
only one for hire. It turns out the woman who
destroyed his cousin's life isn't who Rand thought
she was. And now she's all he can think about!

"Pamela Britton writes the kind of
wonderfully romantic, sexy, witty romance
that readers dream of discovering
when they go into a bookstore."

—*New York Times* bestselling author
Jayne Ann Krentz

Cowboy Vet *is available from*
Harlequin American Romance in December 2006.

REQUEST YOUR FREE BOOKS!

2 FREE NOVELS PLUS 2 FREE GIFTS!

HARLEQUIN®

Super Romance®

Exciting, emotional, unexpected!

HARLEQUIN®

Romance®

From the Heart.
For the Heart.

Get swept away into the Outback
with two of Harlequin Romance's
top authors.

Coming in December...

Claiming the
Cattleman's Heart
BY BARBARA HANNAY

And in January don't miss...

Outback Man Seeks Wife
BY MARGARET WAY